Advance Praise for
*Concerning Everything That Can Be Known
and Certain Other Things As Well*

It turns out that Ron Gillette, poet, journalist, performer, deep thinker, CharlieMilesDizzy fanboy, coffeehouse raconteur, and all-around bohemian extraordinaire, is also a remarkable writer. These twenty-six stories, many of which Gillette admits lean heavily on autobiography, range from the heartbreaking to the hilarious, with stops along the way for scientific explorations, cosmic musings, unlikely epiphanies, evocations of legendary boho hangouts like Urbus Orbis and the Get Me High Lounge as well as perorations on love and friendship and what constitutes courage and how it is demonstrated. There is love and forgiveness—along with an undercurrent of rue—in this book. Gillette lets no one off the hook, least of all himself. But a certain mellowness has crept into his tone. Like Leonard Cohen, he loves the world not in spite of its flaws but because of them. There is something Prospero-like in his current outlook. He remains "nostalgic about the future and hopeful about the past" which, according to Kierkegaard, is the definition of a "disoriented" person—ie, an artist.

Gillette has flown under the radar for so long, mostly, but not entirely, by choice. It is supremely gratifying to see him emerge, blinking, into the clear light of day with this astounding book.

—Robert Sharoff, author (*John Vinci: Life and Landmarks*; *Last Is More: Mies, IBM, and the Transformation of Chicago*), journalist (*New York Times, Chicago Magazine*), and flaneur (Chicago, New Orleans, Los Angeles)

If you find yourself sitting in a café scrutinized by a life-long lover of short stories named Ron Gillette . . . beware! He may observe your slightest eccentricities and transcribe them into a broad saga of *Concerning Everything That Can Be Known*. You'll become part of the multifarious population he brings to life in his delightful collection of humorous, offbeat, and sometimes cynical observations of the human folly.

—Marc Kelly Smith, founder of the International Poetry Slam Movement and author of *Crowdpleaser*, *Ground Zero*, and *The Complete Idiot's Guide to Slam Poetry* (with Joe Kraynak)

It has been said that variety is the spice of life, and this reality is experienced in the whimsical and ever-pivoting collection brought to us by Gillette. How apropos is the title, *Concerning Everything That Can Be Known* . . . when the reader is taken on a veritable journey of locational and emotional vistas. The perspective provided by the author has an element of authenticity not easily attained; herein lies an oft-humorous, engaging, and digestible read that will be sure to provoke a reaction.

—Sean Michael Malone, author of *Spring City Terror 1903* and *Ocean's Grave 1907*

After the knowable, what's left? Plenty! The fossil record is incomplete. The Congressional Record, ponderous as it is, barely scratches the surface. Forensic science only occasionally reveals who dunnit. Q-Anon's wacky pronouncements muddy the waters. And our old friend, the magic eight-ball, passes the buck, saying, "Answer hazy, try again." So I may as well take a shot at the "certain other things as well." If these stories leave you as baffled as you were when you waded in, at least you're no worse off than you were before.

—Ron Gillette, noted author

Concerning Everything That Can Be Known and Certain Other Things As Well

Ron Gillette

Ten|16
PRESS

www.ten16press.com - Waukesha, WI

Concerning Everything That Can Be Known
and Certain Other Things As Well
Copyrighted © 2022 Ron Gillette
ISBN 9781645383970
First Edition

For information, please contact:

www.ten16press.com
Waukesha, WI

Cover design by Kaeley Dunteman
Back cover painting by Chuck Weber

Dedication

To the novelists, playwrights, poets and, especially, the short story writers who fed me and to those who've never written anything but have provided me something to eat.

Contents

Did Comets Kill the Dinosaurs?

"Am I the only one who ever takes out the garbage?" she hollers.

As he is the only other one who might do this chore, Ed realizes that this question is a command. He boosts himself out of the La-Z-Boy and shuffles to the kitchen. He steps on the pedal of the rubber pail and hoists the plastic liner, feeling a certain kinship with the sagging bag.

Moving down the driveway, he can't avoid indulging in his old habit of counting steps. Seventy-five, plus or minus two or three to the curb. Returning empty-handed, he is less empty-headed. He pauses mid-trip to listen to the birds. Some of their multi-lingual chatter emanates from nearby; some, barely audible, from distant yards.

Ed has always suspected the chirps, chucks, warbles and shrieks vaguely define space. He wishes he could define the definition he imagines—give it shape, measure the volume of the air it contains and rope off subdivisions as his neighbors have done with their properties.

The birds, he muses, hold property more lightly than people do. The holdings of one bird overlap with the others. Although they fight with perceived intruders, I'm not sure the boundaries of their invisible turf are forever fixed. Do rainfall, wind or temperature alter the boundaries? Do territories pass from one generation to the next? Is it harder for birds to manage three dimensions than it is for us to manage two? How much air does a bird own?

He has similar curiosities about birds' flight patterns. For half a minute, he watches six sparrows spar on the lawn a few feet away.

1

War or recreation? he wonders, as always. Then, at some cue only sparrows perceive, they scatter in a half dozen directions. One makes a beeline through a thick wall of privet as if it weren't there. One arrows to the northwest and disappears. One gracefully describes a Hogarth curve over the roof. And that's all Ed can keep track of.

Is this an avian form of writing? he wonders. If so, what's the message? And how long does it remain legible? Can other birds discern the text after the author has disappeared?

He knows full well that these considerations differentiate him from the mainstream of suburban thought. He knows he must never reveal what's on his mind if he's to be accepted as a sane member of the community.

Am I a scientist, stolen at birth from my real family? he wonders. Am I a misplaced poet suffering the birth pains of metaphor? Or am I mad—an alchemist conjuring unreal omens and harbingers?

He is happier when his mind isn't on himself. So much more evocative are the pipings of blackbirds. They are rare here, but occasionally they flash in from neighboring farms. Their voices magically deliver to Ed the smells of hay and horse manure. How can sound recall smells? he wonders.

Questions such as these can make a fella weary, as can questions of any other sort—the best way to handle his slacker employees, whether or not to mention his impotence to doc, how he can afford to reshingle his house? So, Ed sits on the bench under the white oak. A dove carelessly struts within a few feet, doing its neck-walk and bug-eyeing Ed.

If I lift my arm to scratch my forehead, he'll take it as a threat, Ed thinks. So, he ignores his itching forehead and allows a mosquito to drink its fill. He wishes he were Francis of Assisi, his heart able to communicate across species lines. I'm really one of you, he sincerely believes, although, at dinner, he'll eat the ham.

Touch me, please. You won't regret it.

But the dove's nerves are shot from spending time near Ed. Seconds after the mosquito leaves, the dove takes off. To tell its family of its harrowing adventure?

Ed wishes he could escape as gracefully. Especially when it turns out Parisi's been watching from across the street. The old guy ambles across Ed's lawn and says, "Hey, Doctor Doolittle! What's d'word from d'world of birds? J'see d'Open on teevee t'day? Man! Dat Lewison kin really putt!"

And that is the intro to a half-hour lecture on golf, the weather and why Fords are better than Chevvies—each a rehash of Parisi's last visit. It is all Ed can do to politely keep his eyes open.

"Say, I see yer gutters are saggin' over dere. Y'know what you shut do about dat?"

"Mm-hmm. Mm-hmm. Mm-hmm," Ed says, like a lumpen hummingbird deprived of nectar. Eventually, the tomcat goes away, and Ed exhales and returns to reverie.

* * *

Now about robins—not Ed's favorite. He wonders what Darwin would say of the value of mother robins' feisty protection of their hidden nests. Seldom would Ed know where their eggs were hidden if the mothers didn't dart out to warn him away, but their angry squawking makes it clear. You'd think noisy robins would be extinct, thinks Ed in a vaguely critical way. But there must be an evolutionary advantage to making noise.

Also of questionable evolutionary value is the robins' instinct for choosing nesting sites. Year after year for the past five years, a robin has nested in the rafters of the garage. With every arrival or departure of a car, with every tool hunt or stowage of junk, the mother robin would go berserk, tearing out the open door or, if the door were closed, battering herself against walls and windows in the garage prison. If she were out when the door closed for the night, eggs would remain uncovered through eight cold hours. This would happen often enough that, eventually, their potential for becoming robins would be exhausted and mom would abandon. Come July, Ed would climb a ladder and remove the nest and its lifeless contents. But the following year, there'd be another nest in the exact location.

Old *Turdus migratorius*, he thinks. In Latin, the robin's real name. In English, his nickname for Harvey at the plant.

He also sees a parallel between Harvey and woodpeckers. Both hammer their hollow heads against the realities of their worlds attempting to get the bugs out.

* * *

The ham is served with potatoes au gratin and mushroom green beans on paper plates. Paper plates on TV trays. On TV, contestants beg for "big money" as they guess missing letters to fill in puzzles. Ed sits in the same room in which this happens and forks up the meal as he stares at the wall. On the wall is a print of Yosemite.

He's seen a photo of a western bird called a green jay. He muses that, in the Midwest, blue is taken for granted. Both birds are beautiful, he thinks, but whichever bird is missing from a local landscape will always be considered exotic. The jay is always greener on the other side. Or bluer, as the case may be.

"A penny saved is a penny earned," says his mother-in-law.

"Huh?" says Ed.

"A penny saved is a penny earned. I think these contestants must be kinda stupid."

"Yes," says Ed. "I think they are."

* * *

After dinner for about two hours, grackles by the hundreds gather in the giant silver maple, making so much noise that one can't hear the television if the windows are open. Why, wonders Ed, in just that tree? And what's the purpose of their nightly meeting?

They remind him of the city's aldermen, squabbling unto eternity in unchanging syllables, sound on sound to which no one listens. Conditions in the tree change not a bit from night to night or summer to summer, so the point of the noise must be the noise itself—an endless campaign for re-election. Oh, you can throw a handful of gravel to scare 'em off, as Ed used to do. But they come right back to continue the debate. They may be different grackles, but they make the same noise. So what's the point of gravel?

* * *

Far beyond the range of any thrown gravel are the migrating ducks. Not that Ed would ever consider disturbing their travel in any way.

Ducks aren't exactly birds, Ed thinks, not being a hunter and not living near wetlands. Ed lives in the flight path, but ducks rarely land in his yard, so all his observation is of the sky. He appreciates the code their vectors contain, but he cannot crack duckspeak any more than he can the vocabulary of sparrows.

He watches as the leader of an overhead vee drops back to let another duck take the lead. He has read that the changes of position allow lead ducks to rest, as air resistance is greatest at the point of the vee. He wishes that changes of this sort were available to him. Although the leadership he provides is rarely noted by his fellow men or women, he feels the fatigue of struggle and would like to drop back a spell.

He also envies the act of migration that geese dramatize more than smaller birds, which just become absent without saying good-bye. Geese seem to laugh at Ed's stationary state. Be that as it may, their clowny sounds give him the same restless feeling that nocturnal train whistles always do—the strong sense of places over the horizon. In the case of train whistles, the sense of steel or yogurt or giant rolls of paper in boxcars, with people waiting at the other end. In the case of ducks, awaited by marshy subtropical hideaways cloistered by cattails, borders blurred in kudzu. The additional sense that, if something were different, it would be possible for Ed to go to those places.

* * *

But best of all are crows.

On Sunday morning, Ed drives to the grocery to buy a newspaper, more or less brainless as he winds through the side streets. Coffee will come later. Later, a shave. But suddenly, he's awake. In the middle of the street, two sleek crows are pecking at the squirrel guts that God has provided.

Ed, unlike most drivers who wind down these lanes, stops the car and ponders. The muscular birds arch and strut around their breakfast. They stand their ground and their purpose remains fixed. They pause and arrogantly look up at Ed.

Yes? they wonder. What now?

Yes? wonders Ed. He feels their intelligence testing his own.

In the distance, more crows are insisting on something. First a few of them, then several dozen. Suddenly, the air is black with a hundred crows, and everyone but Ed is a lord of creation. There are boasts and threats and calls to action for distant work that demands each one's attention. But there's disagreement about what must be done. Feathered shoulders gesticulate and dangerous pointed faces aim in all directions. Before two diners join the fray, they cast wise gazes at the man in the car.

You will not remember any of this, they direct him. Or, if you do, no one will believe you or understand.

Ed knows this to be true.

The hypnotists take the sky and circle like frenzied witches, gleaming like oiled knife points. For ten minutes, in ever-widening circles, they continue their war dance, cawing, cawing over what now must be a five-mile tract, though the sound of their cries does not diminish.

When the flock finally disperses and the neighborhood is quiet, Ed does not immediately start the car. He sits at the side of Pleasant Drive listening to his own heart pound. His species perseveres, and while it does, he hangs on at its periphery, but, at times, the constant pounding is unbearable. No end in sight.

* * *

But the same, long ago, might have been said of the era of dinosaurs. Until the comet or meteorite, glacier or whatever, nothing changed. Lizards—fingerlings and behemoths persisted, seemingly forever, fitting into their tropical puzzle as best they could. Eating, being eaten . . .

That has all finished. The only survivors are the birds. And, until the next cataclysm, the only evidence of Ed will be that inaudible throb.

Protagonist

Our ritual went back a few years. After work on Fridays, five of us would gather for drinks and sometimes dinner at The Dial—Howard, Lillian, Renata, Frank and me. Everyone in the design department but Phil, who, as a newlywed, had more interesting things to do. Before his marriage, our group, with three men and three women, could have been mistaken for three couples but, by subtracting Phil, that illusion was history. Even before that, there'd been no actual *couples* among us, as any eavesdropper could have guessed from our gab. Nothing romantic, just art talk and discussion of our clients' reasonable or unreasonable requests and demands. Work talk.

Those were the kettles that were merrily boiling last Friday when our routine was interrupted by a stranger who approached our booth. He cut quite a figure—a fashion-model-handsome man in his early thirties (a few years older than anyone in our group), athletic build, a beautiful head of hair, a Caribbean tan and tastefully dressed in clothing none of us could afford. Sort of a JFK Junior. His gaze was fixed on Renata, obviously enough that she squirmed and blushed.

"Do I know you?" she asked.

"I *wish*," he said, smiling. "No, we've never met. I apologize for intruding, but I've been watching you from the next booth for half an hour. You're one of the most beautiful women I've ever seen."

We all looked at Renata to see if we could see her through the stranger's lenses. I mean, she's kind of cute, I guess, but we'd never imagined her as a goddess who could cause men's hats to fly off and make them swallow their gum.

Renata's blush deepened.

"I mean it. Your hair, your cheekbones, your smile . . . You're gorgeous!"

Embarrassment aside, Renata was flattered, of course. Most of us are fairly aware of how we look. At some level, we know if we're misshapen or swarthy, bucktoothed or bowlegged or if we're capable of inspiring the opposite sex's dreams. An irresistible eye magnet. Renata knew she's what most people would call "average."

She began to thank the stranger, but he wasn't done talking.

"Except for your nose. But I can help you. Rhinoplasty isn't a complicated operation and I can offer you an attractive price." He handed Renata a business card.

I gasped. Lillian's eyebrows disappeared into her hairline. Howard's jaw dropped and Frank slid out of the booth, stood and punched the plastic surgeon in the gut. It was quick and, except for an "OOOF," quiet.

Frank didn't wait for a second opinion. His fist remained ready to deliver another etiquette lesson. "The next nose that'll need fixing will be yours, mister. Get the hell out of here and never come back!"

While the doc made his speedy exit, we began trying to console and reassure Renata. Not an easy thing to do without making reference to her nose. We explained that there'd been nothing personal in what Doctor Whozis had said. He was just a tasteless desperado trying to drum up business.

"If he's as lousy a plastic surgeon as he is a self-promoter, he probably turns out nothing but Frankensteins," Lillian said. "What a jerk!"

* * *

Back in my study, I knew how I intended the story to proceed, but I left off there. I had to go to the bathroom. When I'd taken care of that, I was distracted by a phone call. Then I decided to have breakfast, and by the time I finished eating, it was eight o'clock. I cleaned up the dishes and dressed for work. So that was all I wrote this morning. I'll get back to it tonight. No chance it'll fade from my memory.

I'm often asked where I get ideas for my stories. I have various answers, but rarely do I confess that most of them are somewhat autobiographical. Not that they're nonfiction. I'm good at disguising the embarrassing or shameful events with imaginative fictions. In what I wrote this morning, for instance, The Dial isn't The Dial. There *is* no Dial where five fictional characters gather after work on Fridays. Nobody I know works in a design department. Frank isn't Frank, Lillian isn't Lillian, Howard isn't exactly *that* Howard and the me in the story isn't me.

I am Renata, nose and all. The only indisputable truth in the story so far is the incident itself. It happened just like that.

But be assured, I don't think any less of my nose than I did before I was offered the nose job. It's not the most beautiful nose in the world, but 'twill suffice. It's good at sticking into other people's business, good at sniffing out the secret stories that people tend to conceal, and it doesn't get bent out of shape when people insult it. On those occasions, I retreat into fictional alter-egos.

* * *

The alter-egos of the other characters in my fictions are, in their way, as real as I am. They become my friends and I sympathize with them as they confront the difficulties they face, some of which are real, others I've invented. For instance, Howard in the preceding wasn't with our design department for long after my encounter with the plastic surgeon. Our agency lost several important clients and announced that, unless we picked up some substantial new business, they'd have to trim staff. Howard guessed accurately that he'd be one of the first to go. He began actively searching for new employment.

He's young (twenty-eight), has an admirable academic record (an MA in commercial art) and, while at Timmerman, he'd put together an extensive, varied portfolio that, despite some in-house detractors, would wow most pros viewing it for the first time. In short order, those credits got his foot in some impressive doors. Before Timmerman could fire him, the door swung open at Bairsford, Montpelier & Osborn.

On his last day with us, Howard showed up wearing a beret and a florid cravat, meant as signals to those of us he'd be leaving behind that the Philistines at Timmerman hadn't appreciated the artiste in their midst. He was riding high.

His first day at BM&O, though, gave him an early taste of the reality he'd stepped into. While settling into his new desk, he discovered a waxy Q-tip in the middle drawer. The first ugh of many.

His new coworkers treated him as untested metal, as they did all newcomers until they'd been lead on a project. The senior artists regarded drafting supplies, brushes, French curves and other necessities of life as their private possessions. They'd refuse to loan them out or loan them out so grudgingly that, if you were granted a piece of chalk or a pencil, you'd be given the knowledge that you now owed your benefactor big time.

And they were brainless. At Timmerman, Howard had been surrounded by his intellectual peers. At BM&O, most of the artists were young, ranging between nineteen and twenty-four, and they weren't interested in anything they couldn't play on a computer screen. So, one day, Howard was surprised to hear two of his coworkers discussing Michelangelo. One of them asked another, "What was Michelangelo's first name?"

Howard volunteered the answer: "It was Michelangelo. His last name was DiLodovico Buonarroti Simoni," he told them. "You can call him Mike."

He expected their response to be something along the lines of, "Thanks! I never heard that before," or, "Wow! You had that on the tip of your tongue."

But no. The artist who had asked the question was nonplussed. "How do you *KNOW* these things?" she asked. As if no one but a wizard could possibly divine such unobtainable secrets. Howard rolled his eyes and decided that the next time anything similar came up, he'd keep his magic powers to himself.

"Last month," Howard told me, "I thought things were looking up. One of the account reps, Pete Tracas, took me along with him on a trip to New Orleans. His client wanted someone to do a few dozen drawings of some local architecture. There really wasn't any reason I couldn't have worked from photographs, but—what the hell—BM&O isn't shy about racking up billable hours. Great, I thought. And the work was fun. Each of the buildings was fascinating, and the client had allowed me my head as far as what approach to take with each of them. I was proud of the work I did.

"But between work hours, Pete and I did some sightseeing. On Bourbon Street we wound up in front of a jazz club named Jelly Roll's.

"*Jelly Roll's!*' Pete exclaimed. '*The* Jelly Roll's! I can't believe it—*me,* standing right in front of the actual Jelly Roll's!' He went on and on. I said to myself, 'This fool thinks that Jelly Roll Morton is somehow associated with this club. Maybe Jelly Roll himself is inside tonight. Maybe we should hop in and get an autograph.' Pete's phoniness made me want to puke.

"All that idiocy was bad enough, but the next morning, back at the client's office, Pete sought glory by recounting the miracle. He bragged to the client, 'There we were, right in front of the actual Jelly Bean's! I couldn't believe it—Jelly Bean's! *Me,* right in front of Jelly Bean's! Now I've really been to New Orleans!'

"Mercifully, that was the end of Pete's routine. I could see by the quizzical look in our host's eyes that he was wondering if there might be a N'awlins club mistakenly named Jelly Bean's or whether Pete was misguided, perhaps drunk enough to have misread the sign. Maybe Pete was just indulging in a strange joke. I, of course, knew it was just stupid Pete, striving after glory by claiming to be a cosmopolitan and a jazz aficionado.

"I imagined him saying something even worse, like, 'I like all the jelly beans except the black ones.' I stood on the far side of the room, pretending to examine some layouts and hoping my position signaled 'I'm not with him.'

"You know me," Howard said to me. "That kind of evidence of brainlessness always brings me down. I can't seem to ignore it. And it's everywhere I turn these days."

"You've gotta develop an ability to see the other side," I said. "The world is full of stupidity, but it's full of genius, too. It's full of ugliness, but it's full of beauty, too."

"I know you're right, babe, but I fear the dark side puts the bright side in jeopardy. It seems to me that darkness is proliferating. It's crowding out the light."

"Pessimists have felt that way for centuries. I don't know if it'll cheer you up, but I assure you, the balance never changes. Light and dark are *constant* because humans cause both of 'em. Neither the geniuses nor the idiots are winning the battle. Unfortunately, human nature doesn't change."

"Well, let me give you another example I witnessed the other day."

"Nope," I said. "I won't let you sink my boat. Let's go for a walk. It's a beautiful night regardless of what people think or what they do."

* * *

That much of the story jumped onto the page in a flash, mainly because, in that writing, I'm both Howard and myself. Similar arguments with my selves go on all the time. But what I'd written to that point completed that story. There's nothing more to tell. Those two pages express my mixed feelings perfectly. I wish I could put an end to the Howard in my head as easily as I can dump pages in a file labeled "Fragments" and turn the computer off. I took my own advice and went for a walk. When I got home, I felt better.

I changed into a bathrobe and slippers, made myself a cup of tea and sank into the recliner. No idiots there, and my more positive mindset took over.

As a writer, I guess I should be grateful for the stupidity in the world. Without it, fiction wouldn't be able to muster crises, the armatures of our literary sculptures. What an idea! A world without conflict, a world without opposition, a world with nothing but smooth sailing and smiling faces. A world without fiction, I guess.

Later, in bed, I pondered such a world as a way to put myself to sleep. Ten minutes in that crisis-free world were enough to drain my tensions and relinquish me to the agents of Morpheus. I guess that might be considered a mini-resolution to the crises of my waking life.

But I dreamt. Rarely do I remember dreams, sorry to say. The few I *do* remember, are usually useless as material for my writing. They're too disorganized and surreal, and when I dip into the dada world, the result is rubbish. When I try to clean it up by putting it in order or injecting logic, it loses any substance the gibberish may have had. I'm aware that it's usually a drag to suffer someone reporting his or her dreams, so I'll keep this brief and refrain from attempting any analysis.

In last night's dream, a civilization of timid beings, thin, pale and silent were immobilized by an unspecified fear. No dictators, monsters, plagues or impending cosmic doom. Just a population of static beings feeling nothing, staring at nothing, expecting nothing, barely existing, and no one stepped forward to distinguish himself or herself as a character. White noise was the only sound.

At the beginning of the dream, those faceless vacuums inhabited a landscape comprising rivers, lakes, mountains, deserts, jungles— all the physical forms and climates that exist in our waking world. In the dream, though, everything was present in a single location.

The only *event* in the dream was that the landscape changed and, protruding from the sky, extending to the horizons, a device resembling an enormous paint roller slowly moved to the foreground, obliterating rivers, lakes, mountains, deserts, etcetera, leaving nothing but flat, featureless nothing. The people, however, remained. They watched the roller wipe out their world without reacting in any way. They'd felt nothing about that world; why feel anything about its loss?

That's it. All I remember, though it seemed to go on forever.

It didn't wake me, but when I was conscious again, the illogic of the dream raised the barometric pressure in my head. Not pleasant. The dream made as little sense as life itself.

In my writing, I try to bring order and purpose to the haystack of our lives without skimping on their unpredictability. I attempt to clean up the messes of characters' lives and reveal the heroism or villainy that's imperceptible to the characters themselves. I want readers to understand the morals of my stories and see the relevance of those lessons to their own lives. I want them to come closer to resolutions to their problems or explain why none exist.

Rarely can I achieve those goals. Too often, my characters aren't believable and, if my plots aren't forced, they're just as indecipherable as life. Like the dream.

So, I watched about fifteen minutes of TV news, unsuccessfully seeking contrast to the dream world. But there again, gibberish. After breakfast, I dressed for work and put on makeup, being careful not to get any lipstick on my nose (ha ha).

* * *

On the El, I rode for half a dozen stops in my usual early-morning fog of brainlessness but, when we got to Kedzie, one passenger who got on was dressed like Abraham Lincoln, complete with familiar hat and beard. He steadied himself by clutching a pole and seemed to be lost in thought.

And so was I. Why is he dressed like that? I wondered. Is he an actor prepared to portray the ex-president in a play? Is he a lunatic who imagines he *is* the ex-president? Where is he going? What will the rest of his day be like? Why wouldn't Lincoln take a cab? Why aren't the other passengers asking him for his autograph? If he has pennies in his pocket, what does he think about his portrait?

During my workday, my coworkers probably thought my mind was on company business, but my head was full of Abe, and my mental sky was full of trial balloons.

The Dark Side of the Sun

It was 1954 in the suburbs. My Dad was in his forties, Mom in her thirties, furniture was blond and Ike was on the green. The boys were home from the war they'd won and none of the twenty or so who'd served with Dad had come home in a box. I was told there were unhappy people elsewhere in the world, but I was only ten, and distant sadsacks had no effect on me. I hadn't yet become one to question apparent realities.

Even the unpleasantness reported in the fictions I read was distant and, usually, defeated in the end. There were no unmown lawns or unwashed cars in our neighborhood. Adults were as presentable as their properties, and their children were never more than normally naughty. Weathermen could confidently predict eternal sunshine and you could hear a pin drop, though none ever did.

Looking at our world from above (there *was* a God with a capital G above us then), we were as dependable as bacon and eggs before the country was warned off cholesterol and animal fat. Our north-south streets were counted by their numbers, the east-west ones were named in alphabetic order and they were all laid out in regular rectangles so no stranger could get lost in the neighborhood. Dads always found their ways home after work. As Tolstoy said, the happy families resembled each other. That was true of my immediate neighbors, but resemblance isn't congruence. There are no identical snowflakes.

Back on the ground, in any snow that fell, the prints of our many boots hinted at our differences. There were, in fact, no twins. Even left and right feet left distinctive marks. My happiness is *not*

18

the same as yours. And some apparent happiness is an illusion. Tolstoy didn't look closely enough.

How did men of the fifties differ from each other? I'll begin with the man who lived in my own home.

Dad stood apart from the macho standards that governed many men of that era. For instance, he ceded to Mom the role of the household boss. "She's smarter than I am," was his belief. Although true in many respects, he was unnecessarily modest. Other virtues compensate for whatever so-called smartness any of us may lack.

For more than thirty years, Dad managed the local branch of a chain of loan companies. Even in the fifties, few employees remained loyal to a single owner over such a span, and few owners treated employees well enough to *deserve* such loyalty. One transaction between Dad and his boss exemplifies their relationship.

When I entered high school, Dad approached his boss with a request: "My son's going to be going to college soon and I'm going to need a raise." The boss said, "Not now. When the time comes, I'll take care of it." These days, that promise would be heard as a no. But Dad trusted his boss and, it turned out, that trust wasn't misplaced. When the time came, so did the necessary, well-deserved raise.

Now, the loan business has the reputation of being a miserly, squeeze-blood business, often thought of as litigious, property-repossessing operations run by Mr. Potter or Mr. Scrooge. In Dad's hands it wasn't. He viewed his customers as honorable people who temporarily found themselves in need. No shame involved. He was willing to help them negotiate the terms of loans they'd be able to pay back and trusted them to do so. Very few betrayed his trust. Customers were grateful for his help and, if they needed a subsequent loan, there was no question of who they'd go to. It was simply a case of neighbor helping neighbor. Repeat business was good.

Although he took the loan business seriously, Dad's real focus was his family, above even any consideration of himself. He would take food off his plate and give it to his wife or children. He would forego any recreations, hobbies, friendships or interests that would distract him from home repair, his kids' educations, the family's health, their financial security, holiday celebrations or any other components of family happiness.

You could say that his belief in God was shallow. It was based on the fact that my mother believed, and he believed in her. Most Christians believe we rely on Jesus to intercede for man in their dealings with God. Catholics, I'm told, rely on Mary to intercede for them in dealing with Jesus. Dad carried those bank-shots a step farther. He relied on Mom to intercede for him in dealing with whatever supernatural beings there might be and whatever life might come after death.

His interactions with the men of the neighborhood were friendly but limited. He was closer to his ex-military cronies, church members and husbands of his wife's friends—friends the ladies acquired while their men were in the service. He belonged to the VFW and Kiwanis Club and, once a month, he and Mom donned western outfits and went square dancing. Every other year or so, the whole family would take out-of-state car trips. Monday nights, he bowled in a league—the only recreation that was exclusively for him.

During the fifties, Mom didn't have a job outside of the house, but she was the family's social connection—active in the church and the PTA, often serving as "room mother" to my sister's and my grade school classes and she stayed in constant contact with neighbors and our extended family (two aunts, two uncles, four cousins and four grandparents).

She was also an imaginative designer of Halloween costumes, birthday cakes and present-wrappings. Her creations should have been photographed and included in a coffee table book. That didn't happen, but they've certainly been immortalized in my memory.

Before I turn my attention to the neighbors, let me apologize for the lack of detail in and possible inaccuracy of what follows. Ten-year-old kids aren't privy to actions, conversations or emotions that comprise life behind nearby doors. For that matter, even my descriptions of my own family's realities should be recognized as nothing more than a kid's imperfect guesses seen through the admittedly warped lens of long-ago childhood. That's no better than asking a cow to psychoanalyze a farmer. Cows may recognize their farmer's hat but they don't suspect that he eats beef.

Our neighbor to the south, Don Simmons, was ten years younger than Dad. The two of them were cordial, but not close friends. The close friendship of his wife, Betsy, and my Mom was their primary connection. As both women were stay-at-home housewives, they had a lot more contact than their husbands had with each other. More about that later. For now, Don.

Don had a good blue-collar job with the railroad. "Blue-collar" is the relevant part of that description. Differences in collar colors somewhat limit connections between neighbors. In our neighborhood, that was more relevant than income levels. No one felt superior or inferior to anyone else. No one even *talked about* money, perhaps because everyone was more or less equal, at least to our knowledge. Everyone was chipping away at a mortgage, no one took extravagant vacations or looked forward to an early retirement, no one owned yachts or airplanes and no one wondered where their next meal was coming from or how they'd heat their houses next winter.

Still, the world of paper-shuffling office workers is distinct from the world of physical laborers, leaving little to talk about unless two guys are both stamp collectors, tropical fish afishianados, golfers or poker players. Don and my Dad didn't share any hobbies. They might borrow tools from each other or commiserate with each other about cleaning gutters. Other than that, proximity gave rise to not much beyond, "Hi. Howzit goin'?" If one of them bought a new car, his neighbor would come over to inspect or admire the vehicle and offer congratulations, but the purchase didn't give rise to envy or gnawing aspiration. My own family's cars were all owned by my Dad's company, allowed for our personal use as well as business. They were replaced every other year, so new cars weren't a big deal to us.

The Simmons were Catholic, my Mom and Dad were Lutherans. Both families were devout, but not so devout that theological differences caused any rifts between them. They were what they were because their parents had been; their children would follow in the same footsteps because, what other choices *were* there? In our town, there were a few (reform) Jews, but they were generally accepted as similar *enough*—as if they were an offbeat breed of Christians. Probably, there was a handful of atheists, too, but they didn't publicize their lack of faith. Non-belief doesn't leave much to talk about.

Religion often brings out the worst in people. Sikhs vs Shias, Irish Catholics vs Protestants, Jews vs Arabs, Hindus vs Buddhists. My god is better than your god, and he's telling me to burn down your place of worship and spit on your holy books. Our neighborhood's believers didn't believe in any of that. The core of all their faiths as practiced was loosely based on "bein' good"—their imperfect memories of the ten commandments and seven deadly sins. They might take the name(s) of their god(s) in vain, they might covet their neighbors' oxen, they might indulge in gluttony or sloth, but they generally agreed about keeping at least one foot on the path of righteousness, and nobody felt the need to debate their understandings of what that meant.

That's a big deal. It puts duct tape on whatever fractures might exist among neighbors. Surrounded by that tacit consensus, even atheists could sing in that choir.

Politics was another field on which neighbors agreed not to play, possibly because everyone recognized it as a potential disrupter of the peace. So secret ballots remained secret. The only meaningful politics was local, and it differed from other politics in that it was face-to-face. The neighbors knew by name the mayor, the police and everyone else with a hand on the levers of power. If something wasn't functioning properly, one could poke the boss in the coat and tell him about it.

"Hey, Al. This isn't working. *Fix* it."

"I'll see what I can do about it."

In the privacy of our home, though, we knew that *national* politics could rile my Dad. His primary nemesis was Harry Truman. It had nothing to do with Harry having dropped the bombs. Truman's sin was that he'd fired MacArthur. Whatever Don or any of the other neighbors felt about Truman, MacArthur, Hiroshima or Washington, DC wasn't public knowledge. Maybe none of them felt *anything*, but Dad would never forgive Harry.

I'll get back to sketching other households shortly, but before I do, I'll credit another positive force in the neighborhood. It was the women—housewives all back then. Their husbands were, for the most part, absent by day, off minding the store, the factory floor or some other sort of workplace. It was the housewives who wove the fabric of the community, and they wove it tightly. Drop-ins at each other's homes might have seemed casual but, just as water cooler chit chat bonds many companies' workers, the ladies' gatherings provided more than opportunities to drink coffee. In sharing recipes and gossip, they were revealing their commonalities—assuring each other that, whatever differences there may have been among them, they were the same in ways that counted. They were all women who lived in similar homes, had similar opinions, similar duties... There wasn't a yeti, a Martian, a concubine or a communist among them. They formed a quilt of compatible patches.

Another big deal.

Mom's best buddy was her next-door neighbor, Betsy Simmons. They were close enough that their children were allowed to call the adults by their first names—an informality rarely acceptable.

Betsy was ten years younger than Mom with a two-year-old son and an infant daughter. She often sought child-rearing advice from her more experienced neighbor. The two shared an interest in raising African violets. Their south-facing kitchen window sills were mini-greenhouses. And they frequently swapped recipes, so it's likely the Simmons family had the same dinners we did on many nights.

Despite the similarity of the families I've sketched so far and the placid seas on which they sailed, the women weren't reincarnations of the Stepford wives. There was plenty of Brownian movement in our pond. For instance, across the street from Betsy and Mom lived Marilee and her husband, both only a few years out of high school, childless and not yet fully domesticated. The appeal of movies, dancehalls, nightclubs and bars hadn't dimmed since their single days, so their nights "out on the town" were frequent.

Marilee's reports of those nights entertained Betsy and Mom. They regarded her adventures with amusement, not disapproval. Marilee was a funny reminder of their own pasts. When we look back on our youthful follies, hopefully we do so with a sense of humor and a fair amount of self-forgiveness.

The two Moms loved Marilee like a daughter who might occasionally require guidance from the wisdom they'd gained by maturity. But who doesn't admire the exuberance of wild horses running free and feel refreshed vicariously by the wind in their hair?

The house to the north of ours was owned by a university and was the short-term home of a series of professors and their families. None of them stayed more than a few years before moving on. It's probably unnecessary to say that none of the academic residents resembled the wild pony across the street.

The neighbors who lived there at the time of this story were Lydia and Professor (his title took the place of his name) Janus. They were quiet and polite but rarely participated in neighborhood doings. The prof and my Dad would occasionally talk over the fence, but Dad viewed everything the prof said as suspect. Intellectuals, he thought, lived in a world so different from ours that their version of reality was foreign, impractical, irrelevant and often loony. This, despite the fact that Dad also vigorously advocated maximum education for me and my younger sister. Where the boundary between *enough* education and *too much* education lay was never clear. He was proud of the fact that my sister and I were avid readers, but his own reading was generally limited to one book a year. Zane Gray was one of his favorites.

My view of the Prof was antithetical to Dad's. I had no idea of what his job was, whether or not he had a PhD, or whether his university was highly regarded or not, but, in my mind, professors outranked politicians, the clergy, the police or mere businessmen. Dad's attitude about the value of education *for me* was another one I didn't really share. I kind of knew I'd wind up in college, but I didn't strive toward that inevitability. I kept all my thoughts on the subject to myself. Schoolwork came easy to me, so it was as automatic as eating, sleeping or going to the bathroom. But, whatever my friends were up to was more important.

Closely related to attitudes about education was my parents' approach to culture. Both of them wanted my sister and me to appreciate music (classical above the rest, though some popular music was acceptable), the plastic arts and drama. They took us to plays, art galleries and museums. Of these laudable pastimes, Mom listened to a lot of classical music on the radio, and, apparently, she'd been a member of a book of the month club before I was born. A good number of her purchases remained on our shelves. I even discovered a two-volume edition of *Remembrance of Things Past* that I'm positive she'd never cracked.

I've already described Dad's reading habits. He didn't have much interest in the other "highbrow" stuff either. Both Mom and Dad, though, accompanied Helen and me on our cultural outings.

When each of us was old enough, my sister and I began music lessons—elementary school band for me (French horn) and piano lessons taught by the Professor's wife, Lydia, for Helen. Both of us were enthusiastic students. My folks thought music (*classical* music) was "good for" us, but, aside from Mom's radio listening, they didn't consume much of it.

Speaking of music, a neighbor three doors to the north of us, Fritz Smollet, was a composer—not one of the professions elementary schoolers told us about when they discussed careers we might pursue in the future, so we thought of Fritz as being sort of an exotic. To top that off, he owned the only station wagon in the neighborhood—a '49 Buick. Better still, it was a "woody"—cool!

His two daughters, one my own age and the other two years older, were my best friends on the block. Movies were one of our favorite recreations. The theater was close enough to our homes that, in daylight, we could walk there. But, in those days, a day at the movies included two feature films, three cartoons, a newsreel, often a chapter of a serial and several previews of coming attractions. Even in summer, it was dark by the time the fun was done, so parents thought it best that the kids be driven home. Fritz was usually the chosen chauffer.

Next door to the movie house was a tavern, and, Fritz would pick us up and stop in for some conversation with friends and a quick one before going home—my introduction to cream soda and other features of that foreign atmosphere that I'd get to know so well in years to come. There wasn't a lot for kids to do there, but the place had a glorious Wurlitzer juke box. We spent the time there watching bubbles spiral around the electric candles while Perry Como, Patti Page, Teresa Brewer, Johnny Ray and their ilk entertained us.

Fritz wasn't there to get loaded, but he generally stayed long enough for us to get bored. Long enough for me to appreciate the unique tavern fragrance and the aura of adult friendship. And then home.

One more neighbor couple requires inspection—the Waymonts, Florence and Sam, an elderly pair who lived two doors south of us. In place of children, Florence had a dog, Buddy, who she treated like a child. She also treated the neighborhood children like nieces and nephews, remembering our birthdays and throwing us parties, handing out lavish trick or treat goodies at Halloween and occasionally taking us to a local amusement park. That was the good Florence.

Beware the other Florence. If one of the kids got on her bad side, the offender was blackballed, and a pariah was never sure how he or she had offended. At least *I* was surprised, mystified, hurt and, eventually, outraged when found myself outcast. There came a time when Florence threw a party for all the kids in the neighborhood *except me!* I wasn't forgotten, I'd been purposely *excluded.*

I talked to other kids who'd spent time on her shit list and they assured me that, just as mysteriously as they'd been booted out of the charmed circle, they were eventually invited back in. I didn't aspire to readmission. I didn't care to have further contact with *INJUSTICE* regardless of the goodies that came with it. I still gave Sam and even Buddy clean bills of health, but I permanently benched Florence. She don't like me, so I don't like her.

I was too young then to diagnose her motives for the on again / off again generosity but, by now, I've seen the same disease poison other behaviors. It's the lust for power, plain and simple. The aspiration to play God, the giver and taker of blessings and punishments, the unquestionable moral authority, the he or she who must be obeyed. As a kid and, even now, as an adult, that seems to me to be a worthless superpower. But one doesn't have to look far to find people eager to throw their hats in that ring.

One afternoon, I was cutting the grass, pushing the old hand mower that was the work-intensive standard in those days. I had about finished when Florence's husband, Sam, showed up.

"I brought you some scissors," he said.

"Scissors?"

"Yeah. You missed a few blades near the edge of the sidewalk. You can't do a good job with a mower."

This was a typical comment from Sam—not funny ha-ha, but odd. Intended as humor, but not quite there. I appreciated the effort. Funny was (and is) one of my core values, and Sam's sense of humor differed from that of the other adults in the neighborhood. It bespoke a world-view that wasn't dependent on so-called adult values. Dashes of surrealism, cynicism and sarcasm—components of my own mindset.

"Thanks," I said. "When I get done taking a little off the sides, I'll come over to give Buddy a trim."

"You can use the mower on him," Sam said.

Buddy was definitely *Florence's* dog. She knew it, Buddy knew it and Sam was well aware that Buddy outranked him in the family's pecking order. Sam didn't sit high on the neighborhood's totem pole either. His appearances in public were infrequent and brief. The neighbors regarded him as a pixilated character who might be conversing with a puka like Harvey the Rabbit. It was just that quality (and the fact that he seemed so separate from Florence) that I liked about him.

Another time he appeared, I asked him, "I've read that you don't care for green eggs and ham."

"That's only partly true. I'm actually kind of fond of green eggs. Eggs of *any* color. My favorites are the purple ones. It's the ham I refuse to eat.

"By the way, do you know how to make a British omelet?"

"No."

"You use only England's best eggs."

Always the unexpected from Sam. One more example. That same summer, my Dad was painting the exterior of our house. Sam stood nearby, watching Dad up on the ladder.

He said to me, "Y'know, I've painted every house on this block."

"Whatchya mean?" I asked.

"I have about two dozen canvases in my basement with paintings of all of them. Oil paintings, temperas, water colors—you name it."

As far as I was concerned, Sam, despite his somewhat gloomy demeanor, was one of the many pluses of the neighborhood. As I indicated at the beginning of this, we were the people Norman Rockwell imagined us to be.

I was about to glimpse the world as seen by Edvard Munch, George Grosz and Edward Gorey.

The afternoon of a Saturday in October, 1954, three police cars and an ambulance appeared in front of the Waymont house. They arrived with sirens wailing (a sound we were unaccustomed to) and stayed for more than an hour. Curious neighbors gathered to trade speculations. The consensus seemed to be that there'd been some sort of medical crisis. Florence? Sam? Nobody suspected Buddy. Then a wrapped body was loaded into the ambulance. The good news: Buddy was out of danger. The bad news was that it meant it must have been one of the humans on the stretcher. The identity of the victim was slow in coming. It was a week before Florence appeared.

The report she gave was gruesome. She and Sam had been sitting together in their living room the previous Saturday when, without warning, Sam took out a pistol and shot himself in the head, spraying blood and brains on the wall behind the couch. We could only imagine her reaction. Her description of it was devoid of detail or emotion, so we were left with only our imaginations of how *we* would have responded. And our imaginations of what had motivated Sam.

The idea of suicide is terrible enough, but the idea of Sam performing the act in front of his wife was worse. It suggested a desire to horrify his witness—an act of punishment almost equal to killing *her* as well as himself. What suffering had she inflicted on him that caused such vengeance? More than a few of us shuddered when we pondered that unanswerable question. Only veterans of the World War or Korea had had any contact with violence or hells of the human heart, and not even they expected a re-enactment in our sunny suburb.

As shocked as the adults were, the kids were even less prepared to comprehend violent death. Sure, we played guns, but when one of us got shot, the victim would immediately jump up and announce, "I'm a new man." In those happy days, the game could continue. Now we imagined a game that could end. We imagined Sam's brains splattered all over the living room most of us had partied in. Sam, whose face we knew, whose voice we'd heard. His death forced us to imagine the potential death of *other* familiar people.

Unable to think the unthinkable, we excluded thoughts of dead family members. Bad enough to imagine the sudden absence of friends and neighbors.

What none of us—adults or children—imagined was that the idyllic world of the fifties was equally perishable. Maybe it had all been a dream—a thin veneer laid over the rotten underlayment of our true natures. Once the memories of recent wars had faded into history, we were free to fray and fight again and, as Roman Emperor Claudius said, "Let all the worms that are in the wood come out."

Whatever the case, the adult consensus about the value of civility would dissipate; our shared beliefs in religion, politics, education and the military disappeared, and newly empowered young people discovered drugs, created rebellious art forms and dared sass their elders. Just because civilization occasionally seems to work doesn't mean it's a good thing. Let's try something else.

Sam may have had reasons for his action, Florence may have reasons for her unpleasantness, but the end of Eden wasn't all their fault. Collectively, we proceeded to evict ourselves.

Full Disclosure

This story is ninety-five percent true. As is the case in most fiction, names have been changed and some details have been altered to improve dramatic flow. Essentially, it's as true as history can be. However, some of Sam's statements are anachronisms. Dr. Seuss's *Green Eggs and Ham* wasn't published until six years after Sam's death. And Sam's joke about British omelets implies that the brand Egg-land's Best existed in 1954. It didn't. Unfortunately, I don't remember the jokes Sam actually told. As Rudy Giuliani (really) said, "Truth isn't true." The anachronisms I substituted are accurate approximations of Sam's offbeat originals.

While I'm assaulting literature's fourth wall, I may as well admit that the 1950s weren't as idyllic for minorities as they were for a ten-year-old white boy. No minorities lived in my hometown. Until, at the age of thirteen, when I became a jazz fan, my contact with them was limited to that I had with characters like Uncle Remus and Charlie Chan or, worse, Fu Manchu and Little Black Sambo. I was to go through a radical transition in years to come. But that's a story for another day.

Escape Velocity

I'd been teaching high school "English" (grammar or literature) courses for five years when the first of several novels on which I'd been working for that whole time was published. I was gratified by the attention publishers and, shortly afterward, critics paid to my debut. Even more gratifying was the attention the book-buying public paid it. I was becoming if not a household word, at least a financially comfortable entity.

I even grabbed the attention of my school's administrators—not the most attentive population.

I tend to think that it was the publicity surrounding the book more than any qualities of the book itself that led to their suggestion (more of a command) that I teach a course in creative writing.

I wasn't enthusiastic about the possibility. I'd never noticed that students had any interest in literature or in fine-tuning their linguistic skills. Nor had many of them been inspired to imitate the literary masters I'd put in their hands. Maybe those deficits were signs that I hadn't been an inspiring teacher, but, if that were the case, how would I fare as a creative writing teacher?

Besides that, I've always been skeptical about the teachability of writing. No one ever taught *me*. I simply imitated writers I admired and could recognize where my efforts were falling short. I'd fix what was broken and try again. That process, not how-to courses, is, as far as I know, what has fertilized all the writers who have ever bloomed.

So, initially, I deferred. Administration changed my mind by allowing me a month's sabbatical to go on a book promotion tour.

33

They also assured me I'd have complete freedom to devise the curriculum. Now all I had to do was concoct a curriculum I could believe in.

Early on, I discovered that my literary reputation meant nothing to the young. I was no J. K. Rowling, no Steven King, no Jeff Kinney, not even a Stan Lee. I was just another blowhard offering them the key to a door they'd never been curious about opening.

Oh, there were a few kids who, because they couldn't see themselves as rocket scientists, business executives, doctors or dentists, thought it might possible to become writers. Most ignored for the moment that, in order to be one, they'd have to write.

Most of those who'd enrolled in my class had done so merely to fulfill a year's worth of English elective that was required for graduation. Only a handful of them had aspirations of doing any writing. They'd always assumed that writers, even contemporary American writers, were men who were buried in England long ago. I blame that misperception on the curricula of generations of high school lit teachers whose assumptions were similar. Either that or they feared the controversies that might arise from forcing teenagers to mull on the difficulties of life in the twentieth century.

I have no such fear. I've dealt with those controversies every day of my life.

* * *

My first class attracted twenty aspiring writers—two freshmen, seventeen juniors and a senior. I'd had previous contact with only two of the juniors. The rest of them were encountering a stranger who'd be sitting in judgment over them for the next nine months, so they were edgy. As with big cats in circus cages, students experience elements of fear and hostility in not knowing what unnatural acts they'll be expected to perform or the temperament of their trainers. They'd much rather be on familiar turf, stalking antelopes or pizza or lazing in the sun.

I intended my introductory comments to allay their fears, but they had the opposite effect.

"You'll be doing most of the work for this course at home."

Groans.

"*You'll* write the tests, so there'll be no right or wrong answers. All tests will be open book tests—*your* open books. Books *you've* written. Your textbooks will be everything in the library and whatever's in your head."

Blank stares until one kid asks, "What do we have to write about?"

"You tell me. Write about everything you know, everything you don't know, everything you want to know and everything you can imagine."

Another kid asks the question that's been on all of their minds: "How will we be graded?"

"Let's hold off on that," I said. "We'll figure that out later."

A friend of mine, a teacher of poetry at a university, once told me, "Everyone writes poetry when they're young, but they don't have much life experience, and they assume that they're the first humans to have had such powerful experiences. Occasionally, a Rimbaud comes along, but little juvenile poetry is worth much. Then, usually in their twenties, the would-be poets stop writing.

"Late in life, when they lose a job, get a divorce, a spouse or a parent dies, their children leave home or life, for some reason, begins to seem meaningless, they get the urge to try again. Unfortunately, they haven't practiced. They lack the skills to play the game."

It made me recall my own early writing—a lot of overheated love poems to young ladies and some tormented complaints about how unfair life is, how underappreciated I was or the ignorance of people who didn't agree with me. I didn't quit, but I switched to prose. I plowed ahead, still lacking life experiences and writing skills but, fortunately, my sense of smell was keen enough to detect the stench of those early efforts.

Those memories granted me realistic expectations of the writing I was about to encounter.

* * *

Before our second meeting, I'd figured out an approximate method of grading. I'd judge each writing sample in four categories: Clarity, imagination, observation and substance, assigning percentages of excellence for each. No totaling, no averaging and no letter grades. The numbers would simply indicate strengths and weaknesses in four aspects of their writing. I ordered rubber stamps of the four categories.

When I announced the plan to the students, they were still mystified. They didn't yet understand the four categories. But they relaxed a bit. Their fears of the dreaded F had diminished.

It was time to get down to business.

"Today, class, I'd like each of you to describe the room we're in. There's no length requirement, but be as thorough as you can. Distinguish it from other classrooms with as much detail as possible. Writers must be observers. They must see things that others don't. Remember, one of the things I'll be considering will be your ability to observe."

Some students began writing immediately, perhaps imagining they'd impress me with their eagerness or industry. Frankly, I had higher hopes for the students whose compositions incubated for five minutes before their pens touched paper. I made a mental note of students who plunged and those who stuck their toes in the water. After all of them had been scratching away for forty-five minutes, I called time.

"Read what you've written. If you feel you've done your best, turn it in. If you think you can improve on it, take it home and fix it." Seventeen essays were passed to the front. Three went home. Three writers who know how it works, I thought. Those three became my night's homework.

Of the seventeen papers turned in immediately, five were worthless—written by students who were too lazy to even consider the assignment. Each of them had handed in a short paragraph that estimated the size and shape of the room (one of which called the room a square but estimated a length and a different width of the "square," making it a rectangle) and the color of the walls. Four of them didn't recognize the presence of furniture or students. No one noticed the clock, the window, the acoustical tiles of the ceiling or the recessed florescent lighting fixtures. They didn't notice *me*. Guess the percentages I gave them in the observation category.

In contrast to the lazy papers, Phillip Arliss, one of the freshmen, impressed me with a paper that included not only the basics, but description and number of desks in the room, the blackboard (green since the 1940s), the number and sexes of human presences, the lighting and temperature of the room, a brief description of the world visible through the window and even the *smell* of the room. He did it all on two pages within forty-five minutes and without revision!

Another paper that stood out was by Marlene Spellman, a junior who's the class beauty and the only writer who paid major attention to her fellow students. Specifically, to the thirteen males. "All of them are toads," she wrote—one of the few subjective assessments in any of the "descriptions." Surprisingly, none of the toads had described Marlene, but I'm sure they'd all noticed her up and down. I'd noticed her too, but my description would be inappropriate.

I had planned to read the class the most notable papers, but Marlene's would not be one of them. I have no desire to publicize a writer's prejudices or degrade her victims. I'm sure both she and the toads are well aware of their opponents' opinions, but it would serve no one's interests if I stoked intrapersonal antagonisms. Instead, I intended to speak to her privately to see if I could alert her to the possible repercussions.

I realized that I'd have to revise my rubber stamp to include a fifth evaluation. What to call it? Revelation? Personal content? Subjectives? No, not subjectives. Most of what we say is subjective. I wanted to credit content that lays bare something about the author—something the author is prone to withhold or disguise or has been unaware of before starting to write.

The next paper I read also seemed to require another category—humor. The best writing doesn't resist handing out a few laughs, even if the subject is death. The funny essay I received was by the other freshman, Al Zelinski, whose friends knew him as Zorro. Here's a sample of his offering:

"Twenty monkeys are confined in cramped wooden desks, awaiting the arrival of their new zookeeper. When he arrives, their chattering dies down and his own chatter begins. The monkeys strain to understand what he's saying, hoping they'll earn a few bananas, but nothing he says makes sense." Al filled two pages with the extended metaphor and slashed a Z as a signoff.

The rest of the papers were about what I'd expected—prosaic observations loaded with wrong-headed grammar and spelling worthy of a foreigner, neither of which was my primary concern. You'd be surprised to learn how many of our most revered writers never mastered those fine arts.

When next we met, I did read Phillip's piece to the other writers (not revealing who wrote it) and asked them to comment.

"I read you this one because it contains most detail. It gets the highest mark for observation. By the way, I'm going to refer to each of you as 'he.' No offense, ladies—the English language doesn't offer us a sex-neutral singular pronoun, and that politically correct clunker 'he or she' is cumbersome and ugly. We can discuss that problem some other time.

"So—back to my topic: The writer of the quoted example—he—is a thorough observer of this room. Take note of all the details he mentioned that you did not. Even so, he missed plenty, including some that you focused on. Now that you've heard an example of how to see, take another whack at doing a portrait of this room. Just shout out what you see. Anyone."

"Flies that are moving too fast to count." "A constant stream of air-conditioned air that's blowing right on my neck." "Somebody who's wearing too much perfume." "A wastebasket full of stuff left behind from the previous class." "A wad of gum stuck to the bottom of this desk." And more.

"Wonderful!" I said. "With your eyes and your brain open, it's amazing how full the world is. With that ammo, you can fill your writing with interesting detail. Thus armed, your next job is to decide what's relevant to your subject and what should wind up in the wastebasket. Don't get distracted by every molecule in the room."

Our time was about up, but I read a little of Zorro's funny essay to leave the kids with the idea that there are many ways to "describe."

They loved it, so I gave the author credit. I handed him a banana and slashed a Z at him with my finger.

"Of course!" one of the guys responded. "The monkey didn't have to sign his name to that. No one but Zorro would have dared."

"And now, may I have the 'homework' the rest of you assigned yourselves?" I said. "Even before reading it, I congratulate you for recognizing the complexity of the task. I look forward to your masterpieces."

I congratulated myself, too, on the day's success.

*   *   *

After school, I was in my office, reading papers by the two students (of the three) who'd taken writing home to improve it. I wished I'd asked them to keep their original versions so I could see whether or not they'd improved the writing or merely changed it. What I had in my hands wasn't any better than the papers that had been handed in right after class.

At some point, I looked up. There was a girl standing silently at the door.

"May I help you?"

"I don't want to bother you, Mr. Fleming," she said. "May I come in?"

"Sure. What can I do for you?

"My name is Toni Jensen. I'm in your creative writing class."

"Oh, yes. I noticed that you hadn't handed in your description of our classroom. Is that it?" I asked, indicating the papers she had tucked under her arm.

She was embarrassed. "No. I ... uh ... I'm still working on that.

I thought if I brought you these instead, I could get some extra time. I don't write very fast."

"What did you bring?

"They're two stories I wrote a few months ago."

"Did you write them for another course?

"No. I wrote them for myself. I wanted to see if you . . . uh . . . think they're any good."

"I like that you wrote them for yourself. You obviously have things you want to say."

"Uh huh." But, whatever she had to say, she wasn't saying it now. She stood, shifting her weight from foot to foot and smiling nervously.

"Well, I look forward to reading them. I'll be glad to tell you what's good or bad about them. Usually, there's some of each. And yes, I'll accept them in place of the assignment for now, but keep working on that and turn it in when you're ready."

"Okay, thank you. Sorry I bothered you, Mr. Fleming," she said, and, quickly, she left.

I immediately put aside what I'd been reading and picked up one of Toni's stories. It was a science fiction story—one of my least favorite genres, but I approached it with an open mind. Frankly, I couldn't make sense of it. The main character was a teenage girl named Noti who was living among aliens on another planet. Why she was there wasn't explained. Neither the aliens nor their world were described, possibly because both seemed to be in constant flux. Noti didn't communicate with the creatures, and she either didn't understand or couldn't hear their conversations. What did they look like? Sometimes they seemed to be the same size as our heroine, but sometimes they were only a few inches tall, and, at other times, they were invisible.

After reading three pages of the story, I started over to see if I'd missed any facts that might help me understand. There *were* no facts, and, as I read further, the contradictions, lacks of information and physical impossibilities proliferated.

I guessed that the aliens were either unaware or dismissive of Noti's presence. They weren't hostile to her. They simply lived their inexplicable lives without interacting with her. As a non-entity among them, Noti herself was rendered vague and floaty except that she was clearly unhappy, alone amid strangers she didn't understand.

I got through fifteen pages of the most undecipherable prose I've ever encountered. It was exhausting, so I took her second story home. It was remarkably similar to the first. Science fiction again, again a young female protagonist struggling but failing to prosper in an unfamiliar setting peopled by unpredictably supernatural creatures. It fell so short of being a coherent story that it was more like one of those dreams from which you awake dizzied by nonsense and non sequiturs. What could I possibly offer Toni that might help her improve the unimprovable?

* * *

For the next week, my comments were directed to the other students, but Toni's problems were never far from my mind. I hoped that she'd understand that the general principles I was discussing applied to her own writing. She never joined in discussions, so I couldn't tell whether she did or didn't. I plunged ahead, beginning with Toni's most serious problem: clarity.

"Regardless of what you want to say, it's meaningless if readers can't understand what they're reading. Now, *you* know what you're trying to say. That, in a way, is a problem. It's so clear to you that you assume your readers know it too. But they don't know *anything* unless it's on paper. They don't know your characters' names, their ages, their sexes, what they look like, what they think . . .

They don't know anything about your characters' friends, families, what if anything they do for a living, their health, the crises they're facing . . .

"Maybe some of that information isn't needed to clarify your story. If it isn't, leave it out. Too *much* information can confuse your readers as badly as too little. In the exercise we did on the first day, I asked you to describe this room and, on your first try, you didn't describe much. When I asked you to be more thorough, you included a *lot* more. Even the flies in the room. Were the flies important? There are flies in every classroom.

"If you're telling a story about an eight-year-old orphan, I can't tell you what is or isn't important to include. Is it important to name the orphan's teachers, relatives or friends? Is it important to tell what happened to the child's parents? Is it important to specify the child's hair color, shoe size or height? I don't know. If you spend any time talking about hair color that doesn't have any relevance to the story, it will confuse your readers. It'll lead them to expect an explanation of *why* that was included. Does the orphan grow up in a Democratic family? Who cares? Unless she later becomes a union organizer or a senator.

"Another important factor that affects clarity is the *order* in which you inform your readers of important information. Usually, it's crazy to mention the character's Democratic leanings before the orphan grows up. But not if the adult orphan's political life will be important to the story.

"Finally, even a single word, if it has two meanings, can destroy clarity. Look for words that mean only what you want to say—not the other."

Part way through this sermon, I had to ask myself if I was losing track of my own story. Was I overloading the message? Was I omitting important information? Was I preaching the sermon upside down or inside out? Time to shut up and hope for the best.

"Okay. Pencils ready? Or, I probably mean, pens? This time out, I want you to write, as clearly as you can, a story about *yourself*—a subject that you know too well, so be careful not to include useless trivia. If your brother, your grade point average, your love life or your health is important, include it. If not, don't. I warn you, this will be a tough assignment, so I won't expect you to turn it in until next week Monday, and I expect it to clarify whatever you want to show me."

* * *

Two days later, as I was leaving the classroom, heading back to my office, one of the girls followed me.

"Mr. Fleming," she said, "may I talk with you?"

"Sure. What can I do for you?"

"Well, it's not for me. Toni told me she gave you some of her stories. I'm kind of a friend of hers and I've read some of 'em. They're kind of strange. I think I can tell you a little about Toni that'll help you understand the stories."

"C'mon to my office," I said, anxious to receive any help she might give me. "Let's see, you're . . . ? I apologize. I haven't learned everyone's name yet."

"Sandra Frithjof. Which stories did Toni give you?"

"Did Toni ask you to talk with me about her stories? I feel funny about discussing her work without her permission."

"I don't really want to talk about her stories. I just want to tell you about Toni," Sandra said. "We're not exactly friends, but I'm probably the closest thing to a friend she's got. She's pretty lonely. We've known each other since seventh grade, and she trusts me enough to let me read her stories.

"Do the stories she gave you have a character named Noti?"

"One of them does."

"Does the other story have a girl with a funny name?"

"Yes."

"All her stories do. All of those characters are her. I'll bet both of the stories you read have a character whose names are spelled with the letters of her name. Either Toni or Jensen."

She was right. How could I have missed that?

"And I'll bet both characters are unhappy living in some kind of fantasy land."

"That's true."

"Well, Toni's unhappy. At home and at school. Her parents have an older daughter who's a real successful dentist. Rebecca's rich, she's beautiful and she's married, with a two-year-old son. Toni's parents give Rebecca all the attention and they're always asking Toni why she can't be more like her sister. I've been to her house and I've heard how they treat Toni."

"Why is she unhappy at school?"

"That's why I wanted to talk to you. Writing those stories is what she likes to do best, but nobody who's ever read them praises them. Nobody understands them. I don't either, but I know she's trying to imagine worlds that treat her better and she wants to get other students to recognize her skills as a writer. I just thought that, if I told you what she's trying to do, you might be able to show her how."

"Well, that's very kind of you, Sandra. I'll see what I can do."

"You probably can help. She really respects you."

After Sandra left my office, I sat in silence for half an hour feeling the weight of my newly assigned responsibility. What *could* I do? I didn't feel I could do much to minister to her special needs within the context of the group. But, even with individual attention, how might I be of service? I'm no psychologist. It seemed to be a story that might be beyond my ability to write.

* * *

In five assignments written during the first three weeks, the writing of many of the students was showing improvement. During that same period, Toni failed to turn in a single piece of in-class or take-home writing. I used that as a justification to ask her to meet with me after school.

"What's up, Toni? Are you writing? I haven't received any assignments in three weeks."

"Oh, I'm still working on several of them. I told you, I'm pretty slow. Did you like the stories I gave you?"

"I'll get to your stories in a minute, but first, I have to say that it's no shame to be a slow writer. I'm a pretty slow writer myself. Are you slow because you don't often sit down to the task, because you're being extremely careful about your choice of words or because you don't know what you want to say? Or for some other reason?

She thought for a minute. "I know what I want to say, but I can't seem to put it into words. I do spend a lot of time trying, though. I've finally finished your first assignment—the one where we were supposed to describe our classroom. Here it is."

"Good. I'll look at it tonight. But let's consider your stories this afternoon. You asked if I liked them. I give you points for imagination, but I have to say I didn't understand the stories. They inspire me to ask questions, but I can't find the answers. Let's look at the story called *A Strange Place*. I certainly agree that the setting of the story is strange, but *strange* is an empty description.

It doesn't say anything more than 'unfamiliar.' *How* is your setting strange? I suggest you change the title to give your readers a more specific sense of the place you're writing about.

"Your characters aren't described either. I don't have a clear picture of the creatures Noti sees. How big are they? What color are they? Do they resemble humans? What do they eat? What are their homes like? What special powers do they have? What do they care about?

"It might be a good idea to write little answers to questions like that—for yourself—before you begin work on the story. As in the description of our classroom, you should include as much detail as you can. When you include some of that information in the story, don't pack it all together in one place. That would make the story seem like an essay. Let the facts pop up slowly—as slowly as we unravel the mysteries in our own lives. And remember what I said in class: Don't tell us anything we don't need to know.

"That's plenty to think about for now. Let's meet again Wednesday after school. When we do, I want to see descriptions of the strangers. And I *do* want to see them by then. No excuses."

Toni left without saying anything but she seemed to understand my critique and accept it. We'll see, I thought.

* * *

Wednesday found Toni back in my office, descriptions in hand. In itself, a good sign.

"They're the same size as we are, but they can change. They can disappear when they want to and they can look right through you.

They speak a language that we can't understand, but they don't speak much. In most other ways, they're like us."

"Are they friendly? They seem to be mean."

"Well, they don't *hurt* Noti. They're not violent. But . . ."

"But what?"

"They aren't very friendly either. They act as if she isn't even there. Noti wants to help them. She knows things that they don't, but they don't pay any attention to her."

"Why did she go to their land and how did she get there?"

"I went because I was hoping to find people who would understand me and would be my friends. People who would think I have good things to contribute and are willing to listen to . . ."

"You mean *Noti* was hoping for those things, don't you?"

"Uh . . . yes."

"But let's be honest, Toni—the story's about you, isn't it?"

"Well, yes. In a way."

"Every story anyone writes is partly about the author. I don't know if you know it, but I've written a novel. Many people who've read it ask me if this character or that character in the book is me. I don't quite know how to answer that. In a way, *all* the characters are me, but, it's also true that *none* of the characters is me. If I were some of the characters in the novel, the school board would fire me. Parts of me are attributed to even those dangerous characters. In every character, there are parts of me combined with aspects of other people I've known. I try to see things through their eyes as best I can. That's where my observational powers, guesswork and imagination come in.

"In many ways, each of us is nothing more than just another human being. We're not the only brave individual, not the only coward, not the only genius or ignoramus, not the only Adonis or gargoyle. Revealing any of those aspects of ourselves isn't doing more than admitting membership in the human race. Hopefully, our writing will lead our honest readers to recognize the strengths and weaknesses in themselves.

"So is the main character in my novel *me*? Maybe it's your dad, who I've never met. Maybe he's your mother, who isn't even the same sex as the character. Maybe it's someone I knew in my youth. Maybe something about him reminds you of Mr. Abbott, who I hadn't met when I wrote the novel. I hope that makes you more comfortable with writing about yourself or about someone else you know. And include more detail. Feel free to disguise the detail, but don't leave it out."

I could see Toni's tension ease. She actually smiled for the first time since we'd been meeting.

"Thank you so much," she said. "You've given me a lot of ideas about how I can rewrite my story. In fact, how I can rewrite *all* my stories." She hurried out, forgetting to leave any of the new samples she may have brought.

* * *

I didn't expect to see any writing from Toni any time in the near future. To incorporate even half of what we'd discussed at our last meeting, she'd have to recast her whole story. If *I'd* had to make such drastic changes in one of the early drafts of my novel, it would have taken me a year. So I was astounded that, two weeks later, she handed me a stack of pages. I was even more astonished when I read them. The new manuscript bore no resemblance to the mess she'd originally titled *A Strange Place*. It had become an actual story titled *Escape Velocity*.

The heroine (it was now accurate to call her that), was now

named Sara Clausen. She had aged twenty years since *A Strange Place* had hit my desk, but she was recognizable as Noti, now Communication Officer Clausen, the only female member of a NASA crew heading for an unnamed exoplanet in the Andromeda galaxy. The fictional character had, in several senses, traveled light years.

Many other characters made their debuts in the newborn story. In the first version, they were merely the collective they. Now, individuals appeared among them: Spelios, an uncooperative alien whose views were the same as those of Sara's misogynist crewmates; Melmoth, a more open-minded alien who, unfortunately, was too low in the pecking order to affect his compatriots' behavior, and Dalmanios, the first alien to perceive Sara's potential to benefit the planet. All three individuals spoke a language that she, eventually, could understand and, with some difficulty, speak. Her speech was hindered by the marked differences between her vocal physiology and that of the aliens, both of which were nicely described.

The NASA crew and the aliens gradually came to respect Sara because both groups were forced to rely on her translations. Her linguistic skill even allowed her to befriend those aliens whose problems with their group resembled problems *she'd* had with her fellow humans. That shared experience granted her insights into both sets of interactions.

Most surprising to me was the fact that, among the NASA crew members, I detected aspects of Toni's classmates' personalities, indicating that she'd focused on humans other than herself. One of the men, despite his sex, was reminiscent of Marlene Spellman, our class beauty queen. Or was it, perhaps, Toni's sister Rebecca? It was a computer guidance specialist named Thor Nillson, whose primary attention was always on himself. Despite that, Toni gave the character credit for having valuable skills. She also saw the world through *his* eyes.

The revised story also modified Sara's (nee, Noti's) characterization of the Toni alter-ego. She understood the crew's treatment of her, admitted to her own flaws and worked to correct them. I know from personal experience that a writer can portray a healthy attitude in a character without immediately being able to make positive changes in his own life, but such changes sometimes ripen slowly. I had hopes that, sooner or later, Toni would recognize that Sara's attitudes were preferable to her own.

Escape Velocity exhibited so many of the qualities of good writing that I'd been trying to teach that I couldn't resist reading a large chunk of it to the class, allowing its author to remain anonymous. Not wishing to interrupt the story's dramatic flow or influence the class's reactions in any way, I read it without pedagogic interjections. It was apparent that Toni's creation was winning the class's involvement. Except for a few students who felt obligated to effect disdain (fearing that any appreciation of a rival's writing might put them at a disadvantage in the dreaded grading curve), most of them were silently attentive, caught up in the story. Toni herself was smiling. As she left the room, she waved at me and said, "Thank you."

* * *

The months of my first year as a creative writing teacher rolled by and, as they did, I changed my mind about the impossibility of the task. I was seeing marked improvements in the work my students were showing me. It was less self-centered, more observant of the diverse aspects of the world, more imaginative and much clearer than it had been at the beginning of the year. Bad grammar and spelling persisted, but, as I've said, those weren't high on my list of priorities.

My meetings with Toni continued too, and they were most gratifying. She ceased insisting on science fiction and fantasy once she recognized the fascinating variety of her fellow earthlings. When I noticed that trend, I felt I should soften my earlier denigration of that genre.

"The best science fiction uses extra-terrestrials and their far-flung habitats as refractions of human characteristics," I said. "Think of how Aesop used animals. You don't think he was explaining the behavior of foxes, crows and mice, do you?"

I never knew which of my comments would go into Toni's blender and come out as cake, but her creations were tastier and tastier.

* * *

When the school year ended, I picked up my own writing, neglected while I'd been learning how to teach. Rereading the year-old false starts and rough drafts that had been gathering dust, I found that I no longer found them worthy. My new points of view were incompatible with those of the previous Mr. Fleming. I deleted thousands of words and turned hundreds of pages of hard copy into origami boulders. The Rockies had crumbled, Gibraltar had tumbled and Ozymandias was busy feeding the worms. My second novel had turned to blank reams of paper and an empty head.

I told my students about that experience at the beginning of my second year in the classroom.

"Erasure is a major activity of every serious writer," I said, giving myself a high grade for my non-productivity. "All first drafts are nothing but kindling for what may become bonfires. Many may wind up as smoldering embers or cold ashes." I stopped myself. I realized I was being too metaphorical for the tenderfeet in my audience. Few of them had ever tried to rub two sticks together.

I guess I was really reminding myself that one step backward is often the only way to make progress. At any rate, at home, I continued to rub my sticks and, eventually, my sparks began to catch. The embers, much to my surprise, revealed a thinly disguised Toni and her inattentive family, who I knew only through what Toni's friend, Sandra, had told me, so my imagination was the only armature for the sculpture that was emerging. And even that sculpture was about to go back to the drawing board.

* * *

A regular ordeal in the life of all teachers is the open house, when, twice a year, doors are thrown open to parents who want to check on their kids' progress or problems. Parents of kids in kindergarten or the early grades are the most inquisitive, and traffic is heavy. By the time students reach high school, most moms and dads have resigned themselves to the fact that years of their offsprings' grades are proof enough of how it's going. The only folks who tend to visit *me* are the helicopter parents, all of whom fancy themselves uncredentialed but superior educators.

At the first open house of the new school year, none of those parents appeared, so I sat alone in the classroom, able to give full attention to whoever might show up. Almost an hour of solitude had passed when a beautiful young lady appeared in my classroom. She was too young to be a parent of one of my students.

"Mr. Fleming?"

"Yes?"

"I'm Becky Wohlters. I'm the sister of Toni Jensen who took

your class last year. I've looked forward to meeting the man who has meant so much to Toni."

"I was very happy to have her in my class. She was very receptive to everything we discussed and her writing proved it. She's got real talent."

"That doesn't fully explain what you did for her."

"I don't get all the credit. I may have uncapped the bottle, but the carbonation was already in there."

"You don't understand. I'm not talking about her writing ability. At least, that's not the main thing. I don't understand the first thing about writing, but I know that Toni's new ability has transformed her. Before taking your class, she was hard to get along with. She always wrote stories, but they didn't make any sense, and when she showed them to me or our parents, she thought that, because we didn't like them, we didn't love her. Of course, she was unhappy, and the unhappier she got, the more she thought we were her enemies.

"No matter what we said or did, she took it as a judgment against her, and the ways she reacted made her harder and harder to get along with. She was resentful, uncommunicative and unhappier by the day."

This was getting uncomfortable. Nothing in Toni's writing had led me to believe I was entitled to root through her family's underwear drawers, medicine chests or psychiatric histories. I wasn't qualified to analyze anything I might find in those locations. I remained silent.

"But her stories changed," Becky went on. "How can I put it? We *understood* them. We could honestly praise them. When we did, Toni was clearly overjoyed, and she stopped treating us as her enemies. I'll just talk about the way she treated *me*. For the first time ever, she began to ask me about my work. I'm a dentist, and whenever our family conversations had anything to do with that, she'd react as if we were telling her to shut up. She'd storm out of the room. The same reaction when I'd say anything about my son.

"Suddenly, Toni began to act like a loving aunt, and positively glowed when Wally cuddled up to her. It was the family feeling I'd always been hoping for. The same kind of improvement showed in Toni's relationship with our folks. She showed me one of her new stories that had a character who, I could tell, was supposed to be our dad. I don't know if she showed him that story, but I hope she did. Her relations with him have always been particularly rocky, but in this story, he was a heroic character."

Becky went on describing the changes she'd noticed in Toni (and her stories) until another set of parents wanted a shot at me, so Becky thanked me again. Before she left, I demurred credit for having been the evolutionary force and gave my attention to the newcomers.

During Becky's report, I'd figured out how the principles of writing had transformed Toni. She'd acquired the ability to see the world through other people's (Becky's and her parents') eyes.

She was seeing herself through their eyes, seeing Becky through their eyes, seeing the world not as a competitive gameboard, but as a field in which one generally gets what one deserves. The sun had risen on Toni's dark night and it became safe to bring the starship out of the black hole.

I wish I could say that the art of living becomes clear to anyone who masters the art of writing fiction. 'Tain't so. I know that, in my own case, publishing a best-selling novel hadn't filled in any spaces on the mysterious Bingo card of my life (except the financial space). Literary success certainly didn't save Fitzgerald, Hemingway, Joyce,

Kafka, Plath or ... For all I know, the Venerable Bede and Chaucer were both nutty as fruitcakes.

As I began again to write that second novel (no longer a mere revision of the novel I'd tried several times to write), I felt certain that, this time out, I knew what I was talking about. I hope the feeling lasts.

Get it?

Dead Again

Aaron Weber. You probably don't recognize his name. You might not recognize his face either, but in the fifties, he appeared in dozens of movies. He specialized in playing those disposable characters whose deaths, early in the movies, serve to get plots rolling but whose absence in the rest of the story isn't noticed as the stars go on to triumph over whatever killed him.

Aaron played the farmer who winds up in the jaws of a giant grasshopper, the gas station attendant squashed under the feet of dinosaurs, frogs or lepuses; the office clerk trapped on the top floor of the blazing skyscraper; the soldier machine-gunned by Nazis, or the pedestrian run over by villains fleeing cops. In the following scenes of those movies, he was often a mass of mutilated goo.

Directors could depend on him. He always knew whatever few lines he'd been given, could hit his marks and could lay real still in his last moments on screen. And he was patient during his long stints with makeup people as they prepared him for his gristly final scenes. None of those movies required more than a few weeks on set, so it was off one assignment and on to another with lucrative frequency.

Ironic as it may seem, he made a good living being type-cast as a deadguy, and his kids were proud to point out to their friends that the body discovered in the barn was their dad. He was a superhero of sorts in their minds—immune to every imaginable fatality.

After years and a few dozen terminations, he was getting bored. There wasn't much variety in his resumé—little participation in the setups, little interaction with other cast members and nothing to do with any post-mortem action of the films. It was up to others in the cast to enact fear of what was to come and horror at what, inevitably, would happen. Only occasionally did Aaron's characters have an inkling that death was in their immanent futures, so he rarely had an opportunity to portray fear.

A movie he did late in his career made him optimistic that it would improve his chances for expanded roles. It was a zombie movie in which he'd have *multiple* death scenes. No dialogue, but more action than he'd been assigned in previous films. He threw himself into preparing for the part. At home, he practiced the zombie stagger until he perfected the shuffle-stomp of a soulless hulk.

But, exemplary though his portrayal had been, it failed to "breathe life" into his career. His name wasn't even mentioned in the few, mostly negative reviews *Empty Men* received. Nor was his phone ringing off the hook with job offers. He let his SAG membership lapse and threw in the towel. No one even heard it hit the floor.

* * *

So, by the early sixties, Aaron was in the market for a new line of work. His experience as a corpse didn't turn out to be the foot in the door he had hoped. No Show Business glamour had rubbed off on him. Occasionally, there'd be a potential employer whose interest in showbiz trivia enabled him to recall Aaron's previous life, but that small group remembered him as a member of the walking dead—hardly a recommendation for any other sort of employment. No stiffs need apply, it seemed, even though there was a lot of dead meat already on the payrolls of the firms to which he applied.

Finally, after six months of staggering from one interview to another, he landed a job as the night watchman at Green Machine, a manufacturer of agricultural equipment. A month prior to Aaron's hiring, one of Green Machine's competitors had been robbed of a combine worth hundreds of thousands of dollars. The thieves had disabled alarms prior to the theft, so Green Machine's management decided to augment their electronic surveillance with a pair of human eyes. Aaron met that requirement.

Manning his post for eight hours a night in the cavernous dark facility made Aaron feel he was back on a soundstage, waiting to be killed off. The industrial jungle was silent as a tomb. The atmosphere in the vast emptiness reminded him of his work in the movie *The End of It All*, a post-apocalyptic tale with a cast that reduced to zero before theramin music played over the closing credits. Aaron's character, of course, had been snuffed long before that.

His new assignment required him to travel the factory from one end to the other every two hours, making sure that each of the fifteen employee entry points was properly locked, then taking a quick look in the storage area where completed machines awaited delivery to customers and inspecting the alarm system to be sure it was functioning—merely a glance at the control board to be sure all the green lights were blinking. Completing those duties took half an hour. Then it was back to his post, where he'd sit reminiscing until time for the next round.

One might say he spent twenty five percent of his nights surveilling and seventy five percent dreaming, but it's hard to divide his worknights precisely. Surveillance time was mixed with reminiscences of Hollywood. The big hollow industrial space reminded him of the imaginary jungles, deserts and swamps in which he used to be killed. One never knew what sort of death was in store for him or from whence it would come, so best to stay alert. He never fully neglected his watchman duties. Employee entrances, check;

shipping and receiving docks, check; executive offices, check; storerooms, check; alarm system, check. And back to home base. Reshoot those takes three more times a night and that'd be a wrap.

* * *

He'd been working for two weeks when life imitated art. As he was between rounds, there was a sound in the industrial jungle. Not an animal sound, but a loud clang and the sound of metal scraping metal. Aaron snapped to attention. He shined his flashlight around the assembly lines. Nothing amiss. He passed the executive offices and walked to the loading docks where, he could see from a distance, four men were busy loading tractors onto a semi that was backed into the room. One tractor was already strapped in place and a second was being winched into position behind the first. The thieves, thinking they were alone in the factory, weren't being stealthy in their work. Apparently, they'd cased the factory before there'd been a human on the scene.

"Make sure you don't leave space between 'em," one thief hollered to another. "If y' don't keep 'em close, we won't have room for four."

"You won't get four of 'em on there no matter how close they are," one of his associates answered. "Three at most."

"An' make sure y' strap 'em down tight. I don't wanna create a scene while we're drivin' down the expressway."

Without any script, Aaron reacted. "*Hey!* What d'y' think yer doin'?"

The surprised intruders froze for a few seconds. Then all of them scattered like a disturbed nest of fire ants, jumping off the truck, dropping their tools and ducking behind crates for cover. One of them took out a gun and fired a wild shot at Aaron. It hit him in the left shoulder, close to the body, spinning him around. That, he recognized, was his cue. He fell, artfully, so that he wouldn't be hurt falling to the ground. And he lay there, motionless.

"*Jesus Christ!* What'd y'do *that* for?"

"What was I supposed to do? He prob'ly had a gun! An' he definitely wasn't gonna let us finish loading the truck."

"Well, finish securing that last tractor fast. We gotta get outta here immediately!"

The shooter gave a quick glance at his target to be sure he was dead. Sure seemed like it. A minute later, with a grinding of gears, the semi sped out with its partial load of tractors, leaving the door of the loading dock open and Aaron laying in a pool of blood.

His acting experience had come in handy. In his role as one of the victims in the movie *Plague,* he'd fallen dead in the street and landed in an awkward position that was painful to maintain for the five minutes required. He wasn't about to make that mistake again. This time, he didn't land on his wounded shoulder and his face wasn't mashed against the concrete. His good arm wasn't uncomfortably pinned under his body. He could have stayed convincingly dead for however long the scene demanded.

* * *

Cut. That was a take. He remained realistically immobile, despite being in quite a bit of pain, until his attackers were a few miles away. Finally, he slowly boosted himself first to his knees and then to his feet. He lightly touched his shoulder, got his first experience of what a bullet wound and real blood feel like and realized there'd be no one waiting in makeup to get him cleaned up. He got back to a telephone and dialed the police.

The hospital scene that followed wasn't in Aaron's wheelhouse.

Animated grasshopper bites had never required medical attention.
The doctors reviewed his portrayal of a gunshot victim as "Ade-
quate." A broken clavicle, some bruising and a fair amount of blood
loss. He was treated and released two days later. The police interro-
gation, likewise, was brief, and Aaron was back home sooner than
he'd expected. And, the size of the insurance settlement meant that
his most recent death was more rewarding than any of the ones that
had been captured on film.

But he had no experience playing the role of the wounded husband, so he wasn't prepared to respond to the scolding that Teresa
had been too hysterical to express when she'd visited him in the
hospital. When Aaron arrived home, she let it all out.

"This is just what I was afraid of when you told me about that
job," she said. "I *told* you it was too dangerous. They send you in
there without a gun, without any instruction about how to handle
intruders, without any plan whatsoever . . ."

"But honey, I needed a *job!* What was I supposed to do? Who
would figure that anybody would shoot someone to steal a buncha
farm equipment?"

"You *knew* someone had just lifted hundreds of thousands of
dollars' worth of machines from the same kind of company a few
weeks before you were hired. That's why Green Machine hired you
in the first place."

"I'm just glad I was able to convince them that I was dead. They
might have shot me again."

Aaron's kids paid no attention to their parents' squabbling.
They were more involved in a game of Cootie, ignoring their
wounded dad. They'd seen him killed so many times that this latest
mishap was no big deal. Good Old Dad always made it home safely.
In fact, the novelty of his arm being in a sling was kind of cool.

Aaron, though, wasn't wearing the sling as anything like a red (or white) badge of courage. When Teresa retreated, he slumped in a chair, wondering if all his cinematic death scenes had been harbingers of his encounter in the factory or, worse, omens of things to come. He watched the kids rolling the dice and assembling their plastic bugs. He shuddered as he envisioned the role he'd be likely to play if someone decided to film *The Night of the Giant Cooties*.

The Last Days of Mount Bobby

When children enter school, most of them shed the diminutive labels they wore since birth. Susies become Susans or Sues, Jimmys become Jims or Jameses. Gone are the Kippies and Katys, replaced by Keiths and Katherines. They take the first steps toward becoming Mister This or Miss That, Doctor Eminent or Judge Wise but, for now, it takes effort to convince everybody that they're no longer little kids.

But there's no new name for Bobby Munson, betrayed by his body, for, at the age of fourteen, he's only five feet one and built like a sparrow. Even surrounded by girls, he's small. So Bobby he remains.

Making matters worse, his croaky Georgie Winslow voice makes it hard to take seriously anything he says. He wears glasses with flesh-colored frames and is the only high schooler who carries a briefcase—traditional hallmarks of the class "brain," but average grades deprive him of even that uncomfortable label.

By high school, hierarchies that began to be established in elementary school are firmly locked in. Six-year-olds have formed opinions about who their classmates are and have received their first lessons in how each one fits in the crowd. They've learned who can build a tall tower of blocks and who cannot. They have watched to see who colors in the lines, who can throw a ball farthest, who can coax a tune out of a recorder, who has mastered jump rope skills. They can tell who has the brains or patience to learn what adults are trying to teach them.

It's time to focus on matters more germane: the ranking of

neighborhoods of origin, churches attended, parents' positions of power or powerlessness, who is attractive and who is not? Who wears the nicest clothes? Who is strong and who's weak? Answers to such questions eventually boil down to the nub: Who is better—you or me?

Bobby doesn't hold any winning cards. He's deemed not as good as you, not as good as me, not as good as anyone else. So he becomes the high school goat.

In the lunchroom, everyone's status is apparent. Fat kids sit alone if not with other fat kids, dummies sit at the dummy table, bullies jostle to see which of their lunchmates deserve to be alphas and the handicapped sit wherever they're allowed. At other tables, royalty sits preening on their thrones, sneering at the plebeians. The brutal game of musical chairs is relentless. Bobby eats with a handful of his fellow goats, all of them painfully aware of what they have in common.

* * *

It wasn't always like that. Although Bobby's grade school experience had gotten off to a similarly rough start, in seventh grade, there was a glimmer of hope: the science teacher to whom our class was handed off was Mr. Palendar, a teacher whose greater-than-expected empathy was shaped, perhaps, by the fact that he was the father of six. Mr. Palendar recognized Bobby's isolation at the bottom of the pecking order and granted him some extra mercy. He encouraged Bobby's apparent interest in science and Bobby responded.

In science class, he became his teacher's go-to guy. With Palendar's encouragement, Bobby began creating rather spectacular extracurricular projects. One week, he brought in a plexiglass case filled with numerous strata of differently colored sand. Buried here and there in the sand were paper cutouts representing various species of fossils to explain to the class that, by measuring fossils' depths, paleontologists can approximate the age of a specimen. It was Bobby's debut in the spotlight.

As Bobby walked to the front of the room the class rolled their eyes as if to say, "Oh no! We're going to have to listen to *this* guy!" They giggled at the prospect of a nobody having anything to say that might be worth hearing.

He launched into his talk, wisely keeping references to the Cenozoic and Mezozoic Eras brief before zeroing in on the seven periods of the Paleozoic Era, delineated by different colors of sand. He spent most time talking about the four periods that gave rise to familiar plants and animals—sharks, spiders, starfish, cockroaches, early reptiles, ferns and such—realizing that only he would be interested in earlier developments. He did make an exception. He dipped into the Jurassic Period for the appearance of dinosaurs. Who doesn't like dinosaurs?

The talk wasn't as boring as the class had feared and Bobby's performance earned Mr. Palendar's praise. He experienced a rare moment in the sun. He wanted more, so, in following weeks, he presented a crude model of a not-to-scale solar system, introduced his pet iguana and brought in a store-bought plastic skeleton to identify a few human bones.

The parade of scientific show and tell began to wear thin on the class. The educational toys were no longer welcome breaks from official curriculum. They were seen as more brown-nosing by the little squirt. But, with Mr. Palendar as a safe haven in Bobby's stormy social sea, life became bearable. For the next two years of grade school, Bobby was more comfortable with his newfound bit of identity.

* * * *

It was at this point that I could afford to associate with Bobby. I wasn't near the top of the class pecking order, but I wasn't near the bottom either. If I watched my step, I wouldn't acquire a pariah stink by being seen walking with or talking to, in moderation, a goat . And we did have some interests in common. Science was one. My own particular interest was astronomy. Bobby was more of a generalist, but I could identify with that.

Besides that, Bobby's life as an outsider had imbued him with a sense of humor typical of contrarians, of which I was one. In those grade school years, *Mad* magazine taught me well that the so-called sensible world was laughable more often than not. Consensus, Bobby and I agreed, was often senseless. The two of us were given to drawing cartoons that depicted jesters' hats on our classmates and both of us could laugh at our own similar headgear. While our classmates were "paying attention" to what they were supposed to, we were often doodling and sharing our upside down insights.

So, largely unnoticed by the others, we became friends. Not *best* friends, god forbid, but better friends than some. I even visited him at his home and got a peek behind the scenes at some of his more elaborate science projects. In public, though, I remained careful to maintain some distance and, mercifully, Bobby seemed to accept that. He had acquired a fair-weather friend behind the scenes.

That was where our situations stood as grade school came to an end.

There is a chasm that lies between grade school and high school—one that many youngsters find intimidating as they leave the known world behind and prepare to make the leap. I have no idea whether Bobby was one of those or whether he imagined he'd permanently left the discomfort of earlier days behind him.

He had not. Worse times lay ahead.

* * *

When we arrived in high school, we were all, for a moment, equals, for, in the minds of the so-much-more mature sophomores, juniors and seniors, all freshmen were little children, despite the fact that only the previous year, as eighth graders, they'd been kings of the hill. They'd imagined themselves grownups.

Bobby arrived wearing a *new* "kick me" sign on his back—his bike. As I said, he sometimes was able to wear those signs with a shrug, concealing any pain he felt—a tacit recognition that his was just proper attire for one of the many clowns.

The rest of us were aware that high schoolers regard it uncool to ride a bicycle to school. Some of them rode bikes around town, but Bobby's was one of only two bikes in the high school bike rack, and the other one belonged to a tough guy who rode it as a sign that no one dared challenge his freedom to do whatever he damned please. Bobby, of course, enjoyed no such freedom, but he ignored the mockery the bike earned him. He lived more than a mile from school—a long trek for someone with short legs and a heavy brief-case. So he continued to ride the stigma.

He ignored it until his bike turned up missing one afternoon. The next morning it turned up at the bottom of the school's swimming pool. The janitor fished the bike out and returned it to Bobby, but the psychological damage was done and the act remained a laugh at his expense for a long time. I wish I could say that I expressed some pity or, at least, that I didn't find the event funny.

My tentative "friendship" continued during those early high

school years, but Bobby began hanging around me more often than was comfortable, testing the boundaries. Often I would find an excuse to cut our contacts short. I'd claim to have to have unavoidable commitments that would prevent our meeting when, in fact, it was my concern that spending time with him would jeopardize my image of being just one of the "normal" guys. But Bobby noticed.

One day, he said to me, "You're really a great actor."

I wasn't a member of the drama club. "What d'y' mean?" I asked.

"You're good at portraying whatever character you want," he said, and he gave me a funny look. "You're always playing to the audience."

I didn't pursue the subject. I'd been caught being a phony friend. I was ashamed of my role playing, but I wasn't sure enough of my social standing to change my ways. I continued to limit my friendship to what I felt I could afford. Better a phony, part-time friend than a vicious tormentor, a category that wasn't in short supply.

While everyone was dressed in street clothes, bullies were somewhat subdued. When we were all in gym clothes, it was a different story, for Bobby was, without a doubt, the least athletic student who ever entered a gymnasium. He couldn't shoot a basket, he couldn't do a pushup, he couldn't run and, worse, he wouldn't try.

Physical education teachers look down on such specimens. They admire macho, and many of them torture those who don't agree. So bullies used gym class as time to throw balls at Bobby's head and the gym teachers used it to loom over him, yelling at his inability to do forward rolls, climb a rope, do a chin-up or lift a weight. Some teachers were rougher than others, but none of them was a gentle drill master.

Then there was Bill Brady. He wasn't a physical education teacher, but he was a wrestling coach with many of the same characteristics as the P.E. guys. In fact, he topped them all with his snarling, no holds barred, militaristic approach to education. Bobby was in no danger of encountering Brady on the wrestling mats but, unfortunately, Brady also taught earth science, a sophomore-level requirement. Standing at the front of a classroom, he didn't moderate the approach he used with the grapplers.

As one might imagine, Bobby had been looking forward to a new, more advanced science class. It promised to be his terra firma in the swirling sea of high school. He knew what it would take to thrive in that environment. So, on day one, he arrived in the science room early and deposited a handmade papier mâché volcano on the teacher's desk. He took a seat in the front row and sat, hands folded, waiting for the teacher to arrive and invite him up to prepare Mount Bobby for eruption, using vinegar and baking soda.

Enter Brady—often an event that preceded some sort of eruption, and today was not to be an exception. He looked at the mountain before him and asked, "What's this crap?" With a sweep of his arm, he knocked the volcano into the wastebasket at the side of his desk. This is how the world ends—not with an eruption but a loud clank.

Bobby cried.

A few vengeful students in our midst laughed at seeing Bobby suffer a spiritual whupping, but most of us were horrified. We shuddered, realizing that this was the dawn of a new day. We knew we were in the presence of a monster unlike any we'd known in grade school. In the painful silence that followed, we watched to see how the victim was faring and hunkered down to see what would happen next.

Eyes They Have but They See Not

Perry McFadden, Pedestrian

I wasn't an eye-witness. I heard the gunfire, but I'd been in the dentist's chair at the time, mouth full of tools, being thoroughly distracted. By the time I was back on the street, ambulances and cop cars were all over the place. And, of course, news trucks deploying armies of cameramen and reporters. To find out what had happened, I muscled my way through a crowd to eavesdrop on one of the newsmen as he questioned a witness. We were surrounded by a lot of background noise, so I can't guarantee I got the whole story. And my lip and cheek were still numb.

The basics were that Federal Trust, around the corner, had been robbed. The thief and four police officers ran down Diversey, trading gunfire. The thief and one of the cops were wounded. Both were scooped up and loaded into ambulances, stolen cash was recovered, crime scene tape was draped around the neighborhood and shoppers began jabbering about the adventure they'd just survived and collecting their wits.

That was enough story to tell my wife so she'd feel "in the know" while we watched the story on the nightly news. Elaine was excited by the fact that one channel's cameraman managed to include a shot of my hat in the crowd. "Yes, dear, that's me alright."

I can't say that television's version of the event was any more informative than what I'd heard on site, but it took longer for television to tell it. And longer still as the story was repeated four times without adding anything throughout the evening. It's funny—despite having been present at the scene of the crime, after hearing the story told over and over, TV repossessed the event. It was as if I hadn't been there. It became just another news story, like all the others that fill the time.

Conrad Pellatier, Paramedic on Call

As we were rolling the gurney toward the ambulance, I happened to hear a guy in the crowd say, ". . . and off he goes in the meat wagon." Stuff like that really pisses me off. It objectifies the poor victim who my coworkers and I regard as precious, delicate cargo. The crew is one hundred percent focused on saving human lives, our minds full of every bit of medical training we've ever had. It's got to inform our hands instantly. I feel nothing but contempt for any cynical lummox who finds our function funny.

On today's trip, that was especially true. The wounded officer was still conscious and was able to talk with us as we stanched his blood flow, hooked up the intravenous and administered anesthetic. He groaned whenever we hit the street's many rough spots but was still voicing concern for his fellow officers. Meat doesn't do that.

Sergeant Frank Gibson

Assuming it's pain killers they're pumping into me, they're not doing much good. I continue to feel a sharp stab somewhere in my middle. If I'm being fed some sort of mind-numbing juice, that works fine. I'm aware that I'm in a hospital—the telltale smell is powerful—and whenever my eyes blink open, I can make out someone in a distant visitor's chair and two medical people hovering around my bed, mumbling.

Even in the warm hospital room, I'm cold. My mouth is dry. I've heard the word, "blood" several times, but nothing else makes any sense. Those are the boundaries of the world I'm aware of. Doped up as I am, I feel as if I'm observing someone else stretched out on a slab—a specimen being studied, and I have no stake in what my observers may discover. Is the inert subject of their investigations an interesting or a boring case, a common puzzle or a rare one? Will the patient live or die? Or is he already dead? Does it matter?

Whoever's sitting at the side is silent. I can't make out if he or she is a friend or relative, a well-wisher or a duty-bound cleric, waiting to administer some religious sacrament. I may as well sleep. At the moment, there's not much difference between reality and dream. I'm a floater, anxiously awaiting unconsciousness.

Unnamed Witness

Last Thursday, me 'n' Stu was sittin' on the bench in front of the post office, havin' a smoke when all of a sudden we hear gunshots. About a dozen of 'em. One of the shooters runs around the corner, turnin' around an' firin' behind him. Then comes four cops, all of 'em sprayin' bullets in every direction. Me an' Stu an' about half a dozen other street folks ducked into a store as fast as we could. We all hunkered down behind a counter, just peekin' up over the top to be sure no one else was gonna follow us in there. A clerk quick locks the door after us. We were in there for about five minutes before the gunfire stopped.

We carefully stuck our noses out to be sure it was safe and then slowly stepped out front to see what had happened. There were bunches of people, mainly cops, crowded around two guys layin' on the sidewalk. There musta been ten cop cars an' a couple ambulances on the streets. Everybody was yellin' an' runnin' around. It was chaos.

One of the guys on the sidewalk was the shooter the cops had been chasin' an' the other one was a cop. I guess both of 'em had been shot. When I started t' calm down, I start gettin' pissed off about how cops are always so trigger-happy, shootin' all over a street fulla people. Who knows how many innocent citizens coulda been hit! That's always the way. 'S one reason I always cross the street when I see a cop comin'.

Well, the ambulances hauled the bodies away an' the crowds broke up. Things went back t' normal an' me 'n' Stu decided t'go t'th' Hole f'r a beer. Stu's different than me—he doesn't see anything wrong with the way cops handle trouble. He's defendin' 'em 'cause the way he sees it, they pertect the population by gettin' rid of a bad-guy, so anything the cops do is okay. Not in my book. I resent havin' t'dive f'r cover to avoid gettin' shot. Not my idea of a good day.

Victoria Slattery, an Officer's Wife

Visiting hospitals! I hate it, hate it, hate it! Under any circumstances. The disinfected smell of these places immediately sets my nerves on edge. But today is worse. I probably shouldn't even be here. I'm fairly confident that Roger has been glued to his desk, but if he were to see me here, there's no telling what he'd do.

So here I sit, watching Frank sleep, thumbing through the hospital's boring magazines. One called *Bass Fishing*, one called *Street*

Rod and half a dozen shelter magazines for the ladies. Not, surely, for this lady. They're filled with photos of homes that've been attended by fastidious homemakers and professional gardeners, reminding me that I've always been a less-than-ideal homemaker. A nurse made the mistake of calling me Mrs. Gibson. I hid my face behind a copy of *Street Rod*. I wonder if Bondo could be used to patch Frank's belly.

How many lives have I destroyed? The guilt I feel over my selfishness keeps me awake nights. Life with Roger was far from pleasant, but my decision to sleep with Frank made everything worse. Even now, I have no idea how our problems *should* have been solved, but the route Frank and I took was obviously the wrong one. How will any of us salvage a happy end? Will Frank overcome his wound? Will he hate himself or me? Now that reparations are impossible, should I break things off?

Will Roger spend years in prison? How will he think of Frank or me if the cops conclude the shooting was intentional and he winds up behind bars? How will the kids think of their mom or dad? What a mess! And it's all my fault.

I try to imagine the road ahead—what I might do to fix things, but it's a jumble. Everything I consider is nothing but pitfalls. I wish I could trust some third party to advise me, but I can't even trust myself to explain the problems clearly enough to set the scene.

Felicia Hochstra stopped by this afternoon to offer her sympathy and see if there was anything she could do. I was tempted to confide in her and ask for advice. A few years ago, her husband was killed in the line of duty, but that's not the same. He hadn't committed a crime and she hadn't played any role in his death. She never knew anything about Frank and me, and she and I have never been close confidants.

Felicia's a fundamentalist Christian, which I, to say the least, am not. I don' wanna hear her repeat all the dogma that was formulated thousands of years before I was born to restrict the lives of people I've never met. She'd lay "thou shalt not kill" on Roger and "thou shalt not commit adultery" on Frank and me and never have any curiosity about mitigating circumstances. I couldn't have faced any of that. And, frankly, I didn't really care what she thought. All my own judgments are in shades of gray—the good and bad content of each of us are thoroughly mixed, and there are no means of atonement or clear paths forward. I just wish I could erase the past year and start from scratch. And, of course, I wish I knew whether Roger shot Frank on purpose. I'd feel so much better if I was certain it was an accident.

Why oh why did I ever confess to Roger?

Daniel Markvart, Pedestrian

Yeah, I was there, sort of. But, as usual, my mind was on Mom. Six months ago, her oncologist gave her six months to live, and day-to-day lately, it looks to me as if he was right. Consequently, all my thoughts, all the time, wherever I am, are centered on her. All events seem to warn me of changes in her health. So that morning's street horrors seemed portentious. I was terrified. Like the people around me, I began to run. I was almost entirely oblivious to the chaos around me. It was nothing but an omen of distant trouble. I had to rush home to see if Mom was okay.

But suddenly, something changed. I hadn't run far before I thought, the chaos is *here*, not there. These people have *deflected* death. Mom is safe. I stopped running, recognizing that loss can be present in only so many places at any given time.

I guess neither conclusion was sound. Chaos in one place isn't indicative of peace or poison in another place. I calmed down and slowed my pace. I continued walking toward home as if nothing had happened. And, in fact, nothing had.

Patrolman Anthony Buonaroti

Until the docs dug the thirty-eight caliber slug out of Gibson, none of us considered the possibility that the bullet had come from Slattery's weapon, much less that Slattery meant to shoot him. Roger and Frank have been partners for years. Buddies. But Internal Affairs thought the incident warranted further investigation.

Whenever a cop shoots *anyone* it troubles all of us. When a *cop* is shot, we feel it personally. This time, it's like the brotherhood's been bitten by a belovéd family dog or your kid's been molested by the parish priest. But Slattery's statement revealed a backstory none of us had imagined. I must say Gibson's affair with Slattery's wife sure makes me wonder if the shooting might have been intentional. I don't think much of a guy who'd ball his partner's wife.

So, Gibson's in the hospital and Slattery's on desk duty, his gun and badge in a drawer until IA concludes its investigations. We're short two men and wondering what to think about it all.

Even given the facts as we currently know 'em, y' gotta wonder why Slattery even mentioned his wife's affair. Makes even other guys on the force wonder. There'd been bullets flying in every direction, and it would be understandable if, in the heat of the moment, an accident had happened. I remember that once, a few years back, my then partner came pretty close to shooting *me*, and I *know* that was accidental.

Eleanor Peebles, Not a Witness

I didn't see anything. I was home all morning. I get all the news I need and lots that I *don't* need from my older sister, Edna. Where *she* gets it, I have no idea. Today's scoop involved a mass shooting downtown. The news was, as usual, accompanied by a heap of editorial comment.

According to Edna, a gang of masked stick-up men hit the Federal Trust bank on Racine. They made off with thousands of dollars, running on foot down Diversey. Fortunately, there were two cops patrolling the neighborhood at the time and the bank teller had sounded the alarm, bringing two more officers within minutes. Gunfire was exchanged and ambulances carried at least four victims—officers, robbers and maybe some innocent bystanders—to St. Francis Hospital. How Edna determined the bystanders were innocent, we'll never know. I guess they always are. One never hears of guilty bystanders. I'm surprised Edna even recognizes the *existence* of innocence.

Then comes the commentary. "That's what life downtown is like," Edna says. "You can't go there anymore. Criminals are out of control. The police can't handle them. Nobody's safe. There are so many guns everywhere and people have no sense of responsibility. It's a godless mob."

And that's what life in Edna's head is like. So, she rarely ventures out in the turmoil. She remains a prisoner of the turmoil she imagines. I don't know how she'd get by without me to buy her groceries and medications or post her letters.

Sergeant Roger Slattery

When I think of all the scumbags I've collared, the atrocities they've committed and the slap-on-the-wrist punishments they've received and compare those to my own circumstances, it's hard to believe in anything like justice.

Did I shoot Frank on purpose or not? I'm not sure. Probably some of each, despite my certainty that he deserved to be shot. What greater betrayal can there be than fucking your partner's wife?

My defenders go farther to say I should have shot Victoria too. I don't think so. I know I've treated her like dirt, losing my temper about trivial stuff, ignoring the kids, moping around the house without talking . . . I can understand her turning to another lover after all she's had to put up with.

Frank, on the other hand, had no beefs with me. No reason to betray me. I've saved his ass on more than one occasion, backed him up in his decisions even when I would have handled things differently. I stuck up for him even when I thought he was being a pussy. But when I think of him undressing Victoria and rolling around on top of her, my thoughts turn violent. I replay everything I said to the IA guys, realizing I easily could have lied about what happened or at least left out the emotions that were burning me up. I know full well the types of bullshit laid out by perps who've preceded me on the grill. I prob'ly coulda sold some "fog of war" excuse. I shouldn't have even *mentioned* Victoria.

So here I sit, waiting for some uninvolved assholes to make decisions about what the rest of my life will be like. Justice? For who? Me? I doubt it. Frank? In my opinion, a bullet in the belly is justice enough for him. Victoria? Unless you count having to do without Frank, she gets off with less than justice. The kids have the best chance. They'd get rid of me, maybe Frank too. The possibility of a new and better life for them.

Sergeant Frank Gibson

Feeling better today. Belly still sore, but it's not so bad that I'm counting the minutes until the next morphine. I sure could stand some orange juice. Or even some ice water.

I'm thinking like a human again and remember why I'm here. At least the bullet. Not much beyond that. I thought I had sufficient cover and backup during the shootout. I guess I was wrong. I have no idea whether any of the other officers were wounded. I wonder if Roger's okay. I haven't had a chance to talk with the doctors, but I expect a visit soon.

I hear Victoria spent some time here yesterday. Strikes me as her presence here would be dangerously incriminating, but I suppose she's capable of concocting a cover story. She's been pretty devious covering for us till now. Still, I wish she wouldn't go out on such limbs. I wouldn't trust Roger not to do something ugly. He's got quite a temper.

Sergeant Roger Slattery

My lawyer seems to think that none of the history of Frank, Victoria and me is relevant. It doesn't preclude a not guilty plea—that the crime scene was chaotic enough that it might clear me of criminal intent. I would. of course, be relieved to avoid a prison sentence, but sitting at this desk, I'm feeling less justified for what I did. Much to my surprise, I'm even beginning to feel some sympathy for Frank.

I think back to all the times in my life that I lost my temper and did something stupid. There've been more than a few things I now regret. Some of them I can explain, remembering why I did what I did. Other things just happened. Who knows why?

I've also been comparing my own idiocies to those of the criminals I've apprehended over the years. If I'm honest, I'd have to say that I rarely knew or cared what led them to commit their crimes. I guess most of them had their excuses, just as I have mine.

Whatever. I had the gun. I had the badge. On the street, I have the duty to be the judge. Now I have to sit and wait to see who'll be appointed to judge *my* crime and my excuse. 'Course, no matter how I paint it, I know I shouldn't of shot Frank.

Captain Raul Estaban

My thoughts are foggy with gun smoke. Purchasing bullets and supplying them to the troops are just a matter of budgets and paperwork. It's after a bullet get fired that the trouble begins. Justifying each bullet fired, analyzing the rifling that marks it and matches it to the weapon that fired it, laser tracing the path it followed and, of course, the unpleasant investigations that always follow, especially if the bullet hit an "important" person. That stuff is my headache. Especially this thing between Slattery and Gibson. Jesus! When Mrs. Slattery's possible role was revealed . . . Well, I don't even want to talk about it. That turned what might have been a simple story into a nightmare.

Unnamed Pedestrian

I wasn't downtown during any of the gunplay. I'm downtown only once a week or so. I read about it in the paper and thought I'd go down to fix the scene in my mind. Get the lay of the land, so to speak, and see if there was still any evidence of what had taken place.

Finery, the women's clothing store that was more or less at the center of the fray had its main display window boarded up and, three doors away, a local icon had caught a bullet in the leg. The barbershop, formerly a tobacconist, had retained the wooden Indian who'd stood guard over the former owner's pipes and cigars, and on the day of the shootout, the ol' chief had been in harm's way and now bore a huge scar. Three days later, splinters on the sidewalk still hadn't been swept up.

What goes on in the mind of an innocent wooden figure?

Rodney Treville, Owner of Finery

I've always believed in the second amendment. I'm a gun owner myself. But when I got the bill for replacing that window, I wasn't too happy. Twenty-five hundred dollars, and insurance didn't cover *any* of it! I have no idea how much money the crooks got from the bank, but I doubt it was much more than that. And I have no idea whether it was the police or the crook who shot out my window. It doesn't make any difference. The repercussions come out of *my* wallet.

Besides the initial cost, there's also the sales I'm losing. Until I get the window replaced, no one sees the merchandise. Foot traffic since the gunfire is way down. No one wants to shop in a war zone. It's as if I'm out of business. Is this the cost of freedom?

Rustling Branch, Cigar Store Indian

My days are numbered. For the past few months, Brent has been pressured by a group of citizens to get rid of me. They claim I'm an insult to native Americans. I don't get it. I am who I am and have always been. I'm no more insulting to my race than Brent is to his. I guess my people and I have been politically incorrect ever since the Europeans arrived.

But my wound is probably the last nail in my coffin. I doubt townsfolk want my shattered leg around to remind them of the violence they continue to inflict on my people and others.

I doubt Brent is likely to pay to get my leg repaired. I imagine he'll replace me with a striped pole—a totem more symbolic of barbering than I ever was. That may serve him professionally, but it will never be the companion that I've been.

Over the years I've been standing out front, Brent and I have developed a relationship that's rare between white and red men or between men and pieces of wood. We've felt it most in those sometimes long stretches between customers when the two of us have no one to talk to but each other. I'm handicapped, of course, by my voicelessness and immobility, but those inabilities make me a better listener. I'd like to think of my silence and the melancholy that's carved into my face as an eloquent expression of sympathy.

But I've also been amused by the fact that Brent has never thought about barbering's relationship to scalping. It's true that my tribe never offered their customers hot towels, but neither did we take as much hair as Brent does every day.

Freddy Balaban, Local Kid

You shoulda seen it. It was real neat. Just like on TV. There were bullets flyin' everywhere an' two guys got shot. I just come outta the drugstore an' cops chased a guy right past me. The first guy almost run me over. The cops were chasin' the first guy who was runnin' t'get away. I think a cop was one of the guys who got shot.

I'm not old enough to have a gun, but my dad's got one. I'm gonna ask him to teach me to shoot. It was real neat.

A Straight-Ticket Day

Wuzza wallpaper in here always brown? If not, they're all dead who recall the first color. Bedsheets are the brown of love imagined and badly laundered. Don't bet on the cum. Or on the departed. Scuzz on the window's the translucent brown of a thousand lonely smokes. A nicotine lens. Through it, I see the world's a dingy smear an' each survivor who staggers past is dressed in fatigues, camouflaged for the muddy war of nerves.

Ev'ry brick of the buildings across the street is aged into gray, brown or black. I expect a Russian tank t'come rumblin' down the block. Budapest, 1956. I observe the scene and get the sense that all of us are livin' in a pop-up book an' the town'll fold up when the page gets turned. An' ev'ry window is just a black square through which a giant kid's about t' poke a finger 'n' wiggle it around inside our hollow rooms tryna get at the people cow'rin' in the corners.

Here I am, finger—Here in this hole, standin' f'r hours, cigarette behind my ear, pushin' glasses up on my broken nose, shiftin' a tightly rolled-up copy of The News from armpit t' pit, tryna under*stand*. Tryna work up some *motive* t'get my ass in gear. Tryna work out from under the barometric *pressure*, but thirty-one inches of mercury or *some*thin', I dunno, is bearin' down hard, makin' me sweat. Oily caffeine's leakin' outta my pores. An' the city's pores are leakin' too.

Ol' Desoto out front's been waitin' f'r days f'r someone t' take it *outta* here. Maybe drive it around in downtown Havana, that museum of automotive memories. Broken axle doan make that seem likely. It's been sittin' there lettin' the once-bright colors of the fifties fade inta who we've become.

A radio tower inna distance is waitin' f'r a message worth sending through the empty air but no, mom, I can't say I wish you were here. An' acrossa way's a rooftop rezzavore, its ancient legs sagging. Gonna drop its empty head inna tar. Anyway, I doubt it very much there's any water innat rusty tank.

The hotel's called The Prospect. That's a laugh. Add up the prospects of the residents an' y' struggle t'make zero. Step out in the hall an' squint through the gloom of yellowed sconces where flies have met their ends. Shuffle along the threadbare hall carpet t' spend whatever's left of *your* life waiting for the elevator. Down to the lobby, where hopeless lobby zombies doze, gathering dust in prehistoric chairs under the disinterested gaze of the semiconscious deskman. We're exhibits in a wax museum.

Better to stay in my empty cell. From up here, I look down at the street. It happens today's election day, and down there is a guy who's holdin' onto hope in the gray November haze. He's a foot soldier in some political army, marching through the crumble, slapping up posters that promise new tomorrows: "VOTE FOR X AND THE SKY WON'T FALL!" But the sky always punches its ticket for the opposition, so tomorrows turn out like our yesterdays.

Big jowly, unshaven face smilin' lotsa teeth, promises flowers're gonna bloom on the dark side of the stony moon. I remember the posters from four years ago, when X was a different candidate but the promises were the same. Poster man was marching then, too, an' he nailed down a cushy job for his efforts.

I'll say this much: It's a straight-ticket day—a day t'pull the lever f'r nunna the above, 'cause the citizens of Brownout don't have minds t'spare for figuring out which circuit court judge or alderman's less useless than the next. The public opinion is gray and slumped over—a nation fulla spinal injuries. I expect a light turnout in this heavy weather, an' at most, the voters who show up might have the strength t'pull the lever that opens the trapdoor in the gallows floor.

But down there, there's one guy who has one more day in which to believe in the future before ballots get trampled into status quo. Then there'll be time to hang the black bunting. That's the view of this absentee.

If y'look at me standin' at the window from over by the bed, I'm just a silhouette—a backlit, two-dimensional man. If y'look up from the street . . .

But no one looks up. They're like bugs afraid t'see the approach of a shoe, the mindless descent of fate, size thirteen. It ain't on *my* foot, Bud.

Maybe it'll rain. I wish it would. *Bust* an' wash us. *Anything* t'make a difference. I dunno.

I'm afraid Henry Ford was right when he said, "Any color, as long as it's black."

Thanks, Hank. Thanks f'r nothin'. Black an' gray an' a dropped transmission.

Now d'hubcap falls off.

Just Another Guy from Olduvai

Ostensibly, Dr. Langerfeld was at the University of Pittsburgh to discuss the footprints discovered at Laetoli. He was, after all, one of the paleontologists most familiar with the find. But he was wrapping up an eight-university tour where he'd been over and over the subject, and the talk and the questions it elicited were becoming a sleepwalk. And he was becoming more and more frustrated at questions from the audiences for which he had no answers. Therefore, he was in a defensive mood from the get-go.

"Everything is knowable," he began. "The truth is out there, challenging us to acquire the ability to reveal it. As we struggle, so-called truth keeps changing as we get closer and closer to ultimate truth. Scientists before Galileo didn't have telescopes, so it was 'true' that Jupiter didn't have moons. In 1610, with telescopic insight, it became 'true' that Jupiter had four moons. Today, it's 'true' that Jupiter has sixty-seven moons. We'll find out how many are really there if we keep asking the right questions. So, feel free to ask questions as I go along."

In the past thirty years, he'd made that promise on campus after campus, generally to students of paleontology. Once again he faced a group of roughly a hundred students (in an auditorium designed to seat six hundred) and a handful of professors and visiting scientists, most of whom had some knowledge of his topic.

"I'm sure you all know Lucy, the *Australopithecus afarensis* who has become the world's most famous hominin, or you wouldn't be here. I was in the field two years too late to be in on her discovery, but, in a sense, both Johanson and I were 3.2 million years too late to meet her.

"But in 1976, I was working with Mary Leakey's team at Olduvai Gorge in Tanzania, when another earth-shaking discovery was made at Laetoli, about 30 miles south of Olduvai.

"Millions of years ago, Laetoli was wet and covered in patches of grasses and small trees except where volcanoes had deforested it. But by 1976, Laetoli, like Olduvai, was dry, hot and mostly barren. Unlike the romantic vision of paleontologists' work, it often comes down to tweezers, whiskbrooms, microscopes and notebooks full of measurements, often in dusty 105-degree heat. It's uncomfortable and tedious to say the least. Scientists will find relief wherever they can.

"During a not-so-serious break in the work, a few playful scientists were ducking behind sand hills, playing a game of elephant dung dodgeball. Suddenly, the game stopped. Before them in the volcanic ash, they saw a seventy-five-foot trail of footprints. These definitely weren't ape footprints. There were no knuckle impressions, and the feet that left their prints didn't have the mobile big toe of apes. They had arches typical of modern humans. Humanin footprints, made 3.2 million years ago!

"How could footprints last millions of years? Because the 'soil' in which they were made was a fifteen-centimeter thick layer of volcanic ash from the eruption of Sadiman volcano, twenty kilometers away."

A boy in the audience called out, "Dr. Langerfeld, you say the footprints were made 3.2 million years ago. How do you date a footprint? And 3.2 million years? I thought radio-carbon dating was useless for dating materials more than fifty thousand years old."

"That's true, but potassium-argon dating and single-crystal laser fusion dating can date older materials." Langerfeld enjoyed answering questions for which he had ready answers.

The boy wasn't satisfied. "But footprints aren't even materials. How can you date an impression? How do you date an indentation in the soil?"

"Because, shortly after the footprints were made, rain turned the ash to a substance not unlike concrete, preserving the prints. Had there been any substantial time lag between the ash deposit, the footprints and the rain, wind would have erased the footprints. And we know it was rain that solidified the ash because we see the prints of raindrops.

"We have another method of dating the soil. We have the footprints of many animals we'd previously dated—hyenas, wildcats, baboons, wild boars, Deinotheriums—an ancient relative of the elephant—and many kinds of antelopes. Not a bad question. But it's one for which we're confident of the answer."

Langerfeld had encountered questions from every breed of skeptic in the past. From scientists who were invested in opposing theories of what had happened at Laetoli, from students who had absolutely no background in paleontology and from religious fundamentalists who believe that dinosaurs roamed the earth 4,000 years ago. Consequently, they believed that Lucy had no place in the Garden of Eden. Adam and Eve couldn't possibly have been *Australopithecus afarensis.* Although he always began a seminar by encouraging questions from the audience, there were many questions with which he had little patience. He was anxious to get on with his exposition and to use it to dramatize science's ability to penetrate the seemingly impenetrable.

"The news of those footprints traveled fast. It took me only a few days to make my way to Laetoli from Olduvai. When I arrived, I walked into a swarm of scientists arguing about who had made the footprints. There was general agreement that some *Aus-*

tralopithecus species was responsible, but there were a lot of species that were contenders—*boisei, africanus, robustus, aethiopicus, animensis*...

"But none of those species were found at Laetoli or Olduvai. And, ever since the discovery of Lucy, more and more *Australopithecus afarensis* bones have been discovered. Not only at Laetoli. We have samples from seventy African sites. And, by 1976, we'd reassembled about forty percent of Lucy's complete skeleton. I was getting to be pretty familiar with the species."

"Was the *Australopithecus* foot so distinct from other genera?" the skeptical boy in the audience called out.

"It wasn't the shape of the prints that led to my certainty. It was also the length of the stride, the length and width of the feet and the reconstructable body height that distinguished the prints from those of other species, and everything was consistent with the Lucy I knew. And, most telling of all, we never discovered the bones of any other *Australopithecus* species at Laetoli.

"There were three individuals who made the prints, but only two were easily legible because the third individual was walking in the footprints of one of the others. The two readable sets of prints were made by a larger individual and a smaller one, and the smaller one seems to have been burdened on one side—maybe a male and a female carrying a child. Perhaps a family group, but we have no firm evidence of that."

The skeptic in the audience, apparently the only brave spokesman for the rest of the group, asked, "Why were the hominins traveling in the direction they were? Were they after food? Shelter? Were they fleeing a predator? Were they pursuing prey? It seems to me that from these rare evidences of behavior, we should be able to learn more about *afarensis* than size and shape."

Langerfeld smiled. The questioner, like paleo-traveler number three, was following in the footsteps of many questioners who'd preceded him.

"You're asking me to read ancient minds based on their footprints. We haven't yet discovered how to do that. Social behavior doesn't fossilize. Eventually, by combining other physical evidence of *afarensis* and our knowledge of other animal species' behavior patterns, we may be able to answer your question."

Questions about the print-makers' motives and destination or purpose were a sore-point with Langerfeld. He, too, had curiosities science couldn't satisfy.

"I *can* tell you that our ancestors weren't fleeing a predator or a volcanic eruption or pursuing prey. They weren't running. I know that because of the length of their strides and the depth of the heel and toe impressions. And, there are the footprints of birds walking in the same volcanic ash. Birds fleeing a danger would be flying.

"But there's no reason to suppose there was some abstract motivation for the travelers' route. Their cranial capacity would have limited them to rather basic purposes—food, water, shelter, reproduction and so on. And, because we know the Pliocene terrain at Laetoli, it's doubtful that shelter would have been more available at one location than another. Pursuit of prey would probably have been faster. It will require a new investigative technique to decipher the reasons our three *afarensis* characters were traveling in that direction. I can tell you that the walkers were traveling from south to north and that, midway in the 75-foot journey, they paused and seemed to look to their left. What were they looking at? Again, there's no evidence."

That didn't stop the questioner in the audience from pursuing the matter: "Couldn't they have been going to get this?" "Might they have been seeking that?" Frustrated at his inability to get to know more about the daily agendas of *afarensis*, the boy finally allowed Langerfeld to move on to more resolvable topics—teeth, legs, brain size, brain-to-body ratios and the methodologies by which various facts were determined. Dates, locations and other topics of which paleontologists were relatively certain.

"The placement of any piece of a puzzle makes every other piece easier to place. When a paleontologist determines the age of a specimen, it narrows the possibilities of that specimen's species. Or, if the species is known, it narrows the age range. The degree of sexual dimorphism focuses guesses about mating behaviors. *Any* known aspect of a specimen—the climate in which it lived, its size, diet, skeletal configuration, soil samples from its environment, cranial capacity, contemporary fauna . . . Know one fact and truth begins to emerge. Know another and it'll resonate with the first. You'll take a step toward confirming or refuting the first and, eventually, the puzzle forms a picture and one can say, 'This is so.'"

*   *   *

"I'm afraid it's also so," the seminar host interjected, "that Dr. Langerfeld must return us to the 21st Century and take his leave. His footprints will move toward Columbus tomorrow. We thank him for passing through Pittsburgh on his way."

Langerfeld left the auditorium, but a few steps down the hall he heard a voice behind him. It was the inquisitive boy from the audience.

"Dr. Langerfeld. You say that the *afarensis* cranial capacity wasn't sufficient to harbor abstract thoughts, but its brain-to-body ratio was greater than in other hominins and greater than in most animals. And even in animals, we've recently discovered some indications of abstract thought. How can you rule out that possibility in *afarensis*?"

"I like your questions, son. They're just the kinds of questions that will drive science forward. I'm curious. What are you majoring in?"

"Philosophy."

"Obviously a philosopher who's ready, willing and able to look in the horse's mouth. I would have guessed you'd be in one of the sciences—one that would give you better access to concrete answers. I wouldn't be surprised if you switch majors somewhere along the line. But, whatever—you've got a sharp mind. What's your name? I'm sure I'll hear of you in the future."

"Owen Yeiser," the boy answered.

"Well, Owen, it was nice meeting you, but I've got to be going." Langerfeld took his leave without answering Yeiser's question. It was a question for which he didn't *have* an answer.

It was five o'clock, so Langerfeld opted for a night's sleep before leaving the campus. A good night's sleep, a good breakfast and a few visits with faculty friends who he hadn't seen since Tanzania. The next day, one stop was at the office of Theo Samuels, a geologist who'd been a fellow grad student at Laetoli back in the '70s.

* * *

"You know," said Samuels, "I heard your talk yesterday. I wish I shared your optimism about science's ability to unearth every truth."

"Well, if anyone can 'unearth' truth, you're the man," Langerfeld joked.

"It's just that the deeper I dig—no joke intended— the more strata I uncover, the fewer answers I'm confident of. There are no ultimate truths down there. The earth moves, the waters recede, the mountains rise, but I don't feel closer to the certainties I'm seeking. I would like to find more connections to the human mind—more purpose to our existence. I think it's likely that I should have chosen a field other than geology."

"What? Psychology? Ethics? Some field that's even less concrete? A field riddled with impenetrable strata? My premise holds, even in the social sciences. If we ask the right questions long enough, light will shine in the darkness. But the social sciences' tunnel is a lot longer than that of the physical sciences."

"My skepticism is more pervasive than yours," Samuels said. "Whether we're talking about rocks or souls, I doubt that the scientific method will get us to bedrock. Think about all the work we've done in our chosen fields, all the discoveries we've made that the world regards as 'important.' What has all that revealed about who we are? How has any of that helped us to proceed in life? These are some questions that remain large in my mind, and they're questions on which we've made no progress."

"You're just racing ahead of our current capabilities," Langerfeld argued. "Eventually, the answers we're discovering now—the answers about our pre-human ancestors, the answers about plate tectonics, the answers we're finding in all the supposedly separate disciplines will contribute to the whole of the answers you're asking for. You don't expect a jigsaw to reveal a picture of cows when you've just completed the border of the puzzle."

Samuels harbored real doubts about whether the cows could ever be revealed. He wasn't sure there *were* any cows. If Langerfeld had any such doubts, he'd long ago decided to ignore them and, as a matter of faith, preach the gospel of the almighty scientific method.

In the late afternoon, the men parted friends, agreeing to disagree. Langerfeld left the campus and was soon on I-70, headed for The University of Ohio.

* * *

Langerfeld had had more than his share of time on the road in the past few months. For the first twenty miles or so, his conversation with Samuels kept his mind occupied, but as their talk faded into the past, boredom took its place. His method of coping with it was to turn his mind almost completely off. The unrelenting sameness of interstate scenery aided him in that process, and Langerfeld augmented the stupor by watching signs that counted down remaining miles to Columbus.

After two hours, with about an hour and a half to go, he switched the radio on to one of those call-in shows. "An outlet for people who don't know anything to share their ignorance with others of their kind," Langerfeld said to himself. But the white noise of the inconsequential was somewhat soothing. A little distraction.

Callers expressed their outrage about various celebrities' behavior. Fifty miles to go. A variety of plans were offered to set America's misguided government back on track. Forty miles to go. Autobiographical tidbits—something amusing that grandma did, an uncle's achievements, tales of embarrassing neighbors. Thirty miles. Solutions to other listeners' domestic problems—rabbits in the garden, stubborn carpet stains, obnoxious teenagers ... Twenty miles.

As Langerfeld approached Columbus, the topic turned to another earth-shaking matter: Callers were responding to the question, "How do *you* eat peanut butter?"

"I like it on rye toast with orange marmalade," one listener contributed. The host of the show approved. "Sounds good. Maybe washed down with a cold cream soda."

A caller from Chillicothe liked peanut butter with bananas, but a caller from Zanesville preferred peanut butter with marshmallows. A Circleville caller cast her vote for peanut butter with raisins—a combination she claimed to have invented.

"Well, *I've* never come across it," the host confessed. "Sounds kinda weird."

A caller who chose to remain anonymous just spooned it out of the jar.

Langerfeld didn't pay conscious attention to any of this information. He hadn't paid attention to the past half hour of programming. But somehow, the words "peanut butter" managed to penetrate the traveler's trance.

Peanut butter! My god! One of the curses of fieldwork, he thought. It was an almost daily item on the menu while in Tanzania. One reason: It doesn't suffer in the African sun. Also, it wasn't an item likely to be pilfered by light-fingered locals who were always poking around in the scientists' supplies looking for snacks. But peanut butter, in the natives' estimation, looked like what the animals leave behind. They wouldn't touch it.

I was so sick of peanut butter by the time I got back to the states, Langerfeld thought, that I haven't eaten the stuff in decades. I haven't *thought* about peanut butter!

But he was thinking about it now. A Proustian nostalgia for the taste and smell washed over him. It brought back memories of sitting with his fellow paleontologists on the rocks of Laetoli, discussing the morning's finds, gnashing down peanut butter sandwiches and swigging bottled water in the Tanzanian heat. It was, unquestionably, a good time—one of the highpoints of his life. The mental stimulation of the work in progress, the companionship with others who fully understood the significance of the discoveries, the physical challenge of working in the tropics . . . Exotic experiences available to few grad students in Ohio. In short, it was the moment in which Dr. Langerfeld had solidified his professional path and acquired the self-image that he'd maintained ever since. And, at the moment, memory of peanut butter almost liquefied in the African heat seemed a path back into the thirty-year-old experience.

It was 4:30. Langerfeld was due to speak at 5:30. But the campus, he knew, was only a few blocks to the left. He also knew there was a grocery store just a few blocks to the right. There'd probably be time to pick up some peanut butter and still make it to the lecture hall in time.

Where the road branched in a vee, Langerfeld had planned to turn left, but, in a split-second decision, he jerked the wheel to the right, causing a tire to hit the divider. The impact of the car hitting the curb at high speed momentarily lifted the car to a forty-five-degree angle before it tipped and skidded, turning on its side and scraping the pavement for twenty-five feet before colliding with a light pole. At some point during the skid, Langerfeld's door popped open and ejected him.

The professor was still alive when the medics loaded him into the ambulance, but he didn't survive the trip to the hospital. During the trip, within minutes, as he lay dying, the accident reconstruction team arrived at the scene and was gathering data.

* * *

The basics weren't hard to unscramble. There were no skid marks before the car had hit the curb, and the skid marks beyond that point revealed that the vehicle had begun to spin around its center of gravity, leaving the marks of the back tires inside the tracks of the front tires. Given that spin was in progress, the driver would have been unable to steer.

From the damage to the curb, it was possible to determine that the speed at the point of impact was about forty-five miles per hour—the speed limit on the street that led to the vee, so, apparently, the driver had been traveling at the posted speed and there'd been no attempt to brake before hitting the curb.

Assessment of the vehicle's brakes would have to wait for examination by the boys in the shop, but on the scene, there was no reason to suspect mechanical failure, particularly as the car was only a year old.

The length of the scrape on the pavement between the curb and the light pole and the estimated speed of the car when it impacted the light pole verified the speed of the car when it hit the curb (original speed minus the friction factor over twenty-five feet—the length of the scrape).

Those were the basics of *what* happened, but the *why* was still a mystery—always more difficult to decipher when the driver is deceased. And in this case, none of the so-called eye-witnesses had focused on the event until the car was already on its side, skidding toward the light pole or crashing into it.

There was no reason to suspect that weather (clear) or road conditions (dry) were contributing factors nor, at 4:30, was darkness. Traffic at the time of the accident had been moderate and one-way. If any other vehicle had been involved, there'd been no contact.

The driver's blood alcohol and signs of drug impairment would have to be assessed later, but, if neither was found, the likely cause of the accident (of which there was no evidence) was driver distraction. Cellphone? Radio? Smoking?

Dr. Langerfeld's accident was far from the first for which no causal factor or condition could be determined. All the accident reconstruction team's speculations merely ruled out possibilities, which left them no closer to the ultimate solution than they'd been when they arrived on the scene.

But at some time in the future—perhaps the distant future— new techniques or tools may become available that will reveal the truth, and scientists will have the interdisciplinary wisdom to connect events to peanut butter and the powerful pull of nostalgia. For who can say that similar tropisms weren't in play as long ago as 3.2 million years?

Envoi

No language interposed between the humanins and their direct experience of what their bodies were telling them. They felt what they felt. Sensation informed them that the day was more comfortable than the past few days, when temperatures had risen above a hundred degrees. On this day, gentle breezes in their hair and on their skins were so pleasant that they tipped their heads back and closed their eyes, though their eyes had no need today to squint out the light of a too-bright sky. The cooler air encouraged them to move about a bit. "A good day to go for a walk," as we humans might have said. So, they ventured out of the shade, where, experience had taught them, it was better to be on hot days. On cooler days, they did what they could.

They could just wander around, of course, looking at whatever there was to look at—a frequent activity. There was nothing specific to accomplish today—absolutely free. North was as good a direction as south, east or west. Back and forth was good as well. One foot in front of another and then they stepped into soil that wasn't soil. It was powdery and soft. Their feet sank deeper than usual into the surface. It felt strange and pleasantly cool. They wriggled their toes in the novelty and decided to keep walking, enjoying the new sensation.

They stopped a moment and looked to their left. To the left was water. Near those acacias. Maybe it was a good time for a drink. Or maybe, they decided, they should go back where they started.

Soon they found themselves in a place that was once "over there" but now was "here." Now, where they'd started was far away. Looking back, they saw a long trail of prints they hadn't noticed when they began. How did the marks get there?

The journey had been pleasant. How much pleasure lay ahead? Why not keep going until the ground changes? Who knows what they'd find later on? Finding out is always surprising. It's sometimes good to be alive.

And not a thought to distract from the sensation. At the moment, no fear of the future.

Other animals continued to go about their business. Irrelevant clouds drifted across the sky. Their passing shadows left no record. In that sense, the shadows were less than we were or would be. Less, even, than trilobites.

Fame in the Rearview Mirror

"Tom?"

"Who's asking?"

"Tom! Don't tell me you've forgotten. It's Riley Sams! Your long-lost TV brother Barnaby!"

"Oh. Sorry, Riley. Sit down! Sit down! I haven't ordered yet. My God! How long has it been? Four years? No. Five."

"It's five. The last show aired in June of 2013."

"No, I haven't forgotten any of it, try as I might. You expect me to forget a stone in my shoe?"

"I've got a few blisters of my own, but at least I can afford a podiatrist."

"A podiatrist and a psychiatrist, no doubt. Based on the few other *Crowded Nest* birds I've bumped into since the *Nest* was bumped, I find that there isn't a cast member whose brain survived intact. Some of it's minor damage. The smaller one's role, the less the damage done! Take it from the guy who starred in that mess, the other extreme of that formula is equally true. By the way, thanks for not calling me Bixby Fallows. Even after five years, it seems no one remembers that Bix was played by an actor named Tom Valley. I know my former so-called manager didn't."

"So what. Bix earned the bucks. The fact that you're still living under the shadow of the character is a tribute to the fact that you nailed the role! There isn't another actor in the biz who could have saved those scripts from the shitcan."

"Thanks for the rave review, but most days, I'd rather have passed the baton to someone who's immune to embarrassment.

Some people—even some of the network guys—still imagine that it takes a goof to play a goof. They don't think it was acting. And, despite the fact that the kids knew *they* were acting—that they had to memorize scripts, hit their marks, take direction—some of 'em imagined that everyone else really *was* the characters they were playing.

"And a lot of the fans too. Idiots! Can't tell reality from fiction, even when the fiction is half-wit humor cribbed from a dozen other shows. Don't even get me started on the *Crowded Nest* writers!"

"Whew! I had no idea you'd come away so bitter. Anyone hearing you spout off like that would quickly forget loveable old Bix!"

"It even pisses me off that an empty-headed buffoon like Bix is considered loveable. Why does America fall in love with characters like that? I'm embarrassed to be associated with that Yahoo. Let's change the subject. What have *you* been up to since?"

"Well, at first there were some summer theater gigs. You know—productions that hoped Barnaby's appeal would rub off on them. I took 'em, thinking I'd better cash in on what might be the last of my glory years. The real value of that was that a few decent paychecks kept my manager believing that I'm not dead and that was what got me the emcee slot on *Joker's Jest.* That's probably ended my acting career but, frankly, I don't miss it. *Joker's* ratings aren't fading, so my immediate future is solid. As I say on the show, 'You wanna take what you've won or grab even more?' Me, I wanna take what I've won. I've watched too many grabbers lose everything.

"Besides that, hosting a game show is a dream job in a lot of ways. No rehearsals, no need to learn lines, and studio after studio filled with fans who imagine that you're *doing* something. All I have to do is show up, put on the makeup and smile. It's like the bank is paying me to show up and ask for money. I ask! I ask!"

"So Brother Barnaby is as dead as Brother Bix? Another actor bites the dust."

"Barnaby and the whole lucrative family. Just old photos in the family scrapbook. Speaking of the family, have you seen any of 'em?"

"Well, of course I see Linda in the newspapers regularly. I'm surprised I haven't seen cardboard standups of her in the liquor stores or mugshots on the post offices' most wanted boards."

"Yeah. Or in a starring role at the mortuary. You know she's got a star in the sidewalk in front of the driving school? But no. I haven't seen many members of our fictional family. I assume most of them and their brainless smiles are working for Hallmark Cards now. I wish them all a very Merry Christmas and a fabulous fuck you."

"Excuse me a moment, Riley. Maitre d'! Yeah, *you*! Does this place employ any waiters? If so, I'd like to volunteer to train one of 'em."

"I'm so sorry, sir. I'll send one of them over immediately."

"If he happens to be dozing near a water faucet, wake him up and have him bring me a glass. Better specify *with water in it*. See, Riley, Bixby Fallows may be a name in lights to this day, but Tom Valley is just an ugly face in the crowd. He can't even get service in a restaurant."

"I'm sorry, sir. We had just changed shifts and I thought the previous waiter had already taken your . . . Bix! Do my eyes deceive me?"

"Your brain deceives you. My name isn't Bix and if the previous waiter took my order, he took it to his hometown in hell. Listen. I'm sick of hearing that 'Do my eyes deceive me?' line. The show has been off the air since you were in high school and my name is

Tom Valley. 'Sir' to you. If your eyes deceive you again, you'll be deceived through a black one."

"I apologize, Mr. Valley. Are you ready to order?"

"If your eyes hadn't deceived you you'd have noticed that I was ready half an hour ago. You've given me time to change my mind. I've decided to give up eating forever. At least eating at this dump. Just bring me a Manhattan with no fruit. How 'bout you, Riley? Wanna take a chance on the house glassware being clean?"

"I'll have a rum and tonic with a splash of Rose's lime."

"Got that? And now, why don't *you* take a turn at being the waiter. *We're* tired of waiting.

"You've just witnessed one of the low points of my post-*Nest* life, Riley. It's that damn catchphrase, 'Do my eyes deceive me?' Fans think it's the height of comedy to quote it at me over and over as if I'd never heard it before. The wit of the masses and also most parrots. It's crossed my mind that the best response would be for me to carry a tape loop of canned laughter and whenever anyone asks if their eyes deceive them, I'd give 'em a blast of the same sound that followed my line on the show. It's what the fans are accustomed to.

"Sorry, Riley. What were you saying before we were so solicitously interrupted?"

"I was wondering whether you've seen any of the rest of the cast."

"Right. Lemme see . . . I bumped into that Bellamy kid. You know—the kid with the Georgie Winslow voice who played Flippy. He's in his early twenties now, looks like fifties, smells like a long stay in the unemployment line. I can't explain his upbeat attitude. To hear him tell it, success is just around the corner from skid row.

"And there've been a few other kids from the show. Some of 'em are working, some still nursing hopes of returning to their glory days. But their cute is history. Most of them have come to their senses and are selling insurance or used cars.

"I've also seen a few of the crew. They're not as painful. They were never as confused about the difference between actor and character as the rest of the world seems to be. Everybody who was on-camera was just another schmuck as far as the crew were concerned, bless their hearts. They knew the difference between a prop and a human being. Props don't necessitate retakes."

"So if I hear you right, if there were to be a *Crowded Nest* reunion show . . ."

"AAARRG! Tell 'em Bixby Fallows has decided to devote the rest of his life to playing Lucky in *Waiting for Godot*. If they ever darken the airwaves with more of that *Crowded Nest* drek, I'll put a brick through my television and all the televisions of the world."

"Back in the day, I wouldn't have guessed you were so unhappy, Tom. You turned in performances that pleased the network, the directors and the writers. The whole cast looked up to you."

"While the show was running, I was happy enough. It was steady work, good money and it was just another job. It didn't particularly bother me that the show was crap. Sure, I was aware that most of the cast should never have been in show business and I cringed at the mindless scripts, but none of that ever kept me from trying to do my best. *Crowded Nest* wasn't the first stinker I'd ever been in. But I didn't realize at the time that the stink of the nest would follow me for years. Television is indelible!"

"So why are you . . . ? Oop. Here come our drinks."

"No. That one's mine, sonny. Me being . . . ?"

"Excuse me?"

"Do you remember my name?"

"I'm sorry. I don't."

"Never mind. You may come across it in your film studies text-book or in a 'Where Are They Now?' column. Beat it."

"I was just about to ask if you were so content at *Crowded Nest*, what turned you so bitter?"

"Look. In any workplace, one has to put up with stuff they can't relate to. No one's surprised about that. Eight hours a day of 'Yah, boss, right away boss, you're the wisest man on earth boss, the cus-tomer is always right, I'm in the mood for meaningless paperwork, I love raking manure...' It's what we get paid for. But when the day is done, most workers get to take off the masks and go home to a beer, a piece of ass or a walk with the dog. They get to reunite with their real selves and apologize to themselves for the way they earn their daily bread. Didn't you sometimes wish Barnaby Fallows had never been born so you could enjoy similar freedoms?"

"Only occasionally. Usually I got a kick out of being greeted by strangers whether they called me Barnaby or Mr. Sams. Barnaby got me better tables, a place at the front of the line, invitations to the best parties and all the beautiful women I could eat, despite the fact that Barnaby was as big an idiot as Bix. That told me that, at some level, the public recognized the difference between the actor and the act. I signed all the autograph books I was handed as 'Riley Sams,' not 'Barnaby Fallows,' and my paychecks were made out to the real me. Barnaby was worth two extra zeros at the end of the amount on the check."

"Well, I guess there was a short time—maybe during the first season—that I felt the same way. At first, Bix was mildly annoying, then he was maddening. And when, years later, it became clear that he was *permanent,* he was infuriating!

"Although he never said so in so many words, Thornton Ever-ly, my manager, thought of me as Bixby too. At least he stopped sending me to any auditions that were looking for anything but Bixby Fallows clones. Everly couldn't wean himself from those ten-percent-of-Bix bucks paychecks. After a few years of my having to reject those roles, I fired him.

"So, what have I been doing? Not a lot. My nest is still fairly well supplied with *Crowded Nest* feathers, so I'm not forced to do a hell of a lot. I spent about a year optimistically going to tryouts for real acting jobs, but after about a dozen showdowns with casting people who couldn't see me as anything but Bix, I said fuck it. Why don't they go home and watch the *Nest* reruns?

"I've done voiceovers for a couple cartoons. I can alter my voice enough to portray little forest critters. You may have heard me chewing the scenery or hiding my nuts. But I'll tell you, Stanislavski doesn't help you transform yourself into a frog or a chipmunk. Once you're there, though, you're safe in the woods of anonymity. No one thinks, 'Hey! That's Bix on that lily pad!' And my real name appears in the credits."

"See, Tom. That was another benefit of working on Nest. It prepared you for appealing to the minds of six-year-olds. I trust the 'toons haven't got you working for peanuts."

"Very funny. No, the pay is OK. I wouldn't have done them if the lettuce wasn't decent. I'm not that kind of bunny.

"The most satisfying job my new manager landed for me was another off-camera voice job narrating a *National Geographic* documentary on the Atacama Desert. I'm kind of proud of that. It went well enough that I'm hoping there'll be similar gigs. I have to say that, although I didn't appear on camera, I really got into portraying a serious, scholarly-though-rugged adventurer. At least I found *myself* believable. Which is a laugh. The real Tom Valley would die in that desert.

"I'd love to see the newspaper coverage: 'The remains of Bixby Fallows, formerly of *Crowded Nest*, were found near the salt flats in Chile's Atacama Desert. He'd been partly eaten by buzzards. Identification papers belonging to a Tom Valley were found on the body.'

"Say, I'm ready for another drink. How 'bout you?"

"Sure. In that sense, I'm ready to grab for more. Maybe with a twist of lemon instead of the lime this time out."

"Waiter! You've got two famous thespians at this table who are dying of thirst. Bixby and Barnaby Fallows will autograph your dickey if you rescue them. Ah! There you are! By the way kid, did you know that Chile's Atacama Desert is the driest place on earth?"

"What?"

"Dry and cold. You should go there."

Danny's Star

The sameness of weekdays is a burden. My job's okay, I guess, but the half-hour el trips to and from work, the repetitions of the paperwork I have to deal with, the endless reappearance of familiar office faces, the pathetic variations of our cafeteria's limited menu offerings . . . Staying awake for eight hours a day, fifty weeks a year isn't easy. I'm yawning as I write this. I know it's my attitude that's the problem. Not all my coworkers suffer the malaise that I do and most of my neighbors live lives they consider stimulating. At least they're more content with the sameness they face. In fact, they don't seem to experience it at all. Rather than watch current television shows, many of them will opt for an oldies channel to watch an *I Love Lucy* or *M*A*S*H* they've seen dozens of times.

At the end of my evening el ride on the Green Line, I get off at Pulaski and walk the three blocks to my two-flat apartment, often counting my steps—a long-time habit. It takes between seven hundred and sixty-five and eight hundred and twenty steps, depending on how weary I am on a given night.

The counting fills my otherwise empty head and passes, in a way, as entertainment. There's no purpose in the counting, but I'm always annoyed when some neighbor, recognizing a face he's seen pass by hundreds of times, makes me lose count with a pointless interruption.

"Hot enough fer ya?" "The end of another day, eh?" "Think it's gonna rain?" "How's it goin'?"

I bring that up because tonight, just as I had reached my four hundred and thirty-seventh step, a guy who was hauling a garbage can to the curb asked my opinion about whether it was hot enough. I answered, "Yup," without losing my count. But then, at step six hundred and five, a guy who was playing with his dog asked the same question. That was one more repetition than I could handle. I lost count of my steps.

Interruptions don't bother me when they happen close enough to my place. Then I can estimate the number of remaining steps with some accuracy. Interruptions happen almost every night because I rarely get near my apartment before six o'clock and, by that time, my neighbor, Danny, is always (and I mean *always*) planted on his front stoop.

"Hullo, Randy," he hollers. "What's new with you?"

"You got it all, Danny."

"Nothing happening here."

"That's life in the circus, Danny. Keep up the good work. What's new in the neighborhood?"

"I haven't seen anything yet, but I'll keep an eye on things. Ya never know."

What I do know is that Danny will be at his post tomorrow and tomorrow and tomorrow unless it's raining or snowing. Not eventful evenings, even for a kid, but even less so for a guy in his late twenties. Nothing significant changes from one day to the next. And I know our exchanges will be just as insignificant every day. Neither Danny nor I require or expect more.

There sits a guy, I think, who isn't pressured into a routine but chooses to lock himself in as tightly as the rest of us.

But I never give him much thought beyond that until, one Saturday afternoon, on my way home from somewhere else, I found myself in a grocery store farther down Pulaski than I usually shop. I was doing the sleepwalk I usually do in grocery stores as I pass through the checkout line. I was sparked awake when I saw Danny bagging my groceries.

"Hey, Randy!" he yells. "I never seen *you* here before!"

"Never *been* here before. I usually shop closer to home. I didn't know you work here." I had never imagined him working at all.

"Oh, yeah! I been working here about five years. I ride my bike over."

"Y' like it?"

"Sure. It's steady work an' the people here are real nice t' me. They always say hello an' they give me time off when I need t' take it."

"Well, keep up the good work."

"Uh huh. You always say that t' me. Well, I'll prob'ly see ya t'night."

"Maybe," I said, but I thought, not for sure on Saturday. "I know you'll be keepin' an eye on things,' but I can't promise I'll be there to check on you."

Carrying my groceries into my place, I passed Danny's old man on the way to his car.

"I just saw Danny at the Fresh Express. I didn't know he worked there."

"Yeah. For years. It's a good fit. Gives him somethin' t' do b'sides his other job."

"Other job?"

"Yeah. You know—watchin' the sky. You prob'ly seen him. Ev'ry night, sittin' on the stoop, lookin' up, hopin' f'r a clear night."

"A clear night?"

"Yeah. It's a long story. About ten years ago, when Danny was about eighteen, I drove the family up t' the Upper Peninsula—t' Gwynne, Michigan—t' visit my older son, Richie, who was in th' Air Force at the time. Well, it's a long way, an' Danny was bored by th' whole trip. Read comic books the whole way. So, one night after we got there, while Richie had some duties he hadda take care of, I figured I'd give Danny somethin' different t' do. I drove a few miles away from the base, out where we wz in total darkness. Out there, you could see so many stars, the sky was practically white. We got out of the car an' Danny just stands there with his jaw hangin' open.

"I said, 'Whaddya think of that?' He don't say nothin'! He's like hypnotized! An' then we see those colored lights dancin' in the sky. The auroras, y' know?

"Well, Danny hasn't been the same since that night. All the way back t' Chicago, he's jabberin' away about the stars, askin' his ma an' me questions f'r which we got no answers.

"We get back an' it don't stop. An' after restin' up a bit after the trip, a few nights later, he's out on that stoop, lookin' up."

"'Whatcha doin'?' I ask 'im.

"'Where are the stars?' he asks me.

"'They're up there,' I tell 'im, "but y' can't see 'em here."

"'Why not? Are they all in Michigan?'

"Nah. They're over Chicago, too, but there's too much light an' foggy stuff here, so, most nights, all y' can see is that orangey-brown stuff. Once in a while, y' see a few stars. Maybe a dozen or so. But not often.

"Danny gets real quiet, thinkin' about that. But ever since then, he's out there ev'ry night, waitin' f'r a Michigan sky fulla stars."

I was real quiet, too, thinking about Danny thinking. I'd always figured his brain was shooting blanks. And later, after the groceries were put away, I couldn't stop thinking about Mr. Yost's story. It had the same impact on me as the stars had had on Danny. He hadn't known stars were there. Well, I hadn't really known that *he* was there except as a lump on the front stoop.

I'd never given the stars much thought, either. Or darkness. Or light pollution. Or . . . Well, there's a lot of things I've never given much thought to. Just for kicks, I sat down at my computer and Googled light pollution. Then, more specifically, *Chicago's* light pollution. I wanted to find out how far from Chicago one would have to get in order to approximate the darkness of the Upper Peninsula. I was thinking that I'd like to drive Danny somewhere that could give him the thrill of his first vision.

Not possible, I learned. Chicago spreads its smeary glow farther than I can afford to travel on a whim. The Upper Peninsula would do the trick, apparently, but that's more than four hundred miles away. I did come across the work of a photographer, Thierry Cohen, who was seeking the same thing I was. On the web, one can see a shot from his work, *Villes éteintes* (Dark Cities), that shows what Chicago's night sky would look like without light pollution. To get that shot, he had to travel to Sheldon National Wildlife Reserve near Lakeview, Oregon in the extreme northwest corner of Nevada.

I wasn't about to travel to northwest Nevada, but I must say that Cohen's photo made me feel what Danny felt in the Upper Peninsula. So, after a brief peek out the window at Chicago's orangey-brown sky, I flopped down on the couch. I turned on the TV, hoping something like Nova was on, but it was that damn antiques show. I watched two supplicants ooh and ah at the price estimates they were quoted and turned the thing off. Bedtime!

* * *

The next day, Danny was still on my mind. I was sharing the frustration he must have experienced sitting on that stoop for . . . what? Fourteen or fifteen years, knowing that breathtaking beauty was invisible overhead, leaving nothing but man-made smudge and, occasionally, a handful of stars. I know something about frustration, but Danny had been (and still, at that point, was) fighting the good fight against it. I had trouble dealing with that.

Over the next week, part of my mind was devoted to finding a solution to the problem. Then I hit on it! Chicago may obscure the universe, but it's also home to the Adler Planetarium, the country's oldest such institution. A planetarium isn't a building. It's a complex machine that somewhat resembles a giant insect. That bug houses dozens of projectors that, in tandem, swivel in every direction to project all the elements of the night sky on the interior of an overhead dome. The projections recreate a night sky more awesome than many Chicagoans have ever seen. And the whole thing moves, simulating the motions of the stars as they look on a planet that rotates on its axis and revolves around the sun!

Danny has got to see that thing! I said to myself. I couldn't wait to propose the two of us take a trip. My invitation surprised and mystified him, but he accepted.

To Danny, any old car trip was a bit of a novelty. His dad usually consigned him to his bike. But I can't say Danny was overcome by the delight of fighting traffic on Lake Shore Drive. Even when we were seated in the Grainger Sky Theater, he was kind of baffled about what he was doing there.

"Are we waiting for a movie?" he asked me.

"Wait. You'll see."

Then the room slowly darkened as if the sun was setting and stars began to appear, the brightest ones first, followed by dimmer and dimmer ones until the dome was filled with all the stars you'd see in the middle of the Sahara.

From Danny came the sort of sound one would produce by punching someone in the belly. It scared me. I looked at Danny and saw that he had slouched down in his chair, his legs as stiff in front of him as the seating would allow and his hands clutching the armrests tightly. He was trying to lay flat on his back to take in the whole dome at once.

"You okay, Danny?"

"It's the real sky!" he gasped. "*All* of it! It's just like I remember! Have you ever seen anything like it Randy?"

We were getting shushed by people who wanted to hear the accompanying lecture, so I calmed Danny down. "We'll talk about it later," I said. He was quiet, but I kept an eye on him throughout the presentation. A lot of squirming and twitching, and he was wide-eyed throughout the ninety-minute show. He was breathing hard as we left the theater.

"What'd you think, Danny?" I asked.

"I had started to think they weren't there anymore. I was so happy to see 'em again. How did those guys get rid of the fog?"

"They didn't. You'll see tonight. The fog's still there, as bad as ever. What we saw wasn't real stars. It was *pictures* of stars, moving just the way the real stars move."

"But real stars don't move."

"No. I said that wrong. The stars only look like they move because the earth turns."

"Man! I guess there's a lot I don't know about stars," he said. He probably hadn't known the earth turns, either. After that, he was quiet the whole ride home. Out of the corner of my eye, I watched Danny's face reflect intense, rapidly changing impulses.

What can be going on in that head? I wondered. I hoped I hadn't created a monster. I guessed he'd want to go there every week, and I couldn't afford to take him even once a month. Admission for the two of us had set me back seventy bucks!

I was kinda surprised that, for the next few days, *my* head, too, was full of stars. I'd never had much interest in astronomy. Long ago my grade school class had taken a field trip to the planetarium, but it hadn't had the impact on me then that it did this time. On this trip, the planetarium's simulation of the cosmos had awakened new curiosities in me. I'd never known what "light year" meant. I started to wonder why stars are different colors. I wondered how astronomers can tell a star's real magnitude when some stars are fairly close and others are very far away. I was ignorant about the whole subject.

So I Googled a few terms. As usual, I started down a lot of paths that didn't come close to answering my questions. An aggravating number of clickable guesses just led me to Amazon's offers to fill my cart. Even topics like astronomy, telescopes, photography and stars, were mostly invitations to spend money. I didn't want to buy anything. I kept poking around until, little by little, I learned a few interesting things about what's up out there.

Then I got an inspiration. I'll bet there are some *photos* on the web that would wow Danny. I thought I'd run next door and invite him to my place. Then I realized that I hadn't seen him since our visit to the planetarium. He hadn't been at his habitual observatory. It kinda worried me. I thought I'd better check on him.

Mr. Yost, Danny's dad, answered the door.

"Where's Danny?"

"Ever since you took him to that sky place, he's been in Richie's room, foolin' with Richie's old computer. I didn't think he even knew how the thing works, but he stays in there for hours."

"Is he okay?"

"I guess so. Why?"

"I haven't seen him out front for days."

"Yeah. I dunno. I think he's lookin' in that computer for the same stuff he was lookin' in the sky for."

"Can I go back there?"

"Why not?"

* * *

Sure enough, Danny was seated at the computer. He was even more frustrated than I had been. Danny didn't know any of Richie's passwords or access codes, so he'd been sitting there for four days, punching buttons at random and watching minimal screen activity. He was probing the blankness like an astronomer squinting at the universe, hoping to discover a new phenomenon. I knew there was no point in asking Mr. Yost for help. In one's search for information, he was almost always a dead-end street. And his computer knowledge wasn't any better than Danny's.

Indicating the computer, Danny complained, "I thought this thing was supposed to answer all your questions."

To keep things simple, I just said, "Not *this* one. But c'mon. Let's go next door."

* * *

In my "study," a spare bedroom I used mainly as a junk room, I went straight to a site I'd discovered called Hubble's Top 100. The site opens with a hundred postage-stamp-sized images, but you can maximize each of them to screen size and scroll to the bottom of each photo to get a few paragraphs that explain what you're looking at. Anyone who's not dead from the neck up would marvel at the sight of those photos. You can imagine Danny's reaction. He pressed his nose against the screen.

"Is *that* what stars look like up close? All those little white dots in the sky are really explosions of *color*?" Danny gasped. "How's that possible?"

"Not all of what you see there is stars," I said. "Some of it's big clouds of gas. In these pictures you can see stars being born, stars dying..."

"I thought stars were there forever."

"Nope. Someday, even the sun will die. The sun is a star, y'know?"

Once again, Danny fell silent, digesting the new information that, when we think about it, boggles us all.

* * *

Most of the time I'd known Danny, I'd given him no more thought than I give a neighborhood fire hydrant, mailbox or streetlight. As we became more and more involved in astronomy, I began to realize that Danny's hunger was leading me places I'd never dreamed I'd go. In that sense, he was my teacher. At the same time, *I* was becoming a teacher—a conduit of information and inspiration. Both roles had snuck up on me. It was more typical of me to be a somewhat critical stand-aside observer. Frankly, the change was refreshing.

One night, while we were looking at star photos, I began reading him the explanatory notes that appeared on the screen under the photo.

Danny interrupted. "I *know* that."

"You *do*!? *How* do you know that?"

"I read it before you started reading it."

"You can *read*?"

"Not too good, but sure. If it's something real interesting, I can read. I went to school y' know."

I was apologetic and embarrassed. I'd always assumed that, because of the stripped-down nature of Danny's conversation, his unawareness of a lot of stuff most of us take for granted, and the fact that a guy in his late twenties still lived with his dad . . . Well, I'd just assumed. The revelation of his reading ability gave me another idea. One that wouldn't cost me anything.

"Do you ever go to the library?"

"I been to one a few times."

"Do you know how to find books?"

"That's easy. They're all over the place."

"No, I mean do you know how to find the kind of books you're looking for?"

"I just pick whatever I find."

"Well, I'm sure there are a lot of books about stars, planets, comets . . . Everything you've ever wondered about space. You could find books like that. We've got to go! I have a lot of things to show you."

The following Friday we went.

* * *

Our first stop was the front desk, where we got Danny his first ever library card. Then we spent about twenty minutes at the computers, where I showed him how to find books by title or subject matter. I skipped talking about author searches, thinking Danny wouldn't be needing that, but I did show him how to check his account for due dates. While we were there, we looked up a title or two and jotted down their call numbers. We talked about the Dewey decimal system a little and we were off to the stacks to find our books.

"When we find the numbers the computer showed us, you'll

find the book you were looking for. And, probably, there'll be other books about the same subject right next to it," I told Danny.

Sure enough, we found eight books about either the Hubble telescope or photos it took. "Now that you've got a library card, you can take any of these books home."

"I want *all* of 'em."

"Why not take one and come back in a few weeks and get another one. Or two. Whatever."

"No, I want *all* of 'em."

So the two of us lugged eight books up to the front desk. Each of them weighed several pounds. We checked them out and lugged them to the car. Danny didn't talk during the ride home. He was studying one of the books. And, for the following week, I didn't see him at all. Either he was riveted on one of the books or he was going from book to book. Then he appeared at my door.

"I want to keep three of these books," he said. "I've finished the rest of 'em."

"You can't *keep* library books. We can renew them and you'll be able to have them for three more weeks but you can't keep library books forever. Other people want to read them too."

"I guess that's good enough," he said.

From the tone of his voice, I could tell that three more weeks wasn't really good enough, but Danny accepted the rules. We drove to the library to return the five he had "finished", renewed the three he wanted to keep and picked up two additional books.

On the drive home I asked him, "What did you mean when you said you 'finished' the books we took back?"

"Well, three of 'em were no good. The other two were good, but I learned everything I needed out of 'em."

"You mean you *read* all those books? Those were pretty tough books!" I had glanced at some of them and I wouldn't have understood much if I'd spent a year trying to make sense of all the physics and math in 'em.

"Yeah. It turns out I can read better than I thought if the books are interesting. A lot of the books they used to give us in school were about stuff I didn't care about. They were boring. The library's books are interesting! Some of 'em had more science than I could get. I had to skip a lot of that. But I learned a lot."

In the following weeks, we made several trips to the library, but I didn't see Danny out on the steps anymore.

Why not, I wondered.

Danny explained. "I understand now that I'm not gonna see what I want to see out there. I can get closer by reading the books."

Myself, I was kind of disappointed to find the steps empty when I'd pass the apartment on my way home from work. Danny had found escape from his isolation, but the temporary release I'd found by participating in Danny's adventure had been short-lived. I wanted back in but, by this time, I knew that Danny was orbiting higher than my earthbound brain was likely to go.

* * *

In November, I began the painful process of trying to figure out Christmas presents for my family and friends. I'm never good at that. Everything I think of is too impersonal, too personal, too cheap or too expensive. Suddenly, I realized that, in the past year, I'd made a new friend. What should I give Danny?

Right away I thought, astronomy books, but I knew he'd become pretty picky about what was "good" and what wasn't. And he'd already read so many that I'd never guess which ones he'd "used up." I didn't want to *ask* him for suggestions. That would subtract any element of surprise from the gift. I always get a big kick out of surprising people. Why wrap a present that the someone knows is coming? But, if not an astronomy book, what? A telescope would be useless in our neighborhood.

*   *   *

Then I remembered hearing about a company that lets people name stars. I went to the Internet again and searched things like "star names," "name a star", "your own star," "star deeds" and all the variations I could think of. It turned out that it isn't *one* company that offers the service—it's *dozens*. When I read all their offers, though, I came away highly suspicious of the whole process. Although their offers included official-looking certificates that resemble diplomas, honorary titles, legal documents or recognitions of high achievement, I wondered if the names people were concocting would ever be recognized by the observatories of the world. Would anyone check to see if stars had been previously named? What was to keep people from naming stars Donald Duck or Charles Manson? And who has the authority to attach a name to an astronomical item?

Many of the companies accompanied their offers of star naming with pages and pages of disclaimers, limitations and legalistic mumbo-jumbo that absolve them of responsibilities for fatalities or disappointments or reminders that management wasn't responsible for stolen hats. I got the impression that star naming is no more legitimate than the world's omnipresent claim of "ABSO-LUTELY FREE!"

Still, the idea appealed to me, despite the fishiness of the deal. The only important question that remained was, "How can I get Danny fully involved in the idea?"

And how could I retain the surprise element? How could I allow Danny the choice of stars and the choice of names? I figured he would first pick a well-known star like Polaris, Sirius or Vega. But those already *have* names. How would Danny or any of us know about *anonymous* stars?

I decided to sacrifice the surprise. In early December, I pitched the idea to Danny.

He liked it, but he didn't jump and shout with glee. His response was surprisingly sophisticated.

"How many stars don't already *have* names?" he asked. "How can I be sure I'm not picking somebody else's star? Is this OK with astronomers? What kind of name should I pick?"

As he'd often done before, Danny was rubbing my nose in my own ignorance. I couldn't honestly answer his questions. I did my best to brush them aside and leave the decisions to Danny.

"You pick the star and what to name it and, if your choices aren't okay, the company will tell us." Fat chance of that happening after they have my forty bucks, I thought.

* * *

With millions of stars and who-knows-how-many names to choose from, I wasn't surprised that Danny didn't get back to me the next day or the next. It wasn't until four days before Christmas that Danny knocked on my door.

"Ophiuchus V2213," he greeted me.

"What?" I asked.

"Ophiuchus V2213 is the star I want to name," he said. "It's the dimmest star that can be seen of the eighty-four visible stars in Ophiuchus. I don't think anybody else has named it. I don't think it even has a Greek letter assigned to it."

"What's Ophiuchus?" I asked.

"It's a constellation that's partly in the southern hemisphere and partly in the north. It's a big one. It's got twenty-two hundred and thirty-four stars all spread out. The name means serpent handler. He even has two little constellations that are his snakes."

"I've never heard of it. It's not very famous, is it?"

"Astronomy people know it. Nobody else, I guess. But I know it. And all eighty-eight constellations are famous to astronomers."

"I thought there were only twelve constellations."

"You're thinking that 'cause of the zodiac. There's twelve in the zodiac, but the zodiac isn't exactly a real thing. You know about the Big Dipper. That's not one of the twelve. Ophiuchus isn't one 'em either. And you can't see Ophiuchus this far north."

"Why would you want to pick a star you wouldn't be able to see here?"

"Even if I lived on the equator, I prob'ly wouldn't be able to see it. Like I said, my star is very dim. It only has an apparent magnitude of six, but that's because it's sixty-seven light years away. It's a blue star. That means it's one of the hottest kinds. But I picked it because it looks like it's dim. A lotta people think I'm kind of dim too, but I'm not. So that would be a good match."

My God! I thought. I can remember when I thought that too! I wish everybody could know Danny like I do now. Compared to Danny, everyone else—me included—is kind of dim. And we're right here.

"Do you know all that kind of stuff about *all* the stars, Danny?"

"Heck no! When you told me about naming a star, I looked up a lot of stuff that would help me choose. Before that, I didn't know anything about V2213 either."

"What are you gonna name it?"

"I'm not gonna tell you. You'll know when we get the certificate. You'll find out when we fill it in."

"We don't have to wait for mail to come. The company will let me pay by PayPal and e-mail a form to fill out right away. We can tell them the name you pick, they'll e-mail us your certificate and we'll print a copy that's suitable for framing, as they say. So, we're ready to roll, Danny. What're you gonna name the star?"

"It's gonna be named Danny," he announced proudly. "That way, some people will remember me forever."

"That'll happen, Danny. I guarantee that'll happen." I'm not ashamed to say my eyes teared up a bit.

* * *

I'm still convinced that the company that issues those documents probably files registrations in the circular file as soon as they hit the office. They would, of course, retain customer contact information in case some customers wanted a second bite of the apple. There are a lot of stars waiting to be named.

But I wish Ophiuchus V2213's new name and the man who named it would be better known to the astronomical community. I wish he'd used his full name—Danny Yost—so that everyone would know him more specifically. Also, the name would sound like "Daniost," making it sound like a lot of existing star names.

I know we can't see Danny's star in Chicago, but I see Danny clear as anything. He's a star of significant magnitude in a constellation of the West Side's sky. Danny is a star that has lit my own dark sky with a new glow. The whole world looks and feels different now. I no longer count steps on my way home. I'm no longer annoyed by the neighbors. The sky isn't as dark as it used to be. Starlight!

I'm Pretending Someone Will Understand This

There's so many things I don't understand. What do you ig-spect? I'm only six. Maybe when I'm older I'll figure it all out. But maybe not. Mom and dad are older and they still don't understand a lot about me. Just like I don't understand much about them. Its like we live in differnt countries and nobody speaks Chinese. Everybody has to guess what the other ones mean. One thing I don't think any of us really gets is the differnce between pretending and real. I'll give you some igzamples.

I know my dolls aren't really people but they're not just toys. A lot of times they need me to decide what they do. But when I'm not there they think anyway. I have to pretend I know what they're thinking so I don't make them do things they don't like. I'm sure I make mistakes no matter how hard I try to understand. I wonder what they feel about my mistakes.

Its the same with my parents and me. They do their best to know what I want. When they make mistakes, I guess they have to pretend. I try hard to tell them but it doesn't always work. Pretending can only do so much. I don't know how *dolls* feel when stuff like that happens but I know how *I* feel when it does.

I'm kind of like the middle between dolls and parents. I know a little about both sides. When my parents play dolls with me it's almost impossible to keep both sides happy. Mom says mom things that don't mean much to dolls. She doesn't get how dolls think. She only pretends they think but she doesn't really believe they do. I wonder if she believes *I* think, cause sometimes she tells me stuff that even the stupidest kid already knows and she thinks its something new, exciting or important. Don't get me wrong. Sometimes mom's really good at guessing what I feel or what I want even though I'm not sure *what* I'm feeling.

Dad isn't much good when it comes to understanding dolls. He dresses them clumsy, moves them awkward and pretends dolls are saying things they'd never say. He might as well pretend a block of wood can talk. Hmm. I never wondered if wood can think. I try to imagine I'm thinking like wood. The dolls I have with wooden or hard plastic heads don't think as good as clothheads. Clothheads think more like me. Animals even more. I can see them thinking.

This problem spills all over. Not even mom and dad always understand what's going on with each other. Sometimes one of them tries to listen when the other one isn't making any sense. Other times the other one tries to be reasonable. Sometimes when *both* of them are crazy I can figure out what both are trying to say and I try to explain to them. But especially when they're crazy they don't listen to me. I'll bet they think what does a kid know? She's just a kid.

Those times pretending helps. I pretend I'm an adult and they're the kids. Too bad I can't send them to their room. When they send me to my room, sometimes I change my mind.

Maybe me and my dolls just don't understand each other cause we speak differnt languages. What makes it even harder is that dolls don't speak at all. I have to speak *for* them and I can only make up what they want to say. I'm sure I make mistakes. My parents make mistakes when they're playing with me. Even my friends who are the same age as me don't always understand what I say. They don't even pretend that they do. Sometimes we get in fights over that.

The world would be a lot better if pretending worked for everyone. Like woodenhead dolls adults get stuck on one idea and they can't change around even when they want to.

When my parents play dolls with me they pretend they're talking to the dolls but I can tell they're really talking to me. They say things the dolls don't want or need to know. I bet dolls can tell when it's not them getting talked to. I wonder what they think about my parents when that happens. I hope dolls know that the differnce between real and pretend sometimes isn't much, even to the person who's pretending.

Differnce between knowing and not knowing isn't big either. I know it isn't always clear to me. When I'm doing good pretending, I don't *care* if it's real or not or whether something's a thing I know or don't know. Fooling myself can be a lot of fun, so I don't worry about it. I hope the dolls enjoy it too. There's so many things they don't know.

I'll give you some for instances of things I mean. Food, sleep and reading. Mom and dad think clocks should get to boss when a person should do stuff. They say, "It's time for supper, it's time to go to bed or it's time to get up." It makes more sense to me to eat when you're hungry and sleep when you're sleepy. Who cares what clocks think? In fact I doubt clocks think at all.

Its not only *when* you eat, its *what*. Some of the stuff mom tries to make me eat tastes *terrible!*

She tells me it doesn't and puts some in her mouth but that doesn't change my mind. It tastes bad to me and that's what counts. Do I make the same mistake when I feed my dolls? When they don't like the pretend food I give them I tell them that its something else. I just try not to give them the same thing again but I *never* give them broccoli, grapefruit or stuff with pepper on it. It doesn't really matter because none of them chew. They don't even really open their mouths. Except one doll I had once that really ate. She really pooped too, but that was a mess. I never played with her much. If I want a doll to poop I'll just pretend. Right now I'm pretending I *don't* have to poop.

The reading problem is more confusing. Mom and dad read to me a lot before I could read and were real proud when I learned to do it for myself. None of my six-year-old friends can read. But now my parents tell me I read too much. They always say "Why don't you go outside?" Well, I don't because reading is more fun. I can imagine I'm outside. Maybe in India or maybe on the moon.

I like books that tell real things and books about pretend stuff. I can't decide which kind I like more. And there are so many books! The library makes me dizzy. I can't imagine what's *in* all those books. I think its impossible for someone to read too much. I feel like reading more than I possibly can and my dolls like me to read to them. I would never tell them they read too much.

I think mom should understand me more cause a long time ago she was a little girl and she told me she even had a lot of dolls. One was named Dolly. Maybe for a joke, naming a doll Dolly. Its like naming me person. Mom must of forgotten what Dolly told her. I tell my dolls I'll never forget. It would be like forgetting who my grandmother was when she was alive or even worse forgetting who I am. If my mom's dolls were still alive (I mean like *doll* alive) would they and *my* dolls understand each other?

I wish I had a brother or even better sister. I bet we could understand each other better then anyone and pretend together without getting confused. I've read stories about twins who are so alike they're almost one person. How great! I could have conversations with myself. And we could have fun fooling other people by pretending to be the other one.

But what if we got in an argument like ones between mom and dad. Ugh! That would be terrible. How would we decide who had to be first to apologize? Would the other one forgive me if I'd been the wrong one? Would we have to pretend to be sorry? What if one of my dolls would rather play with my twin? Would the dolls even recognize that there were two of me? Maybe it wouldn't be so great to be a twin after all.

This makes me think of favorites. I try to pay attention to all my dolls and play with everyone about the same but really really really if you want to know the truth Florry is the one I actually love the most. She's got her own bed right next to mine so I can talk with her right before I go to sleep. The other dolls live together in a cradle when we're not playing. Florry knows all my secrets and I know most of hers. I show her an old photo of my mom's doll, Dolly. I tell her this is your grandmother. I don't want to tell her Dolly's dead. I don't really know what dead means except you're not there anymore. Sometimes mom talks to gramma as if she's still here. Is she pretending?

I have other favorites—food, books, animals, movies even friends. Sometimes I make lists of second favorites, third favorites, sometimes up to ten. Some of them change up or down the list and sometimes back. Other times I think that whole thing is foolish and I should just be glad to have a lot of good things around. Even though there's so many things I don't know and so much I know but don't understand, I don't have to pretend I'm happy. Really really, actually I am.

Degrees of Desperation

The hotel is just a hotel, settled in a strip of similar hotels half a mile from the airport to attract business travelers. Just off the lobby, the Laid-Back Lounge is no more distinctive than the hotel that houses it. It's really just a bar—a large room dimly lit by colored lights in sconces that line the wall and back booths around the perimeter. A mirror backs multi-colored bottles that run the length of one wall. A dozen tiny tables are furnished with jarred candles in plastic fish-netting. Carpeting matches the hotel's lobby. If you've traveled for business, you've been here or in one of the ten thousand similar "heres" near the airports of all the nation's hubs.

The only differentiation is their choice of entertainment options. A few house pinball machines, but a more popular choice is a large-screen color television that tunes only to sports. It serves as an icebreaker for devotees of various local teams and opponents from towns only their locals could love. All fans are eager to express their opinions, creating illusions of expertise and comradery. The conversations TV seeds are vociferous and loud.

Anyone who isn't a sports fan is well down the road to defining himself as an outsider, but at least the television provides something specific to look at, saving patrons from the embarrassment of letting their eyeballs wander aimlessly around the room or, worse, making accidental eye contact with another patron.

The TV also prevents the barkeep from nodding off when he's the only guy in the place.

Sometimes—on Tuesdays, Thursdays and Saturday nights—

the only guy in the place is female. As most of the travelers are businessmen, she wears something sexy enough to arouse tips. In fact, she's an alternate entertainment option—the illusion of fleeting and titillatingly illicit friendship far from home and office.

But this is her night off. The only one purveying drinks is a scowling fatman who's spent years telegraphing the message, "Don't talk to me. I've heard it all and I couldn't care less." So he offers patrons no relief other than booze.

Before customers arrive, he has nothing to do but polish the bar, check the supplies of olives, lemons and cocktail onions and watch his reflection move in the mirror behind the bourbon, scotch, vodka, crème de menthe, amaretto and peppermint schnapps. Face in mirror, bottle, face, bottle, face, bottle—the intermittent face seen like a zoo animal pacing behind the bars of its own kind of cage.

Around seven, a lone customer wanders in, having passed a solitary hour over dinner. Malibu steak. Whatever *that* is. He glances around the room, feigning interest in the lounge's décor. He had hoped fellow road warriors would be present to provide relief from being the only voice in his head. But not yet. He sits at the bar and orders a drink to occupy his hands and justify his presence. In the days before America converted to the anti-tobacco religion, he would have smoked several cigarettes in the first half hour, but these days, there's not an ashtray in the room. No souvenir matchbooks either. Nothing to remind him later of where he's been. Of course, in the past ten years, he's been in this room all across the Midwest and remembers it all too well.

He bends a plastic stir back and forth into awkward shapes, covertly cleans his fingernails and tells the barkeep his name: Paul something, which the barkeep immediately forgets.

At 7:30, a man in his late twenties appears. Paul hadn't noticed him come in. The newcomer sits at the grand piano, which Paul hadn't noticed either. He drapes his sportscoat over a chair and puts a drink on the piano. Apparently, he's about to play. He begins with *Send in the Clowns.*

Paul swivels his barstool around to face the piano and, when the number is finished, he applauds. The solo clapping has an awkward, hollow sound in the empty room. No clowns had entered during the number.

The pianist nods, acknowledging the applause and goes into *These Foolish Things*—a tasty version that goes well beyond the basic melody into well-thought-out improvisation. It's good enough that Paul picks up his drink and crosses the room to stand at the side of the piano.

"H'lo," the pianist says. "Haven't seen you here before. You from here?" The pianist knows he's not.

"No, I'm from Chicago. Here selling school supplies."

"Anything for band teachers?"

"Not that I can think of. Unless they use chalk or are clueless about how to conduct their classes. Mainly, I'm pushing various curriculum plans. Administrators are always in the market for new ways to revolutionize instruction methods."

The topic bores the pianist. He barely listens to the response. "I'm Terry," he says, and goes into *More.*

During this, two other customers enter—bored men poking their noses in to see if *anything* happens in this town. Paul glances at them and recognizes fellow business travelers. The pair settles in a Naugahyde booth, then realizes there's no table service. One of them slides out to make a trip to the bar. Once he's back in place, fragments of their conversation drift across the room to mix with the music. ". . . profit and loss . . . an unmanageable number of SKUs . . . airlines' calculations of cube weight . . . alternative commodities . . ." They pay the music no attention. Nor does the pair at the piano notice the fragments of their conversation.

Next, a woman in her forties, made up as a woman in her thirties, takes a stool at the bar and leans back against it, facing the piano, forcing her dress to expose more leg. Terry apparently knows her and nods a minimal greeting. She assumes it's an invitation (it's not) and crosses the room. While Terry plays *The Lady is a Tramp,* the newcomer introduces herself. Christine. Paul reciprocates.

"You a musician?" she asks.

"I play the shoehorn," Paul jokes. "And records. All kinds. Mainly jazz though."

Christine assesses the brevity of his response and correctly concludes he isn't in the bar to meet women. Terry cases the pair inconspicuously. His eyes seem to roam the room, not really focusing on anything. Christine's eyes now are focused on the door.

From the booth, Businessman Number One is heard to say, "My customers' first concern is price. Sure, they're interested in speed and dependability of service and the quality of the products I'm selling them, but if one of my competitors undercuts my price, it's no deal. Everything but price is just parsley on the plate. When all is said and done, *anybody* can promise great service. And everybody does. You can't prove *that* pudding before the sale is made. Our competitors try to bowl buyers over with reams of market studies and demographic mishmash. It's all too complex for the typical buyer. Really pretty worthless as a sales tool. Besides, my company has a great reputation."

Businessman Number Two is in town to sell his firm's legal services to a major corporation. When he gets a chance to speak, he says, "In my case, customers want one statistic: Cases won vs cases lost. And that statistic is a matter of public record. No bullshitting my way around my firm's track record. No excusing losses by claiming extenuating circumstances."

Number One is glad he has fuzzier facts to work with. It opens the door to his polished sales spiel. Both salesmen speak the same language so, although both of them are more interested in talking than listening and neither is interested in his boothmate's life, they furnish the lonely road with sound. Their chatter continues.

The group around the piano continues to grow one or two at a time over the next hour. Six is enough to let Terry feel he's been serving a purpose. He glances at the still-empty tip jar and decides it's time to ask for requests. Requests, he knows, lubricate contributions. They stimulate interactions among the gathered and give them all a sense of membership. They chip away at the surfaces of each other's icebergs and begin to feel as if they're among friends. Terry, Paul, Elaine, Robertson with no first name and a married couple in their late 50s—Rick and Nedra Overman.

Nedra's talky, fueled by a few drinks before appearing, and is the first to request a song. Terry grants her request for *If Ever I Would Leave You.* Her husband smiles and gives her a hug. Their anniversary, Terry, a practiced eye, guesses. Both of them clap.

Robertson's a grumpy guy in his forties whose contributions to the conversation are limited to monosyllables. When the ball's passed to him, he drops it. The others recognize him as not in the game.

Nedra, on the other hand, is a team leader. "I love Broadway musicals," she tells Terry.

"You'll keep me here all night if you keep playing Broadway."

"Tell you what," he says. "I'll play the songs and you tell me which musical they come from. The rest of you can guess too."

Nedra's enthusiastic; Paul, Rick and Elaine are lukewarm, and Robertson acts as if he hadn't heard. He makes a trip to the bar for a refill.

"This is an easy one," Terry says. "What musical gave us this?" and starts playing *If I Loved You*.

Robertson comes back and whines, "If that's an easy one, I'm out of the game." No one imagines he'd ever been in it.

From Nedra: "*Carousel*. I saw *Carousel* in summer tent theater this year."

Terry flinches at her mention of the venue, but says, "Bravo! The music goes 'round and 'round and it comes out *Carousel*. Ready for tougher stuff?"

Back from the bar, Robertson says, "I'm ready for more music. How 'bout you, Elaine?"

She brightens at hearing her name used and scootches her chair closer to Robertson's.

"Where did you say you're from?" she asks him.

"I'm an out-of-towner. Here on business."

"If this is your first time in town, you'll probably think it's a hick town compared to yours. Too much surrounding farmland and too many ag-dependent businesses. We can still have some fun here, though."

She asks him the businessman's icebreaker: "What business you in?"

His answer is vague. "Hard goods manufacturing. I'm a manager."

"Does that require you to travel much?"

"Lately, yes."

Elaine gives him a lipsticky smile.

Terry rolls his eyes and interrupts the game to slip in a musical comment, *Love for Sale*. He doesn't bother to ask if anyone knows it's from the musical *The New Yorkers*. He knows they don't. And nobody picks up on the tune's relevance to anything that's happening in their presence. Robertson makes a trip to the bar for another refill on his gin and tonic and another one of whatever the lady's drinking.

"Back to the musicals," Terry says.

But before he starts the next tune, another newcomer jumps into their circle. "I know musicals better than Oscar and Hammerstein," he boasts, elbowing his way right next to the keyboard.

"And who might you be?" Terry asks.

"Well, I *might* be Carol Channing, but, in fact, I'm Niles Raiment, a local boy trying to make good."

"Well, hello Dolly," snaps Terry, and once again chooses a song that could possibly be sarcasm, this time aimed at the newcomer: *All the Things You Are*.

Niles can't guess the musical. "I have no idea," he says. "I don't even know all the things *you* are!" Niles aims at Terry, who ignores the nuance for the time being.

"I've never been good at Trivial Pursuit," Elaine says.

"Don't underestimate yourself, babe," Terry pops. "I've watched you in pretty hot pursuit." She scowls at him.

At that, Robertson puts his hand on Elaine's shoulder and jerks his head toward one of the booths in a far corner from the piano. She picks up the drink she'd parked on the piano and follows him. As they leave, Niles sings, "Goodbye, young lovers wherever you are," and segues into a reprise of *If Ever I Would Leave You*.

Terry reminds everyone of the game. "*All the Things You Are?* What show?"

Rick knows it's by Jerome Kern, but nobody can guess the musical. Terry tells them, "It's from everybody's favorite musical, *Very Warm for May*. The song is one of the best by Kern and Hammerstein, but the show turned out to be all the things that weren't. Evidence that Liza wasn't Vincente Minnelli's only embarrassment."

Meanwhile, the fatman behind the bar remains a silent, sour lump. His only thought, four hours to go until last call. The newcomers on the scene begin to pair off. The businessmen in their booth talk about money and how to get it. They tell each other how clever they've been to get where they are. Elaine and Robertson fumble for words that will turn small talk to something more intimate or, if not intimate, at least toward something requiring fewer clothes. Niles' chatter is full of code words probing Terry's possible sex preference, but Terry remains steadfastly opaque and in charge of the scene, empowered by the piano. On other islands, the natives carry on in miscellaneous languages.

"Which musical gave us *Smoke Gets in Your Eyes*?" Terry uses to stump them all again.

Because the Overmans were a pair before appearing, they're somewhat immune to the scene's chemistries. Their own fissions and fusions transcend the others in the room. Nedra's involvement in the musical events is stronger than Rick's, but it's partly an avoidance of other topics. "That tune! That tune! It's one of my favorites! I could stay here all night and listen to such stuff!" she repeats her earlier reluctance to leave. Rick wants to believe her explanation but glances at his watch, timing what's left of the night.

Paul remains the remainder, aware of the vectors that zoom

around him but not playing any active role. He's as alone as when he walked in the room, a blank slate wishing to be written upon. It's early yet. There's always hope.

"*Roberta*," Terry answers the question that no one else could.

* * *

Paul's next slim hope for companionship arrives as a group of six, busily in the midst of a conversation loud enough to command the whole room's attention whether they want it to or not. Clearly six friends with no room for more. They push two tiny tables together, effectively forming a fort against outsider intrusions and a base from which to overpower the music. Terry grits his teeth and plays a lot louder than before, abandoning Broadway for Tin Pan Alley, which provides an excuse for Rick to extract Nedra. He tips Terry and he and his wife leave.

About the same time, the two businessmen exchange business cards as if they'll get in touch some time in the future. The cards remind them of each other's names so they can bid each other somewhat personalized farewells. Without the cards, they'd have remained just "the other guy," names long ago forgotten. They don't pass the tip jar on their ways out.

From the sextet at the two-table enclave, snatches of conversation:

"You might as well hand over your keys now, Jack. Assuming we can even find your car, I've just designated myself our driver."

"You think we don't know you're only looking for an excuse to sit next to Edie? Do you even *have* a driver's license? Do you know how to drive stick?"

"If that's the only reason," the lady shouted, "I'll sit in the back with him."

"And *she* knows how to drive stick, if you know what I mean," another reveler joked.

The whole group knows that none of them wants to sit next to Edie, but to keep their social canoe from tipping, nobody says a thing. The topic changes, the current rushes on.

Bradley, a muscly guy among them, uses volume to clarify to anyone who's in doubt that he's the alpha animal in the group. Most of his braying contains references to purchases he's made, prices he's paid for various items or celebrities he's met—most of the few who've passed through this fly-over burg. The other five act convinced by his pose and defer to his pronouncements. Which fuels his ego and cranks his volume higher, but behind their seemingly participating masks, the minds of his five companions have begun to leave. Only their bodies remain.

Terry does his best Jerry Lee Lewis, battling the loudmouth to a draw. Niles and Paul stay with it. Niles wiggles in his seat and waves his arms. He's doing the "look at me" dance. Paul watches his neighbor act foolish and is increasingly aware that he's not part of whatever this scene is. His mind wanders. It drifts back to his dinner menu—back to things he should have chosen instead of what he chose.

From the sextet, a musical request. *Sweet Caroline.* Terry grits his teeth. He's gotten that request more times than he can count and he knows that those who request it are laying in wait to pounce on "So good, so good, so good" when it's time for that lyric. Sure enough, tonight's group doesn't disappoint, although they aren't actually so good.

Paul glances around the lounge. There are a few new faces at the bar, at the tables and in the booths, but none of them seem like potential... What? Friends? Conversationalists? Worthy companions for the last remaining hour? So he tosses a few bucks in Terry's tip jar and thanks him for the good music. Leaving Niles as Terry's only audience.

* * *

On his way out, Paul notices that a briefcase has been left in the booth recently occupied by Robertson and Elaine. No big deal, he thinks. Just take it to the front desk and it'll get back to him. First glitch: No Robertson is registered at the hotel. Maybe the briefcase isn't Robertson's. Fortunately, the case isn't locked. Paul assumes the owner will be identified inside, so he opens it.

It's full of help wanted ads, resumes, cover letters and miscellaneous documents to bolster a job hunt. But the contents don't identify Robertson. The job hunter is someone named Vern Masters—not an out-of-towner as he'd claimed earlier to be. A local boy.

Am I wrong about having seen the case at Robertson's side, Paul wonders. He returns to the lounge to ask some of the others.

Terry's not particularly interested in the whole business, but he verifies Paul's memory. "You're not wrong. That was his."

So it's back to the front desk to see if Vern Masters is registered.

"He is," says the man at the desk. "In fact, I just saw him pass by with a lady. I'll make sure we get it back to him. Thank you."

So sour Robertson, supposed manager of hard goods manufacturing, in town on a business trip, is, in fact, unemployed Vern Masters from right nearby, stopping in at a local watering hole to pick up a stranger who'll help distract him from reality. It isn't hard for Paul to shrug that off. He'd never paid the man much attention or invested any belief in the cover story or what it was meant to conceal. No moral judgment. Who cares?

And who were the others? Also passing ships, leaving no tracks in the choppy waters. Finally, who am I, Paul considers. At least I really am myself, a salesman from Chicago, alone in some other people's home town, letting good music block out the silence. And now I'm tired. Time for bed.

*   *   *

In The Laid-Back Lounge, the fatman issues last call. Whatever the seekers have been seeking has been captured or, more likely, has escaped. Too late to change that, they shuffle into the night. Terry stops at the bar to fill out a time sheet and collects his pay for five hours plus.

"Good take tonight?" asks the fatman.

"So-so, I guess," Terry says, and he splits.

Total tips: six dollars.

Tomorrow night, faces will change, but all the types will be back. Even now, their planes are circling over the airport and the hotel has lit the Vacancy sign.

In the Transcendental Night

Thoreau had been asleep for two hours, working, as always, on emptying his head of civilization's disruptive chatter. That buzz had diminished, night by night, with every sleep, until now, nature's whispers were louder than the sounds he'd left behind. Generally, Walden nights were as quiet as anyone could hope, far from civilization's inherent disturbances, but Nature never sleeps, and Thoreau's ear was tuned to its tiniest murmurs. His sensitized ear whispered, "Be awake." To be awake is to be alive, he had written, and the rest of him remembered that admonition. Outdoors, *something* was sounding.

"Ork . . . Ork."

Familiar though he was with creatures of the pond, the trees and the forest floor, he couldn't name the source of the sound, and it continued for half an hour.

"Ork . . . Ork . . . Ork."

He rolled in bed, switching from pressing his right ear to the pillow to pressing the left."Ork."

Now his curiosity was awake enough that sleep was impossible. He got out of bed and stepped outdoors. Naked in the woods ("Beware of all enterprises that require new clothes."), he cocked his ear, attempting to discover the source of the unfamiliar sound. He approached the pond, imagining that perhaps a frog had awakened him with its incessant nocturnal song. But, in his time living at Walden, he'd familiarized himself with dozens of local frog species and could identify each by its distinctive sounds. Sometimes even individual frogs. Not a frog, he decided.

As he neared the water, the sound seemed to come from behind him. A nocturnal bird? He knew the birds as thoroughly as he did the frogs. Owls' hoo hoo hoorer hoo, sounded like human sobs, expressive of minds that have reached the gelatinous mildewy stage in the mortification of all healthy and courageous thought. Whippoorwills chanted their vespers. Screech owls intermittently voiced their u-lu-lu, sounding the dark and tearful side of music that mournful women fain would sing. "Oh-o-o-o that I had never been bor-r-r-r-n!" came the sigh on his side of the pond, then circled with restless despair to some new perch on the gray oaks, bringing to the forefront of the poet's mind the stark twilight and unsatisfied thoughts which all have.

No, it wasn't a bird. He stood still to subtract the sound of his footsteps from the night, listened for a moment, then walked closer to the pond. The sound came from above, first from the left, then the right, first from nearby, almost directly overhead, then from a distance.

"Ork." But not exactly that, he thought. The spelling of sounds is never exact. The translation of Nature's language into alphabetic formulae wasn't meant to happen. God's wild words resist appearance on paper, in books. One must hear them as spoken or be content with approximation, as one must when deciphering Greek or Aramaic. What would an Arab mean by saying, "Ork" or understand were it heard in the desert? Was that a camel?

Thoreau wondered if what he was hearing might be a solitary insect, hoping to attract a distant mate. He scanned the trees, knowing the unlikeliness of spotting such a tiny speck of music. Bugs there were—plenty of them, all seeking, not mates, but the naked poet. He was soon well-bitten, blotched, but curious still. Deeper into the woods he walked.

"Ork . . . Ork . . . Ork . . . Ork."

His bare feet had been hardened by previous contact with the forest floor's detritus, and a thick carpet of pine needles softened his steps, so no twig or bramble discouraged his search. Deeper he continued into his element, the mystery intermittently sounding, luring his gnawing need to know. He needed at least to see. Science was a distant secondary goal, but if he could name the elusive speaker and then to detail its way of life from birth to death—its mating, diet, seasonality, favored element, migratory paths and strongest sensory modes, each new piece of information would be a pleasure. He stopped again to listen undisrupted by even the softest sounds of his own footfalls.

Nothing but the rustle of wind in the trees. And, softer, his well-suppressed breathing. His eyes, now accustomed to the almost total darkness, saw not much. More, almost certainly, than eyes trained by so-much-brighter civilization, but nothing that revealed the source of any sound.

In the distance, the rattle of the Fitchburg train provided proof that his ears were still working. The train, he knew. He'd heard it pass before and had learned to ignore the evidence that he wasn't alone in the world or even the woods. He felt a grudging admiration for man's imagination, the power of the engine and the invention's ability to further the purposes of commerce, despite his disapproval of those purposes.

Just as Thoreau was about to take another step, almost inaudibly this time, a single "Ork." Then silence. Then he put his right foot down once more. It was the only sound.

In the silence, he shuddered, feeling the omnipresence and infinite variety of Nature. Or God, as he often labeled that overwhelming entity. Surrounded by the tangible darkness of the woods, he was more than engulfed, he was *subsumed*—one of the thousands of units throbbing in the night.

If I am Nature and Nature is God, he asked himself, am I God? He resisted the thought, feeling it immodest, but truly, the physical sensation of such an equivalency was hard to discount. As was his own smallness in the big picture. A leaf of an enormous tree, the bubble of a fish, an atom of God. But modesty had never been one of his problems. He was always quick to argue with those who hold differing views, even if those views weren't all that different from his own.

Too much mentation, he thought. The mind so often interferes with experience. Better to observe without comment. The world is overfull of scientists, philosophers and reporters who struggle to analyze and interpret Nature. Preferable to let it speak for itself. Rather than travel such a path, I should return to sleep to awaken refreshed and receptive in the morning. So back to the cabin.

There, the sound of sturdy pitch pines rubbing and creaking for lack of room against the cabin's shingles; squirrels moving on the roof; under the floor, a woodchuck; a loon laughing on the pond, and the bark of a fox in the distance. Thoreau waited at the door for a recurrence of the other, elusive sound.

Nothing. Back to bed and under the welcome warmth of his coverlet. A minute passed as his breathing slowed to its nocturnal rhythm. He closed his eyes and waited for his mind to empty, but his exercise in the woods had stimulated ideas, and his reinvigorated mind was no longer capable of ending its disturbances. Without actual sounds to draw his attention, his innermost essence fed him memories of things he'd heard at other times, in other locations— even the occasional intrusion of manmade voices—the rattle of carts passing on the nearby road and the roar and moans of a train in the distance. Ah, man and your civilization, he thought. Noise and nothing.

These sounds, as they seem at this moment, thought Thoreau, are imagined, not heard, and he recalled the sound that had awakened him earlier. Had it emanated from Nature or his own mind? Again, that recurring question roiled the very dregs of the poet's mind: Are Nature and I the same entity? Are my observations of water and woods, trees and toads, animals and air anything more than deep looks in a mirror? Does Nature have a mirror in which it observes me?

Nothing is as soporific as imponderables of such scope, and he drifted into sleep. The pen on his desk was out of the question now, the book not a project on God's list of things to do. A larger, less-tangible task of merging with the woods had taken him beyond proximal observations of anything currently available. The elements yet unknown, the origin of the species, Mendel's wrinkled peas, the number and nature of planets, the galaxy beyond Andromeda, the so-called improvements and additions to civilization's arsenal of distractions . . . How keen a waking eye might be required or how deep a sleep? How close a unity to be achieved?

And just before the poet's eyes opened in the morning, before the observer resumed his work, before the sparrows began their trill, his innermost ear detected, "Ork." He awakened and heard, additionally, the gentle whirr of a mosquito's delicate wings in the room.

Miasma

Campbell Timpali's one man show at Surely Enough Easel opened on Friday. I owed him a visit, so I dropped in. As always, his focus was on potential buyers. He paid them more attention than he paid me. He was busy explaining his work to potential customers, so he couldn't do more than nod and smile at me or at Fabrienne, a friend he'd known in New York who, when he arrived here, had introduced him to local artists to give him a foothold in the community. She'd also found him the ideal studio space, which he'd eventually rented. Both services earned his gratitude, but Fabrienne knew the mandatory games well enough that she didn't expect more of a greeting while customers were gathered 'round.

I took off on my own to check out the paintings while Fabrienne and her date, Peter, joined the crowd of Campbell's fellow painters and sculptors in strolling the gallery. Most of them were leveling primarily negative critiques. He was, after all, an opponent in the battle for the attention of monied aficionados. They strolled from painting to painting, sharing their reactions with each other and eavesdropping on critiques being offered by everyone who considered themselves qualified.

At one stop, a fifty-something man dressed in paint-splattered coveralls was telling a similarly attired sidekick, "Campbell is at it again. He claims he's back in touch with the natural world, but everything I see here would have been impossible before the Industrial Revolution. Grinding gears and coal smoke! Dickens choking in factory fog!"

Splatter Man's companion nodded and stroked his chin, pondering the profundity of his pal's insight. Fabrienne and Peter couldn't see the basis for his complaint. The painting in question was done in nothing but soft-edged blue and green pastels.

"I think that guy formed his opinion before he arrived at the gallery," Peter whispered to Fabrienne.

The next painting showed a shockingly orange man emerging from a green haze. The extreme contrast in colors made the figure jump aggressively out of the background. Examining it closely was a grandmotherly woman who was deep in thought. Suddenly, she noticed Fabrienne and Peter standing next to her. She pointed at the painting and said, "Orange," and quickly moved on.

Peter whispered again. "She's right. It's orange alright."

The unpleasant vibe seemed to permeate the room until Fabrienne noticed that Campbell had completed his serious business and was now surrounded by half a dozen of his friends. They were discussing a twenty-by-six-foot multi-colored abstraction. The group seemed pleasant, so the two of them moved in to share a three-way hug with Campbell. He introduced them to the others. Conversation within the group was light-hearted and generally positive, centering more on processes than on the content of the painting. These folks, unlike many artists present, seemed to know what they were talking about, so I joined them and picked up some interesting perspectives.

Peter was distracted by a chimerical woman standing next to a wall about ten feet from our group. She was about seventy years old, very tall, thin and had a four-foot waterfall of whitest hair. She was wrapped in a billowing scarlet theatrical cape and was smoking a cigarette in a long cigarette holder. Once Peter noticed her, he couldn't look away. She was at least as much of an attraction as any of the intended displays. The thing that caught *my* attention was her flamboyant makeup—her eyes were two violet birds in flight, their wings extended an inch to each side.

Embarrassingly, she noticed Peter staring at her. "Do I know you?" she asked.

"Uh, no. I'm sorry for staring. I was admiring your cape."

"Denk you," she said in a deep-pitched burr. And nothing more. No offering of her name or her relationship to the event. Peter, feeling unwelcome, bid her a truncated farewell.

Rejoining Campbell and his friends, Peter gestured toward the wall and asked, "Who *is* that?"

Campbell looked toward the spot Peter had indicated. "Who's who?"

The chimera had vanished. Peter described her and several people in the group remembered having seen her, but no one knew her name. Conversation returned to this and that.

* * *

Who was that addressing the post-concert crowd at the Symphony on Thursday night? It was she of the scarlet cape, dressed this time in a silky, metallic gold evening gown—probably lighter than would be comfortable on this chilly evening. Warmer was her bright yellow tam-o'-shanter.

She herself was warmer, too, than she'd been when I'd seen her at Surely Enough Easel. This night, she'd captivated a circle of music lovers, telling of her past.

"I vus only nineteen, so you ken imachin how impressed I vus," she said, waving her arms to each side. "Stravinski vus in hiss late zixties zen, liffing in New York. I vuss zere viz my fozza. Igor vus zomvut frail, but hiss mind vus as young as ever. He vus vorking on orchestrating two preludes fun Bach's Vell-Tempered Clavier. He vus very velcoming to me, shpentink almost a hef hour answerink z'kvestions uffa teenage girl he'd neffer met."

She was as exotic to me as she'd been to Peter or Stravinski. I wondered if she always wore outfits that bordered on outrageous. I remembered that I'd seen her before at symphonic performances, but I'd never heard her speak before. Her voice, her accent, her gestures, taken alone, would have been enough to attract attention, but to hear tales of a first-person encounter with Stravinski was the capper. I joined the group around her.

And when her performance ended and the group dispersed, I moved to the bar and asked the man who was mixing the drinks, "Who was that woman?" describing her.

"I've heard people address her as 'Magda' and sometimes as 'Princess.' She's attended many concerts and seems to know all the regulars. I don't really know her background—who she is. For instance, I don't know if 'Princess' is a nickname or an actual title."

I couldn't help but be curious about what or where Princess Magda, if that was her name, ate. I couldn't imagine her sitting at the counter of a Dunkin' Donuts or having a Rootie Tootie Fresh 'n' Fruity breakfast at an IHOP. It would be less surprising to see her eating escargot for breakfast or relying on personal chefs to feed her.

Once I started to speculate about so-called Princess Magda, all sorts of questions arose, as they do about other of our fellow citizens. All of us are mysterious if we're thought about at all. Most of us remain non-entities But the Magda image demanded, "Think of me!" her voice wrapped in memorable sandpaper.

I assume she's got money, I thought. Those duds can't be cheap.

And I assume she's well-known in whatever oddball emporium in which she finds them.

* * *

Friday night, Julie, Lisa and I were at *A Child's Garden of Misinformation,* a play written by and starring Julie's friend Glenn Potter. Glenn had been on a roll for the past year. This play came hot on the heels of two big (as measured on the little theater scale) hits. If that weren't draw enough, Julie was well along with stoking her crush on Glenn.

And *Child's Garden* didn't disappoint. It was a hilariously bitter take on the tortuous path children must travel to discover what's true and what's trickery by adults who have all sorts of ulterior motives. The children, in most cases, were wise enough to see through the misdirections and give the audience hope for a better world coming as the children's generation inherits the reins.

After the audience took its leave, a dozen of the performers' friends and family members, Julie, Lisa and I among them, hung around to schmooze with the cast. Also among them, the mysterious Magda, this time dressed entirely in black, wearing knee-high boots and shades. In the dark during the play, she'd been all but invisible except for her long, white hair which was more eye-catching than ever with the house lights dimmed. Glenn was listening intensely to her commentary.

"I dun't anymore enchoy zet Neil Simon sot uff humor. Jokey, joke, joke. So forced! I luff what yoof done viz ziss play. You leaf z'audience tzu discova za trechik comedy uff ow-a efryday lifes vizoudt rubbink ow-a noses in z'opvious," she said. "You gif us credit foah heffink zom brains."

All three of us were fascinated by the speaker, and Julie took advantage of her relationship to Glenn to insert herself into the discussion and pulled us along as she joined the pair.

"Hi, Glenn. You've done it again. We all loved it. Your writing, of course, but your performance too. Ooh, you were nasty. Who's your friend?

"Magda," he said, "This is my friend Julie Robb and her friends, Ron and . . . I'm sorry."

"Lisa Mulay."

"Julie, Lisa, Ron and Magda Fidonia Belzenar Borghezi. Magda, Julie Loeb, Lisa Mulay and Ron Gillette."

"Magda knows everyone. Including some major theater people and the stories they usually hide from each other," Glenn tantalized us. Magda just smiled.

"How do *you* know each other?" Julie asked.

"One night she just introduced herself, I guess because I'm a theater person and she follows the scene," Glenn said. "Well, she didn't exactly 'introduce' herself. She just started talking with me. And again, the same way after a few other shows. She'll fill you with stories about everyone you've ever heard of, but she won't tell you much about herself."

"Vut's to tell?" Magda asked, laughing. "I'm an olt voman. I'fe het es many lifes ezz you might expegt on zumvun my aitch. You vill hef es many ven you're es olt es I."

"If that's true," Lisa said, "I'm off to a slow start."

"I'm zorry," Magda said, "You must excuse me. I promised zom frients zet I voot visit zem zis efening ent I don't vant z'visit zu be zo late. It vus nice meetink you." And she left.

"As I warned you," Glenn said. "You'll never learn much. *I* never have. I call her The Wisp because she comes and goes like the sun on a cloudy day."

"She seemed like she was in costume, too," Julie observed.

"Always is. She's a snappy dresser," Glenn said, and laughed. "A standout in the faceless crowd!"

And I, after waiting so long to hear her name and story, couldn't recall the name I'd heard, and Glenn was called away before I could ask again.

* * *

Last Saturday, I was at Smeary's, a little jazz club on the North side, to catch Johnny Griffin, and there she was again, talking to Griff between sets. I wasn't close enough to catch the conversation, but Griffin was laughing at whatever she was saying. I poked the owner of the club.

"Who's that?" I asked, indicating the Magda figure.

"That's Johnny Griffin. Just back from Denmark. I was lucky to book him. He's really in demand."

"No, no. I mean the woman who's talking with him. I've met her before, but I don't remember her name. I don't know her well enough that I can butt in on her conversation."

"Oh. That's The Wisp," he said, rolling his eyes. "She's in here whenever we book big name talent. I don't know why, but they all seem to know her, even if they're from out of town. I know her by sight, of course. Who doesn't? And I know what she's called. But that's about it."

"Is her name Magda something?"

"Yeah, I think so."

I was up for more answers, but didn't see an opportunity to get them. I hung around for another set and then I split. I stopped in at one of my favorite bars for a nightcap. The bartender who was on duty that night was a pal of mine.

"I got a question for you, Dave," I said. "Several times in the past few weeks, I've bumped into an old lady who's always dressed like a fashion model from another planet. She travels with a hip crowd and it seems that everyone knows her. Do you?"

"Long white hair, has some sort of accent? Sure," he said. "The Princess."

"Princess of what?" I asked.

"Oh, I dunno if she's a princess of anything. That's just what she's called. She's in here once in a while. And, like you say, everyone knows her. Why don't you ask Philo? He's hung out with her some."

So I asked. ". . . Philo?"

"Oh, yeah, man. The Princess? I'm surprised you don't know her. She's always around. Well, where to begin? I understand she's Romanian or, like, Hungarian. Dunno whether she's actually a princess, but I'm pretty sure she's *some* kind of royalty. She's lived practically everywhere in Europe and has hung in royal-type circles. Art circles, too. She knew Dali, Magritte, even met Lady Day right before she died. I think she splits her time between Paris and New York. If I ever see the two of you at the same time, I'll introduce you. She's *out* there! So many wild tales, I can't tell which are true and which aren't. It's fill-in-the-blanks time. Which is the way I like things. Someone even told me that she'd been a consort of *Rasputin's*. I mean, if you can believe that Rasputin *had* a consort."

"Well, you seem to know more about her than anyone else I've asked. I keep running into her everywhere I go lately, but she always disappears before I can manage to talk to her. Is her name Magda?"

"I never heard that one before. Everyone *I* know just calls her Princess."

As in so much of life, the more answers I get, the more questions arise.

* * *

Even in a city of six million individuals are individual thises and thats, and they tend to glump together with those of their kinds. There's fair amount of overlap among the different breeds of culture vultures. The beauty of a big city is that it supplies food for even the most exotic birds. I guess I'd have to include myself in that flock.

So, it happened that, one morning at A Hundred Cups, a variety of night people happened to be awake early and gathered for coffee. I brought up the subject of The Elusive One. I thought the gathered crowd would be certain to flesh out the little I knew about her. But no.

"Whenever I've seen her, she seems to be flying solo, but she's always the center of a crowd of people who, if they don't actually know her, still seem to defer to her plentiful pronouncements. From whence cometh her power?" a dancer asked.

One mystery that bothered all the birdwatchers was Magda's omnipresence. It seems no event is complete until she shows up, and she always does. "Is it possible that she's twins?" a sculptor guessed.

A singer was curious about, "How is she able to evanesce without witnesses to her entrance and dissolve without anyone seeing her go?"

"Has anyone ever seen her in the daytime? In a laundromat? On a bus?" a theater owner asked. "I mean, we've all got mundane things to take care of outside of the world that really interests us. Does she ever shop for groceries? She ever pop into in a drug store for dental floss or a comb? Does she send a servant to buy her smokes?"

Even collectively, putting our artsy heads together, we were peering into a fog at Big Sur.

* * *

Somewhere in the city, in a building none of us knows, a woman we only know *of* makes her bed. She dresses and brushes her hair. She checks herself in a full-length mirror before sitting on the overstuffed sofa that faces the window and thinks, Vut's first? There's an address book and calendar on the table at her side. She verifies the coming evening's offerings and lights a cigarette. The book is dense with highlighted dates, names and addresses. She adds a few notations and goes to the kitchen to get a cup of herbal tea.

Also on the side table, sixteen ornately framed photographs, some of individuals, some of groups assembled in four neat rows, like an acapella choir. All races, both sexes, all ages and the full range of stations in life in attendance. How did a Kazakh Kurd and his camel earn their ways into this collection? Under what circumstances did she meet that sharecropper couple? Is that young Magda herself as the bride in the ancient wedding photo? It's unlikely the groom is Omar Sharif, but there's a strong resemblance. Both bride and groom have faraway looks in their eyes.

Isadora Duncan, the Taj Mahal, two young people making funny faces on a four-panel photo-booth strip, a Burmese cat, General Eisenhower, a banquet table set for twelve with twelve guests awaiting their hostess, the seating arrangement marked by engraved place cards she designed herself.

The rest of the effluvia may resemble our own, none of which is worthy of inspection or comment. Everything in the room—

lamps, carpets, hangings, paintings, sculptures—are the ghosts of an admirably rich life lived, but Magda Fidonia Belzenar Borghezi's active mind has no more time to dwell on any of that. There's the present to fill, collections to add to. Even this early, she begins assembling the public persona. She's due at The Alhambra this evening at nine.

She moves from room to room, gathering items she thinks she'll need before she returns. She fills a sack, makes a phone call, sits and has another tea, stands and removes something from the sack.

We must imagine what the phone call was about. And what was in the bag? What came out? And where is she going?

She's going *out*. To attend to many of the things to which we all must attend, wearing sensible shoes and clothing appropriate to the weather. Nothing remarkable here. But before she left, she fondly rubbed the head of her four-foot statue of Copernicus.

Our imaginations are left in a room empty of explanations of raisons d'être, histories or any preview of parts the props will play in dramas to come. Until the curtain next rises, the theater, for all purposes, doesn't exist, and we're on our own with our pale imaginations.

Reflections on a Floating Head

The group of university students I hung with back in the day wasn't what you'd call serious. True, a few paid some attention to earning their degrees, but many of them spent most of their energy pursuing alcohol, drugs or coeds. Another potential goal—wisdom—is available on campus too, but wisdom isn't a goal that can be pursued. *It* pursues *us*, growing slowly, imperceptibly. Or, rarely, it bursts upon us without warning. What follows is the story of an unexpected explosion.

Among the fun-seekers in my circle was Big Joe, a scholar who, in addition to applying himself to the university-prescribed curriculum, was an outsider studying his dorm mates as we played cards, played practical jokes and drank. To Joe, we were interesting lab specimens.

We lived in a dorm in which the beds, desks and doors were made of metal, designed to withstand whatever abuse the resident chimps could dish out. Big Joe required more comfort than the institution provided for his meditations, so he hauled an overstuffed chair from a yard sale (or a dump?) up three floors to his study room. He'd sit in his throne, a book in his lap, bemusedly observing our hi jinx. Occasionally, he'd join in the foolishness, but even then, it was as if he were an anthropologist studying the fascinating natives.

The whole campus was his field of study. While out of the dorm, he'd root out odd aspects of the academic and extra-curricular environments and report back to his less-observant dorm mates, filtering what he'd found through a quirky sense of humor.

He discovered, for instance, that the town surrounding our campus had gained national fame and whatever fortune it had accumulated from the invention of barbed wire. "The utility of barbed wire," Joe philosophized, "was that it kept academics quarantined from the resentful farmers who lived outside the wire."

Joe also had mapped the campus with an eye toward defending it against military attack. Military history was one of his hobbies. "It's likely that the frontal attack will be by tanks and foot soldiers advancing down Venture Drive and crossing the river in front of Stannard Residence Hall. We'll have to erect blockades and station some heavy armament in Turret Two of the Administration Building." And so on. This was a joke of course—a private joke that was an outgrowth of his political science major.

* * *

Perhaps Big Joe's major find was Dr. Robert Foster, a world history professor who the majority of undergrads found ponderous. Big Joe did not. He recognized Foster as a full-time resident of the world of deep thought and ideas more profound than mere mortals are aware of. Big Joe referred to him as "a floating head," a mind that exists as an organism independent of a body, and he meant that as a compliment.

* * *

At first, the rest of us used the term derisively. "You can always spot a floating head," we said. "When a normal person wears a necktie, the front and back of the tie hang straight down his shirt. A person who's a little off (like a typical professor) will wear his necktie over one shoulder. A floating head will wear his necktie with the front over one shoulder and the back over the other shoulder." We said of floating heads that they lived "over the blue wall," the blue wall being the border between sanity and insanity.

Dr. Foster did, indeed, live over the blue wall—a land where ideas were living, breathing creatures. There, one could converse with the intellectual giants, great innovators and bold adventurers who'd been centuries in their graves. To Foster, they were living companions. They weren't abstractions, they were as tangible as metal beds, as active as our chase after coeds, as much a force of life as grade point averages. Living in the world of ideas, Foster fell somewhat out of touch with life on the ground, making him typical of the class of what's known as "absent-minded professors." When the university campus would occasionally intrude on the contents of his mind, he'd blink back to attention, surprised to find himself on Felton Drive, surrounded by students. But he wasn't absent-minded. He was very much present somewhere else.

* * *

Before quoting any of Dr. Foster's statements, it's important to describe his sound. His voice was a somewhat gravelly baritone, and every word that he spoke was over-enunciated. His mouth contorted to open wide enough to emphasize every consonant and accentuate the "AH" sound wherever it occurred. It was as if his name had been assigned to grant him every opportunity to let the "AHs" roll out: Daahkter Raahbert Faahster.

After only a few contacts with Dr. Foster, Big Joe reported him to his dorm mates. "My history professor is something to behold!" he told us. "This morning, in the midst of his lecture, he began speaking Greek. At first, we thought he was going to give us a brief quote from some ancient historian, but the Greek continued for *ten minutes!* Then, all of a sudden, he caught himself. He said,

'Uhh . . . Don't worry—that won't be on the test.' It was as if he'd left the world for ten minutes and, suddenly, was plunked back to walk among us. I've never seen anything like it."

A few of us who heard Joe's tale had to see this character for ourselves. There was no academic credit to be earned by sitting in. That was irrelevant. This was a free show. (The barker says, "Twenty-five cents extra will get you behind the curtain to see the *real* freaks.")

And we weren't disappointed. Dr. Foster's class was scheduled for eleven a.m. One day, Big Joe and two others (I was one) were seated in the lecture hall at the appointed time. At eleven, there was no Dr. Foster. By quarter past, still no Foster. Ten percent of the two hundred students decided to leave. By 11:20, more than half the class had hit the road. At 11:30, perhaps twenty curious students remained, aware that, with Dr. Foster, anything was possible. Sure enough, a few minutes later, the man appeared, disheveled and breathless. "I'm sorry," he said. "I forgot what day it is. For those of you who stuck it out, I'll try to make it worth your while."

And he did. The lecture contained another memorable Foster moment. The textbook was written by a historian named Crane Brinton. Apparently, Brinton was one of Foster's favorites. The lecture for the day concerned Octavion Caesar, and Foster had a direct quote from another Brinton text: "Octavion had little *potentia* but much *auctoritas*. But *auctoritas* of that degree is *potentia* indeed." After the quote, Dr. Foster laughed: "Haaww haaww haaww! Isn't that Brintonesque?"

I guarantee that none of the undergrads in the hall were familiar enough with Brinton to be able to distinguish his sensibility from that of Soupy Sales. Nor did any of us know what *auctoritas* is. It's the origin of the English word "authority."

Foster's aside came directly from his subconscious without any consideration of our inability to appreciate it, as his pronouncements often did. But Big Joe and the two of us awaiting such moments certainly appreciated the quirkiness of it. We were converts to the Foster cult. From that moment on, we took to following him as he strolled around campus, waiting to witness similar gems that might fall out of his head without warning.

One of the places we encountered him on more than a few occasions was the student cafeteria, a place few of the faculty frequented. Dr. Foster, though, was outside of any class prejudices. In his opinion, anywhere food was available was a place to eat. He didn't even mind if underclassmen joined him at his table. A true egalitarian.

Watching Foster eat was a bit like watching a jackal attack an okapi. His mouth, extremely mobile while enunciating his words, was even more so while gobbling a sandwich, and the gobbling didn't interrupt his speech. The simultaneous activities often caused both words and food to fly, as his spattered clothing attested. His enthusiasms for speaking and eating were intense.

And his subject matters in the cafeteria tended to be even more unpredictable than they were in the classroom. His acolytes' anticipation of surprise was always richly rewarded. His own enjoyment of the subject matters was clear, and a side-effect of that enthusiasm was that we anthropologists were imbued with the man's love of learning. It was kind of a bank shot. None of us, with the possible exception of Big Joe, could have been mistaken for scholars, but we admired our mentor enough that we at least felt the pull of his persona.

It was therefore surprising one afternoon to hear Dr. Foster deliver the following monologue. We could tell right away that his mood was different than we'd seen before. His eyes drooped and his usually mobile mouth was slack. His voice was muffled and slower than usual. Apparently, his mind had wandered back to the 1920s. He put down his sandwich and began.

* * *

"In 1927, two Italian immigrants, Nicolo Sacco and Bartolomeo Vanzetti were electrocuted after having been convicted of murdering a guard and a paymaster during a robbery of the Slater and Morrill Shoe Company in South Braintree, Massachusetts. Prejudice against immigrants of any kind was widespread in the country in the twenties, so many people took it for granted that the foreigners were guilty. And, if the suspects' foreignness wasn't proof enough of their guilt, both men had been active socialists. More proof that they were murderers. Even before the trial was completed, angry mobs were calling for the death penalty."

This wasn't a typical Foster narrative. Perhaps it was the tone of his voice. The story he was telling felt like a contemporary news story rather than a trip down some historical lane or an exploration of an exotic forgotten continent. His audience was silent, wondering what unexpected turn the tale might take.

* * *

"The trial dragged on for months. Conflicting eyewitness testimonies from a handful of questionable characters played a big role in the trial. There were 'witnesses' who claimed to have seen minute details from great distances and the court heard conflicting descriptions of the person who'd supposedly driven the getaway car—he was dark-skinned, he was light-skinned, he was in the car alone, there was a passenger in the front seat, in the back seat. Testimony that the two suspects were in other locations at the time of the murder was disregarded. There was judicial sloppiness—required procedures disregarded and so on and so on. It was disgusting.

"I wasn't the only one who thought so. There was enough public protest over the verdict that the governor of Massachusetts, Alvin Fuller, appointed a committee charged with reviewing the court's decision.

"I was encouraged. The committee was to be headed by A. Lawrence Lowell, the president of Harvard. Samuel Stratton, the president of MIT, and Robert Grant, a former judge, were on the committee too. These were three of the most educated men in the country. I was certain that they would reverse the travesties that had taken place in Sacco and Vanzetti's trial.

"But the committee was, if anything, sloppier and more prejudiced than the court had been. It concurred that Sacco and Vanzetti were guilty and, in April of 1927, both men were sent to the electric chair."

* * *

At this point, Dr. Foster fell silent. He stopped eating and looked down at the table. After a moment, he said, "As a young man, I believed that education was the cure for all man's ugliness. The cure for war, famine, cruelty and misery. The Lowell Committee proved to me that I'd been wrong. Education *doesn't* have power over human nature. The best I can claim for education is that it can wave a greeting to right paths and point us in hopeful directions. But whether we choose to follow those paths is up to us as individuals. Right choices require something more."

There was a thirty-second pause before he added, "I'm sorry to say that, in the forty years since that trial, I haven't been encouraged by the choices mankind has made."

Downcast and contemplative, he was silent again. And so were we. It had always been Foster's *style* that drew us to him. On this afternoon, it was the *content* of his rumination that captured our attention. And, although Sacco and Vanzetti, in the middle of the story, had seemed to be the victims of the proceedings, it turned out that Foster himself was collateral damage.

Immature as we were, we felt the weight of his conclusions. This head, we realized, wasn't floating at all. It was well-grounded in a world independent of politics, opinion polls, public consensus and the tides of common men. Foster's entire life had been devoted to educating himself, yet his moral sense called even the value of education into question. His courage to drill that deeply left us without jokes, without irony, without escapes from our own moral responsibilities.

History, given fifty more years in which to ponder the guilt or innocence of Sacco and Vanzetti, has come to various conclusions—both guilty, both innocent, only one or only the other guilty. Whatever the case, it doesn't alter the impact of that admirable alternate juror, Dr. Foster, on a handful of college students back in the sixties.

By the time of his lunchroom lecture, each of us had already taken more than a few multiple-choice moral tests and, in addition to tests we'd continue to face as individuals, right around the corner were tests that the nation would administer: Vietnam, Kent State and Jackson State to name a few. Over and over, we'd have to decide how to defend our campuses against enemy attacks.

Our parents were spending a lot of money to buy us our educations, but we realized the cost would be a lot higher than that. We'd have to enroll in a different sort of school.

Four Tales From the Dark City

(1) The Lunatic Gambit

More than most of Chicago's coffee houses, Urbus Orbus, in the Bucktown neighborhood, attracts self-consciously artsy twenty-somethings who pay too much for coffee and fussy sandwiches in return for ambience that nourishes their pre-ennui. Very few patrons are over thirty.

What happens to those who exceed the unspoken age limit? Do they run out of money? Do they perfect despair and take their own lives? Are they abducted by aliens? Or do they hit the big time in the art world and move to New York? Whatever it is, they all disappear from the Urbus orb before they're eligible to run for the presidency.

All but the chess players. They're exempt from early expulsion. So, my regular chess partner and I sit among kids and a handful of chess geezers, jousting to the strains of reggae, world music, Eurotrash anthems and industrial noise that the kids consider music.

One night, a ragged little guy of indeterminate age—somewhere over thirty—with tousled hair and half his teeth asks if he can play the winner of the game we have in progress. Usually, we don't admit outsiders to our games, but this night, we made an exception. The guy was so *odd*, we figured he *might* be a genius.

But no. He was a *terrible* player! And he didn't lose gracefully. He blamed bad luck, ill-health, background noise and a pesky fly. He demanded another chance. Again, terrible! It was clear that he'd never beat either of us, and neither of us is a great player. Then he began explaining how extraterrestrials have affected human history.

We began to wonder how the guy gets by in twentieth century America.

"What do you do for a living?" I asked.

"I'm a chess piece repairman." He wasn't joking.

"Is there much money in that?"

"Not much," he confessed.

"What d'ya charge?"

"Maybe a nickel for a pawn, a dime for a knight or a bishop, a quarter for a king or a queen." Rook prices available on request, I guess.

After a moment of silence, during which I imagined his annual income, he added, "I also *make* chess sets," and he dove under his chair for his sample case—a cigar box.

The chess pieces he hauled out were plaster of Paris. All were chipped or cracked. Horses' heads were missing, bishops' miters were blunt, the turrets of rooks were crumbling ... Even the knob-headed pawns had suffered by rattling around in their cigar box. Best of all, every piece was tempera-painted red, white and blue in random splotches. Not red for one opponent and blue for the other, but red, white and blue pieces for you, red, white and blue pieces for me. It was as hard to identify the enemy as it had been in Vietnam.

The repairman wasn't pleased with our response to his color-ful collection. Grumbling, he faded into the mists of the Orb. We continue to see him in various chess venues around town. Some-times, he's in the midst of seemingly normal people, and they seem to treat him as a fellow normal. It's possible, I guess, that he's able to win a few games playing them, particularly if they're just learning how pieces move, but he never travels without his oddball chess pieces or his oral history of the cosmic invaders.

(2) Prince Charles and the Pimp

At the heart of The Green Mill is a stage that offers some of the best jazz in Chicago and the liveliest poetry show in the nation. But, at the far end of a fifty-foot bar, near the front door, is Slime Corner, home of patrons who aren't interested in any of the entertainment offerings. They're the shot-and-a-beer for breakfast crowd.

The informal boundary of Slime Corner is somewhere around the tenth stool back. No one wants Slimers closer to the stage than that because Slimers, whether they approve or disapprove of the night's offerings, tend to disrupt it, particularly if they've spent a few hours indulging in their hobby before the shows begin. Often, they've drunk themselves deaf and are oblivious to their own volume. So, they're kept near the front door for the owner's bouncing convenience.

Thus ghettoized, they've developed something like camaraderie—even a pride in their identity. At one point after they'd been labeled, they even had Slime Corner tee-shirts printed and refused to sell them to anyone but known, full-time alcoholics.

But the "slime" label, whether pinned on the group by an outsider or owned to by one of the denizens, exaggerates the degradation. Within the brotherhood of the bottle, several members maintained a fingerhold on respectability. The group included an architect, the landlord of a twenty-unit apartment building, a Chinese Zen master, a cop and two painters. They read—at least the newspaper— they gathered at each other's homes for holidays and, when they were able to help themselves, they also helped each other. When one of them found himself hospitalized, he could count on Slimer visitors. Good minds and bad, kind hearts and cruel ones shared self-destruction in Slime Corner.

One Slimer who had stumbled farther down the hill than many was a painter known as Prince Charles. Most Slimers shelter under pseudonyms. Outsiders who encounter Prince Charles always find him surly. He is hunched over and cross-eyed. His speech is slurred and his clothes are rumpled.

One night I arrived at the club too late to get a seat near the stage. Finding myself in Slime Corner, I met Prince Charles. His first words to me were, "New York Jew lawyers aren't welcome here."

"Wrong on all three counts," I told him. "I'm not a New Yorker, not Jewish and not a lawyer."

"I don't like you anyway," he said. I didn't take that personally. I'd heard that that was his constant stance.

One night, after knowing Charles for about a year, I saw him on the fringes of Slime Corner, coming on to a good-looking, well-dressed woman who'd come to hear the music. It was obvious that two such disparate characters were never going to connect in this world. Charles' planet had nothing to offer hers. But I was in a capricious mood. I decided to turn up the Bunsen just for an experiment.

I was in a suit and tie, so I appeared to be from her world, not his. I moved between the pair and told the woman, "Listen to what this man has to say. He taught me everything I know. Accurately, he is called a prince by everyone who knows him."

I moved away to watch from a distance. As I suspected, the elegant young lady quickly exhausted her patience with Charles' come-on and disappeared to the front of the club to listen to more-entertaining fare. Soon afterward, Charles joined me. His whole demeanor was different than I'd ever seen it. He clapped me on the shoulder and, I think, looked me in the eye. One could never quite read his watery red cross-eyes.

"Thank you for that, man," he said sincerely, missing the fact that my intercession had been intended as a joke. With that, he settled in for a friend-to-friend evening. In the course of that evening, he told the following story.

"One night," he said, "I was sitting at the front corner of the bar and, out the window, I see this guy kickin' the shit outta this woman. He's holdin' her by the arm an' swingin' his leg alla way back to kick her as hard as he can.

"Well, I was so drunk, I didn't know what I was doin', so I run out. It was some pimp, sore at his whore. She was screamin' an' try- in' t'get away. I hadda do somethin', but I didn't know what. The pimp was real big. He coulda killed me.

"Then I see one o' the pimp's real expensive shoes has come off while he's kickin' her, so I push the shoe in the gutter an' say, 'Hey, man! Yer shoe's in the gutter.' He says, 'Huh?' an' lets go of the whore to get his shoe. That gives her a chance, an' she runs off."

"Charles!" I say. "That was a beautiful, brave thing to do! You're a hero!"

"Nah," he says. "I was drunk. I didn't know I was doin' it."

What can we say when the autonomic circuit is wired for goodness? Are its sparks not good?

(3) Sunset at The Cowpokes' Lounge

The twelve years I worked in Chicago's Loop would have been wonderful years if they hadn't been such *wet* years for me. I didn't think of myself as being a *problem* drinker. Booze seemed to be a natural part of the downtown rhythm—part of being young, vigorous and involved in a world-class city.

It became a habit to end the workday at closest place to start, The Wabash Inn, a quiet, comfortable place that served simple, inexpensive dinners in addition to drinks. But every damnation has a friendly greeting on the entrance—some inviting cheese on the trap. One or two drinks at The Wabash might have been harmless, but not when one thing led to another. If conversation was lively, they led to another and another until the place closed at nine. And when things went *that* far, they went farther—to The Cowpokes' Lounge, three blocks away.

After civilized taverns closed, my friends and I staggered, young and vigorous, past skyscrapers lining paved streets under electric lights to arrive across the street from the Eiffel-like sweep of the First National Bank Building. Then, a dive down a dark flight of stairs brought one to The Cowpokes' Lounge, a Fantasyland for the fucked and far from home.

The room was large. Loaded, it might have held two hundred galoots, but I never saw more than ten. Loaded, the ten always were, and lonely, usually, sprawling at wet wooden tables decorated with cattle-branding motifs augmented by afterthought graffiti drawn by drunken buckaroos and buckarettes. On the walls were wanted posters, the skull of a long-horned cow, brandin' arns, and strands of barbed warr.

Get-ups varied. There were suits, like mine, but there was also a sampling of fringed shirts, chaps, boots and ten-gallon hats. I never saw guns or spurs. Where did those people *come* from? On what sort of vehicles did they arrive? I mean, there we were, in the middle of a city that scares even Milwaukeeans, and suddenly one found oneself bending elbows with the outcasts of Ogallala! The stockyards were long gone. What did those cowpokes *do* during the day?

And, as one's brain washed farther and farther away from recognizable shores, one was entertained by a trio of ancient cowboy musicians known as The Galoots. Electric git-tar, bass and drums plus a gloomy vocalist. If there'd been an announcer, he might have drawled, "Yay-us, folks, The Galoots. Ever' las' one of 'em over sixty-fahv an' the lot of 'em could be the layst of their breed. Lookit them tard red eyes, them saggin' jowls. Fer the las' ninety-eight hours, they bin playin' these same four songs over an' over fer yer ennertainmint, an' they're jis' too raggedy t'quit now. Ah'm not sure they rilly exist, but le's give 'em a haynd."

And over the whining electric guitar would come lyrics familiar from a few drunken minutes ago: "Lay yer haid / upon mah pil-low. / Lay yer warm an' tinder bod-deh nex' t' mine."

No two-steps at this hoe-down! This is the music of floor-burned foreheads and puffball noses! This is flypaper for the soul! And yet, young, vigorous Ron and his friends are now too deflicted to move. Better check to see if I've still got a dollar for the el. Maybe I better eat something. On the menu: chili cheddar, chili mac, venison chili, Mexican chili, *chili perch* . . . This is as good a time as any to heave.

I climbed steep mountains to get home after such an evening. It's a miracle I never wound up under a train. Another miracle is that, despite the self-revulsion that hit after wallowing in the West, two or three weeks later, The Galoots would serenade me again. "Lay yer haid / upon mah pil-low . . ."

My boozy period has been put behind me except for the shuddering realization of how much life—how much youth and vigor—was wasted under its influence. The nineteenth-century-styled hell that was The Cowpokes' Lounge is gone from our city. The building that hosted its *Twilight Zone* has been torn down. The illusions of the cowpokes have vamoosed.

But how does one kill a vampire permanently? Will the world ever be free of its Blue Hotels and Sad Cafés? The Galoots' warm and tinder bod-dehs have reappeared out near O'Hare Airport, where they now serenade suburban sots and the drunks who fall out of the sky.

(4) Butchie Descending

In the mid-nineteen-eighties, a dark, uncomfortable, smelly nightspot popped up like a boil on the fringes of Chicago's Bucktown area. The club nestled, the lone "business" in an otherwise residential neighborhood, coming awake just as neighbors were heading for bed. Fully packed, the room held forty patrons if fire codes were obeyed—about sixty if they weren't.

From the black, graffiti-covered ceiling, there hung a beat-up trumpet, a brassiere, doll heads and posters advertising musical happenings of the past. Jazz LPs were nailed to the walls.

The stage would accommodate about six musicians—about a dozen in the unlikely event they were all playing harmonicas. The aforementioned smell emanated from the club's constantly malfunctioning unisex restroom, accessible only by clambering upstage, disrupting any performers who might be working.

It became my hangout because it was hospitable to poetry readings. Hospitable and, because of its small capacity, it was a room easily packed. It's always nice to read to "capacity crowds." Over the course of my years at the club, the popularity of poetry events outgrew the joint and poets were forced to move to the more commodious Green Mill.

During the club's approximately ten-year lifespan, it was the site of several notable and several notorious events. One night, astoundingly, it was visited by ex-President Carter and his wife, Rosalyn, in Chicago for a Habitat for Humanity event. They stopped in because of the club's reputation as a good jazz scene, and Jimmy was a jazz fan. While they were there, Rosalyn had to use the "rest" room. After their visit, a graffito appeared in the john: "If this place is good enough for Rosalyn to take a squat, it's good enough for *you*!"

But the club's real notoriety arose from its name—The Get Me High Lounge. As one might suppose, the person who named the place was also notable. He was the club's first bartender, Butchie D., an unrepentant hipster, heroin addict and alcoholic nightcrawler. When anyone from the day world would confront Butchie with news of reality or anything he found it difficult to comprehend, it would lay him low. He'd aim a headache squint at the interloper, snap his fingers repeatedly and say, "Get **ME** high!" Note the emphasis. Most denizens emphasized "HIGH," but Butchie's locution (and everything else about Butchie) was other.

Whatever else one might say about Butchie, one had to admit he was *not* a businessman. Although there was a sign behind the bar that read, "No free drinks. No exceptions," by the second set on any evening, Butchie would have broken the rule with his own throat about half a dozen times and, after that, every other drink for every other patron was on the house. Let the good times roll!

So, the house, eventually, fell—not into the oblivion at the end of business road, but out of Butchie's ownership. The owner of the place was a guy named Dave, who already owned four successful Chicago clubs. He was that rarest of his breed, a *humanist* club owner. Musicians, employees, patrons and even the inevitable "bounced" respected him.

Dave mercifully allowed Butchie to stay on as chief (only) bartender at The Get Me High. Which was convenient, since Butchie lived in a hell-hole apartment upstairs. But there was trouble in the nether paradise. While on the job, Butchie continued to drink up the profits, which no longer came out of his pocket. Worse than that, he got thirsty one night after afterhours. In an alcoholic mind, there was only one solution to that problem: He sawed a hole in the floor of his apartment, The Get Me High's ceiling, and lowered himself into his old position back o' the bar, there to get higher and higher. So, finally, he was asked to turn in his bar rag (*Was* there a bar rag?) and his keys. A new bartender was hired.

"Snap! Snap! Snap!" went the fingers of fate and Butchie disappeared totally and permanently. As must we all, eventually.

A Gift from the Ethers

I'm a big fan of Chicago's little theater scene, despite the fact that much of what it offers is crap. When creative people take risks, you have to expect losses. Ninety percent of *everything* is crap. The great stuff makes up for the many nights of disappointment. At least I hope that's true. I've done some little theater myself and almost certainly have been responsible for some of the genre's joys and sorrows.

One Friday night, I went alone to The Platform on Clark to see *Mondo Tomaso*, a play written by and starring Tom Calavero, a friend of mine. The play dealt with various aspects of his relationship to his lifelong alter-ego, the actress Moira Shearer. (Tom is gay.) The play is an outrageous, funny, sad, poignant and multifaceted social commentary that contains both biting cultural accusations and self-deprecating wit. It turned out to be the best night I'd spent in a theater in a long time.

I couldn't wait to spread the word. The first person I thought of was my longtime lover, Paulette Marleigh. We'd been planning to "get together" on Saturday night, so I didn't bother to call her. I just showed up and knocked on the door of her apartment slightly before the time we'd planned.

She answered the door naked—surprising, but she was *always* surprising. We enjoyed a long embrace, but when we separated, I said, "Get dressed. I've got a treat for you. Tom Calavero has a play that's going to be at The Platform on Clark for the next three nights. You're going to love it!"

"So I took a bath for nothing?" she said.

Who wouldn't love such a provocative attitude and a quick response? I followed her into the bedroom to watch her dress and half an hour later, we were at The Platform.

The play, a long one-act, featured Tom himself as Tomaso and a cast of five other actors identified in the program as The Tall Brunette, The Not-So-Tall Brunette, The Perky Blonde, The Spunky Redhead and The Guy Who's Not Tomaso. The women portray Tomaso's casual friends, role-models, adversaries, some exaggerated female prototypes and some innocent bystanders, each of whom offered opportunities for social criticism and jokes about and in defense of Tomaso. The Guy Who's Not Tomaso is a less-judgmental mirror who attempts, not always successfully, to be sympathetic to Tomaso's circumstances.

Paulette was silent throughout the performance but, when it was over, her enthusiasm burst forth.

"That was really something! I loved his ability to laugh at himself and, at the same time, make himself a sympathetic character!" She gave him credit for accuracy in portraying many kinds of women. "Not many men are that fair," she said, "especially when they're being critical. The funny stuff about show business and image-making . . . Wow!"

I had to stop backstage to congratulate Tom. "This is the best thing you've ever written," I told him. But, when coming face-to-face with the author, Paulette couldn't see her way clear to dishing out unmitigated praise. As was usually the case, there was a teasing edge to her comments. She loved playing a rascally devil's advocate and testing the reactions she'd get. She smiled as she poked Tom's coat, looking for vulnerabilities.

"We'd like to know more about the Guy Who's Not Tomaso. How does he come by his liberal attitudes? Were he and Tomaso

childhood friends? Were they ever lovers? Is he a figment of Tomaso's imagination?"

Tom was flattered by her interest and attempted serious answers to her questions, but I could tell he didn't really appreciate
her editorial suggestions for revising his script.

"You've gotta take him as presented," Tom said. "I've given
you everything I care to about the relationship between the two
men. After all, the play's about Tomaso. The other guy is important
only as an illumination of *him*. Nobody spends much time asking
Conan Doyle about Doctor Watson."

"Well, you made him interesting enough that you made me
want to know more. I also think you could have made Tomaso's adversaries more vicious. You let them off easy, I thought. I've known
gay-bashers who go a lot farther."

"I didn't want to turn them into cartoons. Besides, I have a certain amount of sympathy for them. They victimize themselves by
their intolerance."

She asked The Not-So-Tall Brunette whether she shares any of
her character's traits.

The actress wasn't in the mood to interact with an audience
member. "Well," she said, "I *am* a brunette," and she left to take off
her makeup. Her character, by the way, wouldn't have interacted
with a member of the audience either.

Paulette continued sparring for about twenty minutes until
other fans demanded Tom's attention. He was glad of having an
excuse for escape. I made a mental note to explain her to Tom at
some later date. Not *apologize* exactly, but explain that she treats
all poets, musicians, painters and performance artists the same way,
regardless of her opinion of their work. Me included. I've been told
to comb my hair differently than I do, to grow a mustache and to

be more selective about the roles I take. I've come to regard it as her own personal art form—exercising her creativity without actually creating anything. Of course, some recipients of her probing resent such attention.

For example, Matt, a friend of mine who emcees a cabaret series at a nightclub, has been successful enough with his show that he's become a local celebrity. And, because of his success and my admiration of his work, Paulette has mostly been critical.

"He whips the audience into an emotional frenzy, but behind the lather, there's not much there," she says. She's not wrong about the emotions, but I think she's blinded by that quality and misses the ideas. Our difference of opinion on that subject has filled many hours with our arguments. As in the case of our post-Tomaso encounter, she usually debates in a jokey, casual style that's only tough enough to get a rise out of Matt and me.

Once we were away from The Platform, I scolded her. "You were messing with material that I know you admired. He was polite, but I could tell he didn't care for your comments."

"I don't see why not. I was trying to be constructive."

But she hadn't been trying to be constructive. She hadn't been trying to be critical, either. I knew that her only goal was creative conflict. She was just rubbing sticks together to see what would flare up.

Even in bed, later that night, she sought some turmoil. Mine was not the longest penis she'd ever experienced, and she commented on that. "The average penis is only six and a half inches long. By my calculations, that means there are four miles of unused cunt in Chicago."

I never heard her state the average depth of Chicago's vaginas. I'm not even sure she'd ever sat down with pencil and paper to do the calculation necessary to come up with the unused mileage. I've doodled some math on the topic and I think she's exaggerating.

So, our life together was full of sparring. To Paulette's credit, none of our debate deteriorated into the kind of hateful, hurtful destruction that takes place in many couples. Much of it involved disagreements about issues like: Should you use a comma or a semicolon in this sentence? Who's the superior auteur—Fellini or Bergman? How high above the couch shall we hang this print? Are graphic novels likely to offer more than or less than regular novels? We rarely got into the macro-issues that get some couples' underwear into a bundle. Not much religion or party politics, on both of which we were too much in agreement. A little social justice, race and economics, but never did we whip out ripsaws like, "You're fat. You're ugly. You're stupid. You're clumsy, greedy, lazy and useless." There's no fun in hurting each other. If anything, our "disagreements" were part of what unified us. And I was generally a good foil for her game—often losing sight of the fact that it was all a joke.

But there was one subject matter that got me angrier than others.

I'm a chronic disbeliever in all things mystical. I think it started with my break from Christianity and all its holy counterparts. Once I'd purged my beliefs of supernatural beings and life after death, various incarnations of the "I have the answer" crowd were next to be erased from my slate. More suspicion of that than faith in academics, government officials, scientists, critics of the arts, military strategists, evolutionaries . . . If I can't see it, sense it or test it in some way, it doesn't exist.

Naturally, the many varieties of parapsychology drive me crazy. Astrology, communication with the dead, magic crystals, UFOs, psychic predictions, numerology, reincarnation, Ouija boards, tea leaves and other weevils that bedevil human intelligence always disrupt my customary calm.

Now, I can't be sure Paulette truly believed in any of that stuff. She did advocate it to me frequently, but, knowing her enjoyment of playing the provocateur, when she *did* invoke the monkey gods, I couldn't be sure it wasn't just a pose.

"There are two guys who live down the hall from me," she told me once. "One of them invited me to dinner last week. I hadn't known him or his roommate very well before that. I'd never been to their apartment before and neither of them had ever visited me. But when I went to their apartment, I put my hand on the doorknob and, when I touched it, I knew immediately that they're good people. People I would like. People I could trust. I got such a reassuring vibration from the doorknob."

"I get reassuring vibrations from doorknobs too," I said. "Even from doorknobs on doors that lead to unoccupied rooms. I guess it's possible that good people lived there at one time. But doorknobs don't vibrate."

"I'm serious. That's never happened to me before, but this time . . ."

"Paulette! That's baloney! Doorknobs don't analyze people or send messages."

"How else can you explain what happened?"

"*Nothing* happened! What hand lotion were you wearing at the time?"

Well, the back-and-forth continued awhile, but it just petered out without convincing either of us. I never found out whether the guys down the hall turned out to be good people or not. I didn't travel down the hall to get the doorknob's opinion. Nor did Paulette concede her point. Neither evidence nor lack of evidence would change her opinions *if* her real opinions were actually revealed by her outrageous statements.

Despite the games, we were a solid couple. We both knew our unorthodox views were a better match for each other than for anyone else. Outsiders might not have seen us as two of a kind, but we were comfortable in our contrary contentions.

In December of 1994, Paulette turned sixty-three. We always exchanged presents on birthdays, but neither of us made a big deal about them, partly because I was nine years younger and some commentators were critical of that. Some commentators are critical of everything.

The following month, she developed a persistent cough. We didn't make much of it. January was a cold, snowy, windy month. But the cough caused her some pain, so, after a few weeks of that, she saw a doctor. When she reported the diagnosis to me, she treated it casually. Almost as if it was insignificant.

It was *not* insignificant. It was lung cancer. Partly because of her reporting style and partly because my tendency is to deny bad news, my first thought was, it's an early diagnosis. Maybe Paulette has a long, relatively good life in front of her. Maybe it can be cured. Not true. It wasn't an early diagnosis and the prognosis wasn't good. The doctors gave her perhaps a year to live.

Although at one point doctors misled us into celebrating her supposed cure, they soon reversed the statement and gave us even worse news. The cancer had metastasized to her liver. Still, Paulette's demeanor was bright. Although in a good deal of pain by this point, she remained active and cheerful, grocery shopping as vigorously as ever, cooking wonderful meals, going to concerts and shows.

In fact, in February she was *very* upbeat. She got the news that Chicago's Lyric Opera was about to present Wagner's rarely per-

formed Ring Cycle in its entirety. It was planned for four nights
in February and March—Götterdämmerung on February 24; Das
Rheingold, Die Walküre and Siegfried on three nights in March.
Zubin Mehta was scheduled to conduct. Paulette was knowledge-
able about classical music and *passionate* about Wagner. She'd been
a classically trained pianist in her teen years. "I should have been
a cellist instead," she was fond of saying. "It's the only instrument
that's held between the legs."

She couldn't stop talking about the Ring. Her financial situation at the time didn't allow her to dream of attending, and mine
was no better. I could feel that hearing the opera would mean everything to her, but I was helpless. She spent weeks enthusing about
The Ring and the rarity of the opportunity. I wracked my brain
trying to cook up a plan for coming up with the price of a ticket. I
could feel the difference between a casual wish and deep need, and
the imminence of death put teeth in that difference. Then, one day,
Paulette showed up ecstatic.

"I got a call from a guy I went to high school with. He's in Chi-
cago for a business convention and, believe it or not, he invited
me to go to Das Rheingold. He's a dentist back in Minot, North
Dakota, and I haven't seen or heard from him in forty-five years.
Isn't that amazing? We were never close friends, but he knew that
I'm currently living in Chicago."

It was as if the hand of the God I don't believe in had reached
down from non-existent heaven to bestow some grace on my love.
I was almost as ecstatic as Paulette was, relieved that an ear at some
Make a Wish Foundation had heard her beating heart and judged
her deserving.

On March 11, she dressed for the opera and left to meet her
friend.

Any visitation from Paulette's old home town would have been miraculous. She'd escaped the incompatible small-town life of North Dakota at the age of 18. It had been more than the nothingness of the place that she was escaping. Another problem was that her family was one of the very few Jewish families in town.

Worse than that, her father was a notorious "character" in the Jewish community. Even some members of his family told him to keep away from their homes and businesses. He was what's known as a schnorrer—a charismatic beggar who feels everyone else is obligated to give him whatever they've got. He employs guile, a hint of threat and shame on anyone who's reluctant to support him. He was also an unfettered womanizer and a drinker. And some of his stigma slopped over to affect his daughter.

She headed first to the supposedly bright lights of Minneapolis, which turned out to be less exciting than she'd hoped it would be. Then to Milwaukee, where she picked up a college degree in English, and then to Chicago. There she felt the first of what she'd been looking for—a cosmopolitan, somewhat bohemian atmosphere that would provide outlet for, even appreciation of her saucy wit. She got an editorial job on a trade magazine, did some nude modeling at Chicago's Art Institute and hung with a crowd of writers, painters and musicians. She began using the name "Marleigh" because she felt it fit her better than her real name.

There were infrequent trips back to North Dakota to visit her then-widowed mother, but, other than that, there was no turning back, no regrets. And there's nothing in the historical record to indicate that Zubin Mehta ever visited North Dakota.

If Paulette had any second thoughts about her convoluted history or choices she'd made, some of which had gotten her knocked around a bit, none of them were in evidence after Das Rheingold.

"It was more than I could have hoped for. The orchestra, singers, the grandeur of the score ... Not being an opera fan, you can't possibly imagine how thoroughly transporting it was. And the unbelievable coincidence of my old friend the dentist showing up at exactly the right moment and choosing to take *me* to the opera! By the way, this wasn't a romantic encounter. You needn't be jealous."

I wasn't. I was nothing but relieved that Paulette's dream evening had come together. It was like Cinderella attending the ball.

"He's still a dentist in Minot. He was here for only a week for a dentists' convention. He's already on his way back."

And we, unfortunately, were on our way back to being fully occupied with terminal illness. Paulette's breathing was now sometimes difficult. There were frequent emergencies requiring an inhaler and one incident where we were caught without one. Frantic, I had to dash into a drug store and demand that a pharmacist *give* me one and I'd be back later to pay for it. The panic I exuded convinced him to ignore store policy.

Somehow, the fact that the cancer had spread to her liver caused her recently shapely legs to swell up to double their normal girth, and the strength in her legs was sapped to the point that I was required to lift her out of chairs to a standing position.

And her mind was affected. She wasn't always sure where she was, even when in a familiar location. It was that debility that bothered her most and the one that she was most likely to deny. I tried always to guide her without questioning her judgment. Even during this period, our silly bickering persisted.

In late August, for instance, she told me, "I'm going to die on November 11."

"No you're not." I still held on to the hope that she'd last for years. "What makes you say that?"

"Because when I wake up at night and look at my digital alarm clock, very often, it says 11:11."

"Doctor Clock, I suppose," I said, getting angry. "You know why you think that? Because when you wake up at 10:14, 1:03 or 3:27, the numbers aren't memorable. They occur just as frequently as your 11:11, but the four ones stand out in your memory."

As usual, she didn't change her mind. Occasionally she'd count down for me the days remaining until November 11. I will say that, unlike some terminally ill people, she didn't talk herself into declining at a rate that would fulfill her prophesy.

But decline she did. In late September, I got a frantic call from Paulette telling me to get over to her apartment immediately. "I have to get to the hospital right away!"

"Honey! I'm out of town at the moment. I'm more than a hundred miles from Chicago. It would take me hours to get to you. What's wrong?"

"I was cleaning the barbecue grill and a fork that was hanging on a hook pierced my leg. Blood is squirting out of me like a faucet!"

"Call 9-1-1!" I demanded.

For once, she obeyed. Her phone cut off immediately.

As soon as I got back to the city, I went straight to the hospital. Paulette was resting comfortably, the crisis apparently past. The only visible evidence of her accident was a small bandage on her leg. The puncture had been small despite the fountain of blood it had released. But she was hooked to a constant supply of oxygen.

"I guess you can't leave me alone for a minute," she said.

Probably true, I thought. "I will try not to," I said.

For the next two nights, I slept in the hospital, in a visitors' lounge near her room. She was in and out of consciousness, but it made her feel better to wake to my presence.

During one of her waking moments, she began to gasp. I tried to increase the flow of oxygen, but I couldn't figure out how to do it. I ran out in the hall and yelled for assistance. A nurse was there in seconds, turned up the oxygen and the crisis was over.

"You saved my life," she said. I was quaking, unable to respond. I cradled her gently in my arms.

"I don't want to leave you," she said. Tears came to my eyes.

She died the next night, while I was sleeping in the next room. In the morning, I went back to her room, only to find it empty. I ran to the nurses' station. "Where's Ms. Marleigh?" I desperately asked everyone.

"I'm sorry to tell you she died a little after three."

It was October 3. Ten-oh-three on the digital clock and only ten months since her initial diagnosis. I don't remember anything about the next few hours except that I called her adult daughter (from a long-ago-ended marriage) who lives in Alaska. She, like her mother before her had found it necessary to put plenty of geography between herself and her origin and the acquaintances of her youth. She'd known that her mother was very sick and had been planning to make the trip in the next few weeks. She arrived the following day.

We spent a week both living in Paulette's apartment, deciding how to dispose of her possessions, arranging for a memorial service and sharing our very different experiences of Paulette. We also visited the morgue to view Paulette's body one last time. Although the daughter and I had met on several occasions, we'd never been close. Our relationship had been awkward. Being thrown together for a week of bereavement, we each felt the loss the other was experiencing, and the awkwardness evaporated.

At some time during the week, while remembering many facets

of my life with Paulette, I thought to ask her daughter, "Do you happen to remember one of her high school friends who became a dentist in Minot?"

"No. I met two of her girlfriends from high school, but that was when they visited us in Chicago. I never spent time in Minot and she didn't talk about it much."

"The reason I ask is I'd like to call him and tell him how much it meant to your mom that he visited here and took her to an opera that she very much wanted to see. That evening was the brightest time of her last few months. Can you at least give me the names of the girlfriends you met? Maybe they know the dentist."

"One of them was Jean Manville. The other one was . . . I have to think about it. Rose something. If you get in touch with Jean, she'd know."

* * *

"Hello, Jean? I'm a Chicago friend of Paulette Marleigh's. I take it you knew that she passed away recently."

"Yes, I did. I was so sorry to hear the news. She was a wonderful person and one of the world's great characters. We'd stayed in touch all these years."

"I'm calling in the hope that you remember a man who went to high school with both of you. He's currently a dentist in Minot. I want to get in touch with him to thank him for taking Paulette to a performance of Wagner's Ring Cycle at the Lyric Opera. It meant so much to her."

"No, I'm afraid not. To my knowledge, none of our classmates became a dentist. And we had a small graduating class."

"Maybe Rose would know the man." Jean gave me the number, but Rose, too, drew a blank.

"Well," I thought, "how many dentists can there be in Minot?"

More than I thought. In 1996, there were five dental practices in town, and each of them employed multiple dentists. Not knowing the name of the person I was looking for made the search more difficult. I had to run through the whole explanation for five receptionists and wait for them to survey all the dentists in their offices. Usually, that meant making follow-up calls a few days later. In all, eighteen dentists responded that they hadn't known Paulette by either her married or maiden names, and most had never been to Chicago.

I called the high school to see if they had records of a student in the graduating classes of 1944, '45 or '46 who had become a dentist. No, they were unaware of any dentists.

And this, really, is where this story begins. It begins in my head, where the dentist is likely to live for a long time to come. Does he exist somewhere beyond my detective skills? Is he currently practicing in some other little town in North Dakota? Did Paulette know him from some place outside her high school class? Is he currently working for Doctors Without Borders? Did she invent him, hoping to make me jealous, to relieve my guilt at not being able to take her to the opera or to spin an intriguing fiction for my entertainment?

In other words, did he exist? If he didn't, did Paulette *believe* he did? Did she attend the opera or not? Given Paulette's quirky personality, any of those alternatives is possible. I imagine one, then another, then, as I often am, I'm forced to recognize the impossibility of knowing *anything*. I must say that, in this case, Paulette herself created that impossibility. Her ability to blend reality and fantasy continues to rekindle the love I had for her.

Somewhere Over the Overview

Allow me to introduce myself. Even if you *don't* allow me, I'll do it anyway. I'm your narrator. While you've probably encountered a variety of offstage voices, omniscient viewpoints and authors' footnotes, you're probably not used to being addressed this directly in works of fiction, particularly not before the story gets started. Well, be prepared. The following doesn't aspire to being a story, a poem or reportage, and it will intentionally break many rules and frustrate expectations.

"Once upon a time," according to the narrator . . . Actually, it was much more often than once. What follows happens almost *constantly* with minor variations. It happens on all continents. It happens while we sleep. The seemingly disjoint events herein described overlap with and augment each other. They're so multilayered that one loses track of which end's up or what's down. So, let's start again.

* * *

Many times upon a time, there were several people among the others. I'll begin with Dave Montgomery, a forty-six-year-old radio repairman who'd traveled fourteen hundred miles from Minneapolis to see Johnny Vista's Vegas stage show. He was the first fan to approach the star. More about Vista later. For now, he must accept second billing.

What had moved Dave to go backstage? He didn't really know. He wasn't seeking an autograph. He wasn't seeking a memento for a celebrity auction or a contribution to a charitable cause. He really just *found* himself backstage, swept there by a surge of the jostling pack of Vista admirers. The random currents of the mob carried him to the forefront of the crowd, and it was suddenly clear that he might have a chance to speak to the singer. But there were only seconds to consider what to say. Then those seconds ran out and he was face to face with celebrity, nervous about the lack of a script.

Shyly, Montgomery began. "You've always been one of my favorite..."

Bodyguards cut him off. They threw a choke-hold on Montgomery and muscled him past the crowd, down a narrow hallway and out a back door. On the way, they banged his hip on a metal stair rail, providing him a purple souvenir of the encounter. He and his bruise stood in the alley behind the theater, panting, perspiring and trying to reorient himself.

Back inside, the next fan who'd been shoved at Vista was as anonymous as Montgomery had been but, inexplicably, this one was hugged and granted forty-five seconds of good-natured joshing by Vista. Someone handed Fan Number Two an autographed copy of Vista's latest CD before the singer and his entourage squeezed through a doorway and hustled out of sight. All in all, it had been an encounter the fan could report proudly to his neighbors, coworkers and, many years later, to his grandchildren, who likely would wonder who Vista had been before his celebrity had withered. "He was a real nice guy," Fan Two would recall.

Fan Two was a fifty-five-year-old Colorado man, due to retire from teaching high school at the end of the next term. Not that he's germane to our tale. He won't appear in this narrative again. You may wonder what will become of him after his work in this story is complete. Yes, intrudes the narrator, you may wonder. It's a wonder-filled life! But you'll hear no more about Fan Two. He fades back into the crowd.

* * *

However, to return to the other players, we, too, wonder from what tier of seating, from which balcony or box can we best view the left and right hands of God? Is it Vista's voice that calls to the many while thugs are delegated to choose the few? Or are mercy and wrath, giveth and taketh the red and black on the same mystic wheel—a Caddy for the waitress, boils for Job and nothing at all for the faceless multitudes so far in the background that they're out of mind?

Let's forget Montgomery for a moment and shift our attention to Mr. Vista, whose real name used to be Henry Lewis.

Vista had endured ten minutes of backstage worship before retreating to his dressing room. He drank a glass of milk before cold-creaming his makeup and taking a hot shower. Moments later, in jeans, tennis shoes and a tee-shirt, he shuffled wearily to the parking garage, where his driver sat reading a newspaper in the car. The two men nodded silent greeting and remained silent through the short drive to the hotel. What experiences could such disparate men share? There's no such thing as a famous chauffer. So four miles were traversed in silence.

When I say "his" driver, I mean nothing more than what we all mean when we say "my" barber, "my" priest, "my" boss, "my" neighbor. We don't actually *own* any of them. And the designation "my" doesn't distinguish them from the rest. It's quirky lingo that doesn't purposely mean much. And it's vaguely insulting to those on whom we pin it.

Back in his suite, Vista showered again. He stepped out of the steamy bathroom and donned a terrycloth robe. In the kitchen, he picked a jar of green olives from the refrigerator. In the living room, he slid some Debussy piano preludes into the CD player. On the balcony, he fell into a lounge chair, opened the olive jar and stared out at the view he'd purchased: the dark desert, spoiled only by the reddish glow cast by the billion bulbs burning for public consumption. The traffic ruckus, constant in this town but quieter at this hour, was muffled by the piano music. He popped three olives in his mouth and imagined sand giving back to the sky its furious heat.

For, just as Vista can easily afford any sensation he might choose, he also can afford the not inexpensive sensory deprivation of this setting—gauze for a wounded and battle-weary soldier, the blessed moments in which he tunes to the gods outside celebrity; the absence of klieg lights and microphones. No adulation requiring response. Holy the nothingness into which he can sink. He luxuriates in sinking there. Soon enough, the yakkety-yak and hubbub will re-exert themselves, requiring and requiring more than can be given. The price he must pay. But, in this setting, not a thought does he think. Not a thought for the driver, a character who, here, won't even be named. Vista thinks not a thought for Montgomery, who, for Vista, had never existed. Vista's not that kind of guy.

Not a thought for bodyguards, drinking together in a dim-lit lounge where a bare-breasted woman in a feathered G-string giggles as she delivers a tray of Manhattans. Brutus and Bigfoot and Lobo bulge at every double-knit seam and entertain each other with buffalo noises.

"Show 'er yer equipment," laughs a lump to his buddy. His buddy wags a roll of money like a fat cannoli in front of his trousers. This passes for wit among the trio. From the roll, the waitress is offered a bit of cheese. The beefsters and the waitress laugh and laugh together. Even gamblers and diners who pass their table laugh, not really knowing why. But laughing makes them feel that they're included in the seemingly festive scene.

The bells and buzzers of games of chance deafen players' hearts and minds to their own more intimate gains and losses. In the hall are hundreds of the previous generation's zombies, their death stares riveted by the machines that command them. They jam tokens in the slots, pull the levers, jam tokens, pull levers, jam tokens. Rhinestone-studded Naugahyde and rainbows of neon blind all eyes till goodness and mercy seem to overflow from loose slots. Alcohol is the proof. Bugsy Segal looks down from gangster heaven and gloats, "Just as I have foretold."

* * *

Two of those eyes belong to Montgomery, who's thinking of home and wondering if his quarters will last until tomorrow. He's thinking of checkouts and connecting flights, the cost of this vacation, his return to work—the radios that have, dependably for fourteen years, required repair. In the past four days, no doubt those radios have proliferated. Dusty on the counter in Minneapolis, they await the return of Dave like a loving family awaiting dad. Dad, for his part, will ooze relief to be back in their familiar presence, the chore of vacation dutifully completed. The attractions of the surrounding city have become less attractive the longer he's been here. The miracle of their existence has become irritating.

Dave is temporarily distracted from such matters that surpasseth understanding—the possible causes of the evening's unpleasantness, the response he will have from this point forward to the music in his massive collection of Vista recordings.

The distraction: He pulls a lever and hits a jackpot. Quarters droppeth like the gentle dew from heaven into the tray beneath. Smelling more cheese, a feather-crotched waitress hands Dave a drink he didn't want and sticks a nipple in his ear. But Dave is catching coins in his rubber bucket. Nipples and bruises and radios are not, at the moment, part of his conscious universe.

The narrator has a passing thought about Vista, but Vista's no longer on stage at the casino or in this tale. The narrator has nothing more to say. He's arbitrarily separating wheat from chaff, and Vista, so recently deemed wheat, is now, for all his fame, nothing but chaff.

* * *

Till now, the narrator has been focused on a few grains of sand—Montgomery, Vista, his driver, his bodyguards . . . Every protozoan's important, but we shouldn't long ignore the vast animal kingdom. If the narrator is to do his job, he'll zoom in, zoom out, zoom up and over.

Look—the boundless sky arcs over the balcony, bar and casino, ultramarine over desert surrounding. Away from the city, rhinestones give way to stars against the velvet void. Over mesquite, saguaro and creosote bush. Over deer mice, insects and lizards emerging from their rank burrows as life above ground again becomes livable. Even these creatures shake granules of sand from their surfaces and begin in darkness to pursue their tiny goals.

The sky arcs farther over the Mojave. Twelve miles out, it shelters the bones of Bonhamie, Lobo's late lost poodle, long his only friend—the only outlet for whatever gentleness the thug's soul could muster.

Six months ago, through a screen door left open, the dog imagined purpose in a passing iguana and, with a canine's insufficient foresight, chose pursuit over loyalty. As many of us do, he launched himself into the unknown without considering repercussions. Too late, he realized his owner was nowhere to be seen. His became a dangerously godless world.

In private, Lobo weeps, but, for the past six months, the public goon's been meaner than ever. His grief finds relief in others' pain. Few readers will be able to sympathize with Lobo. In his brief time on stage, he didn't inspire us to care about his problems. Another soul lost in a minor role. Is there *nothing* but loss in this accursed desert?

"There are also jackpots," think the carnivores who feasted on Bonhamie. "I've always liked French food," thinks one. But that ends the poodle's time on stage. Another protozoan.

* * *

As far as topography goes (and it goes on forever), very few jackpots equal the Rockies. Their steepness forces water to rush down and down and causes aspiring climbers to weigh courage against foolhardiness. In this, no load of gear has any weight. Nor, while falling, does the snow. Still, they weigh more than what Dave Montgomery, Vista or the waitresses may be up to. And what about the other seven billion? What are they doing?

Tectonic plates crash and wrinkle the continent, ignoring human scale. For those who see beauty in the violence of broken rock, there's beauty to be seen. It lifts our spirits. This is why we call it elevation. It's hard to get closer to the sky than this.

But above the Rockies, an eastbound jet carries some humans above the others. They've concluded their business or pleasure in the west and they've deconvened, making room for the next wave of conventioneers. The next swarm is already on the trade floor, arranging trays of plastic doodads. Amazingly, every one of the previous batch—the homeward bound—is bounding home claiming to have been a winner, though a few confess to having broken only even. In the pressurized cabin, their minds float free, above it all, depressurized.

Boundless, the sky arcs over Denver's tourist cabins, Kansas City's feedlots, Omaha's churches and universities. It arcs over Chicago's Lake Shore Drive. It arcs over you, it arcs over me.

* * *

There was a time when I wore a necktie and you a briefcase in that faraway land. Then you got a phone call that, briefly, seemed important. It turned out not to be. But then, in a restaurant, we were handed menus that begged consideration. I chose the sweet and sour duck, you ordered egg foo yung. They deserved a fifteen percent gratuity. Everything deserves what it gets.

"Please leave a message at the sound of the beep."

Behind us, desert creatures still burrow. And far below them still grind the lower layers of the earth. Like them, our lives are moved by the invisible—ideas simmering in minds other than our own. Some of them are up there, on the fortieth floor, looking down at the tops of our passing heads and dreaming of our next assignments. This year, those minds didn't even deem us worthy of a trip to Vegas for the national convention. While Vista is beginning his European tour, we sit and grumble in our office cubicles.

In the afternoon, before deadline, we conclude the Davis project under budget. We turn our attention to another project and another and another, ad infinitum. Then our attention turns to something else. Attention always is and was temporary, according to the narrator. The only constant is numbing elevator music played by The Eternally Mindless Strings. We ride down.

Midday broils in our slow-moving taxis, our dust storms and dilemmas, our paper pretensions and business agendas: parts of our history we'd forgotten. Did our ancestors do this or that? What was on their superiors' minds as sales forces awaited familiar luggage to appear around the curves of airport carousels? Damn! It never comes. So, aggravated, it's off to the claims office and a confrontation with time-consuming paperwork. These things happen. They must be borne.

How long has it been since our last meal? Even narrators have to eat! How much influence will hunger exert over our impatience with system malfunction? Does that excuse rudeness? Will it clarify to the woman behind the counter that, somewhere in the air, the baggage we long for really does exist?

On the escalator one wonders if the next transportation will require exact change.

The trip into the city is interminable and, by the time we arrive in the so-called gleam of alabaster, a sandwich has assumed significance well beyond corned beef, Swiss cheese or sauerkraut, despite the fact that many others in radically different circumstances have been hungrier by far than we will ever be. But none of them are on our minds as we wolf down our welcome home. Coffee and a burp and travel is complete.

*   *   *

Over the lake, the sky turns purple. In Chicago's western suburbs, one of which is named Buffalo Grove, it's still orange and rose. The buffalos are long ago departed, but tribes of teenagers on their antelopes roam again and again past the franchise restaurants. And locusts, after long songs to heat, fall silent in the dark green trees. After the game that we wound up winning three to two, the softball league organizers pack their bats and balls in canvas bags and wrestle them into their station wagons. Pizza celebrates victory and consoles defeat.

Indoors, those who didn't compete settle in their Lazy-Boys and reach for remotes, preparing for the oblivion that passes for entertainment. They control the controls as if they are *in* control. They pass trays of sweet or salty anesthetic while, outdoors, clouds of insects roil around aphrodisiac streetlights. They (the insects) whirrr the song of the summer night that's concluding in this part of America. The overzealous among them get fried to a crisp.

It's all national and local; indoor and outdoor; manic or lethargic; animal, vegetable, mineral; solid, liquid, gas. It's trivial and cosmic under all three hundred sixty degrees of sky. It's been this way all day and will continue as that dome goes dark and the only remaining light is artificial.

And now you and I are wet with each other, sweetly exhausted, images spent. We're as mindless as we can hope to be in the embers of our ecstasy.

Our luggage is now submerged. If we were capable of describing it to claims, we'd sketch the detritus of all of the above, combined with the desire for that and more. This is luggage we will never lose. Like planets, it circles endlessly the carousel.

But, for now, bedwarm, you throw a leg over me and sleep.

* * *

For those who require a final exhalation, a moral of the story, credits to crawl across the screen at the movie's conclusion, I can pretend that the movie *has* an end, but some protozoans will live happily ever after, while others, just as successfully, will become extinct.

Other narrators will take my place and the story will go on. Until it doesn't.

Pawn Without Sweetrolls

Knob-headed pieces move on the gameboard without destinations. If there are rules to the endless game, they're ever-changing, creating the illusion that there *are* no rules. Some players imagine they have more than pawn power. They hope to discover the game's purpose. At times, some seem to have won or are winning, some seem to be losing or have lost, but one can never be sure until moves have been made. Only then, after rewards have been earned or penalties suffered, do players get any clues about how the game ought to have been played.

Midnight in The Sizzler, a diner on Chicago's near south side, a pawn named Rick Taylor scrapes the grill, getting ready to close. He's been alone for most of the past eight hours. He's served two slouching pawns, both of whom have hung out till closing. Both are regulars who show up for their nightly soup or chili. One of them, about ten years Rick's senior, wearing a khaki jacket and a working man's cap, catches Rick off-guard by doing more than placing his order.

"What's your name?" he asks.

"Why?"

"You know *my* name. I'm embarrassed that, after all the times I been in here, I don't know yours."

"I *don't* know your name."

"Sure you do. You always ask me, 'What'll it be, Bud?'"

"I call everybody Bud."

"Well, this time you got it right. Bud Drapek. And you?"

"Rick." Just Rick, no last name offered, no "pleased t'meet ya,

Bud." Just Rick. Taylor isn't behind the counter to make friends. He isn't *anywhere* to make friends. But Bud Drapek imagines he's made a connection despite the fact that Rick's not a connecting kind of guy.

"Haya doin', Rick? Y'know, I always get a kick outta how, when I ask what's the soup a' th' day, you always say, 'chicken noodle.' What's it gonna be tonight?"

"Chicken noodle."

Drapek laughs. "The soup a th' night's the same as th' soup a th' day, huh? Well, I guess I got no choice. I'll have that. Best chicken noodle soup on Chicago's South Side. An' maybe a Coke. Best Coke on Chicago's . . ."

Rick's heard Drapek run this routine dozens of times. It bores him. He bores easily. Sounds that pour from mouths other than his own are annoying. So are his own words. People who require him to speak ask too much. His private world is *painfully* private, but so, too, is allowing anyone in to see the emptiness. No skills, no interesting hobbies, no fascinating insights to share. He thinks of himself as "self-sufficient," but that's not really enough Keep Out.

He takes shelter in the kitchen and comes back with "One Coke and soup special." In Rick's sarcastic parlance, everything's a special. Meanwhile, another customer—an unfamiliar face—has appeared. Rick moves down the counter.

"What'll it be, Bud?"

Bud Drapek laughs. "Another Bud. Hey, Bud," Drapek hollers at the newcomer. "Ask Rick what the soup of the day is."

The stranger ignores that. Instead, he asks for a menu.

"Up on the wall," says the automaton behind the counter.

"I don't see so good. Do you have any sweetrolls?"

"Out of 'em. They're mainly for the breakfast customers."

"This *is* my breakfast."

"Mmf. No breakfast here after noon."

"Can I get some toast?"

No response, but Rick returns to the kitchen to fill the order. Drapek hollers back at him. "I work second shift at the front desk of the Blackstone. Over on Michigan, y'know?" And he starts a long, one-sided explanation of all the interesting people who've taken rooms at the hotel, room rates and everything Rick never wanted to know about the hotel business.

"You'll never guess who checked in last night," Drapek says. Rick doesn't venture a guess, nor does he care. He tends not to take an interest in human interest.

Twenty minutes till close. He brings the toast. Drapek continues to report the details of his life.

He reveals who came in last night—a name that means nothing to Rick. "Y'know who that is? She was in that movie about the kidnappers. That's why I reckonized her. She was real nice t'me. Humble, y'know. Not at all like the character in the movie. She's in Chicago for . . ."

Rick indulges in his long-standing habit of ignoring chatter. Drapek's monologue rolls on and on. Rick checks the clock again. Fifteen minutes till closing, but Rick exercises his prerogative to dictate house rules.

"Okay, you guys—too long is here," Rick announces. "Time to pay your chef and hit the road. No more nothing till tomorrow." The toast eater has only taken two bites. He gobbles the rest of the first slice and pockets the second slice, intuiting that the joint has never heard of doggy bags.

Once Rick's alone, he shovels a few dishes in the sink and, while they're soaking, gives the counter a cursory swipe of the rag. Back at the sink, he swishes dishes in warm water and leaves them in the rack to dry. Another Sizzling night has come to an end.

"The Sizzler." That's a laugh. If there's any place in Chicago that sizzles less, it would be the remnants of the Robert Taylor Homes or a typical night in the morgue. The name's an ironic tombstone on the long-ago aspirations of the owner, Old Man Syzmanski. Rick knows that, in the past four hours, the place hasn't taken in enough to cover the forty-eight bucks he's earned during that time. Despite the tedium of his shift, he's grateful that Syzmanski never does the math that might lead him to close the joint at eight. Rick needs the hours. One man's subsistence is another man's subsistence.

So Rick's had plenty of time to think. Not that he's *done* any thinking. He's thirty-six now, and, over those years, he's thunk himself out. He's scraped the grill of his life until there's nothing left worth thinking about. His head's as empty as the Sizzler's ten stools.

Ovens are off, the door's locked. He hopes no after-hours knocker will question the CLOSED sign. The man in the glass box is no longer a cook, no longer a waiter and most certainly not a doorman. He's merely the man who has turned out the lights and become a pedestrian—another pawn moving on the dark board.

No latecomers tonight. Nor do any passersby on the street watch Rick fumble with the lock and begin the long walk home. He heads north on Wabash and, after crossing the expressway, moves west to Clark to enter the canyons of the Loop.

A young black guy with a phone at his ear passes him heading in the other direction. As they pass, Rick catches a few words of one-sided conversation:

"We gotta approach this situation very clever." The rest fades in the distance.

Rick vaguely notes that there's something wrong with the grammar of the half-conversation, but he doesn't linger on that long enough to figure out the flaw. He wonders what the "situation" is. That curiosity, too, is fleeting. It's the word "we" that captivates him. That and his vague curiosity about how the speaker defines "clever." His own the lack of a "we" with whom to approach life's situations nags his subconscious.

That lack is painful enough that he wonders if the man with the phone and the person he'd been calling might welcome his assistance in approaching their mysterious "situation." Foolish, he realizes, to imagine camaraderie with a passing pawn. What are the odds? And anyway, he really doesn't have any help to give. *He's* the one who needs the help. Of course, the fact that he's been unable to connect with *anyone* in a city of four million is probably his own fault. Not my fault, he thinks. The menu choices aren't appealing. They're a buncha dullards.

And, at this hour, most of the millions are asleep. The wakeful few don't strike Rick as likely companions. Nocturnal men staggering in pursuit of their various anesthetics of choice. And the women who pass fall into two categories—those seeking customers for their darktime business and those who fearfully hurry past Rick, trying to remain safely invisible. He doesn't want to know the former and the latter don't want to know him. The daylight choices are no better.

As he hits Monroe, he sees four businessmen conversing outside The Palmer House, smoking and enjoying the Spring weather. Businessmen, thinks Rick. What a life! These are the so-called important people. People with skills. People with something to point to as accomplishments. But, as he passes, he catches a fragment of their conversation.

"Man! Did you see the ass on that one in the red dress?"

No accomplishments after all—no more achievement than Rick has achieved. Even the woman they were speaking of, despite what might be considered her asset, is probably nothing more than another person in the red, thinks Rick. Businessmen. *Monkey*-businessmen reminiscing about a monkey woman. Given the fact that there are no females in their midst, apparently, the guys haven't approached their unimportant situation very clever. Still, he thinks, they can imagine their quartet of "we" as being, in itself, a group of "friends." The illusion of strength in numbers.

He encounters nobody else until, as he crosses Madison, an old guy slumped in a motorized wheelchair speedily rolls past without a word. Not much vehicular traffic at this time of night, so the guy might arrive safely at his destination.

At Wacker Drive, there's The Korner Kafé—a Sizzler clone except for its higher-traffic location and the better business it does as a result. And, it's slightly more "luxurious," if four booths along the window qualify as luxury. As he does many nights, Rick stops in for dinner. He sits at the counter. A badge identifies the waitress as "Lois." He grunts her a hello.

"Hi," she responds. "Haven't seen you lately. Been on vacation?"

"I been around. Not every night, I guess. But a couple nights this week."

"I guess it's me who's been missing. I had a few nights off," she says, "'cause I had a busy week at school. I'm taking some courses at the Art Institute." Apparently, the silent lump before her at the counter isn't going to deter her desire for conversation. "Plus, I been working on a project."

"What kinda project?"

"It's kind of a six-foot sculpture made mostly of feathers. It was supposed to be *all* feathers, but it's hard to get hold of that many feathers. They're kind of endangered. And expensive. I had to start using artificial ones. They're made of fabric. I guess that's okay. It's easier to shape fabric."

"In the shape of what?"

"It's not shaped like anything. It's abstract."

Rick's response is equally abstract. He's never been good at dealing with abstractions, and he's never spoken with Lois much. He has no idea what kind of abstractions her mind might contain. He never even knew about her studies at the Art Institute. His own mind is more abstract than anything the Art Institute would recognize. It's a minimalist mess.

"Hmm," he says, and is silent for a minute. "You seem too young to be a college student."

"There are some younger than me."

"How old are you?

"Twenty-two."

"You wanna be a artist?"

"Oh, it's hard to make any kind of living as an artist. It's just something I like doing."

"So you make a living doing this instead?"

"Well, frankly, it's hard to make a living doing this, too."

"You don't have to tell me. I do pretty much the same thing."

"You seem too old to be doing this."

"There are some older than me," Rick says.

"So why do you come in here? Why don't you eat at your own place?"

"First of all, it's not my place. I just work there. And, second, I spend eight miserable hours a day in the place. That's all the nothing I can take."

"What do you do for fun?"

"I come in here," he says bitterly.

"Some fun."

Another customer calls Lois away. Before she goes, Rick quickly places his order—huevos rancheros and a coffee—and sits alone, fooling with the silverware and thinking about artificial feathers. One takes what fun one can get.

For fifteen minutes, he watches Lois down the counter, talking to a skinny old (really old) man with a week-old growth of beard, a shaggy head of hair, ratty old clothes and a Cub hat. Despite all the conversation Lois is sharing with the old guy, Rick doesn't hear him place an order. Then Lois disappears into the kitchen and comes back with a plate of fries for the old guy.

When she returns to Rick, he asks, "What was that all about?"

"Oh, that's Billy. He's in here a lot. Never orders much. I don't think he has much money, so sometimes I give him some fries on the house. I have to be careful about that. Management keeps a pretty close eye on what gets sold. They're always suspicious that employees are dipping into the till or eating the profits, but I figure they aren't gonna miss one potato every once in a while."

"Billy looks like he's more than a few potatoes short of a meal."

"Yup. But he's a good guy. Interesting too. A long time ago, he used t'work at a printer's. He was a typesetter. Y'know that old saying, 'Mind your p's and q's?' That comes from typesetters, 'cause the metal slugs of p's, q's, d's and b's all look the same in a tray of lower-case letters. Especially 'cause they're all backward and upside down."

"I thought it came from bartenders reminding customers to mind their pints and quarts. You sure Billy didn't pick up the saying that way?"

"No. He may look like a drinker, but he's not. He just doesn't spend anything on his appearance."

"Except the Cub hat. Seems like an unnecessary decoration."

"There's a story behind that, too. Before he retired, he lived in Milwaukee. When he got here, he made the mistake of going to a Cubs game wearing a Braves hat. The Brewers were the Braves then, and they were the Cubs' arch-rivals. Well, a bunch of Cubs fans cornered him after the game and beat him up pretty bad, so one of his friends gave him the Cubs hat for protection."

"Ain't life grand? A guy gets beat up for backing the wrong team! The great American game."

"I prefer to think about the guy who gave him the hat. *That* guy was pretty grand. Yeah, people are okay sometimes."

"As long as you're wearin' the right hat, I guess."

"And, you gotta mind your p's and q's."

"Problem is, with all those p's an' q's bein' backward an' upside down, it makes it hard to mind 'em. But I'll try to remember that," Rick says. Unfortunately, he's already forgotten the saying, its origin, its relevance, Billy's life story and Billy himself. Just more feathers, floating through Rick's head. Abstract. He shlurps the dregs of his coffee, leaves Lois his dirty dishes and two bucks. Her biggest tip of the night. The biggest tip *he* got tonight jingles in his pocket.

Woman who gives an old bum free fries deserves a tip, Rick thinks. He heads for home, his lonely head full of self-pity. He fails to take credit for the tip he left Lois. Grand, in spite of his bitter demeanor.

North of the river, canyon walls aren't as imposing as those in the Loop, but Rick remains smaller than everything that surrounds him. Smaller even than everything in the game board's other twenty-four time zones, where billions of pieces are making their moves.

He imagines Lois tomorrow, hobnobbing with her artist buddies, all of them focused on projects of one kind and another. Will those projects provide them reason enough to go on? Maybe, if they can convince themselves of their projects' importance. They're not gonna cure cancer, walk on the moon or discover new continents, but paint and plaster, toothpicks and feathers have a better chance of filling out a life than flipping burgers does.

Rick remembers making a car out of macaroni noodles in his long-ago elementary school class. Easier to see purpose even there than in ketchup and grease. There's comfort in being surrounded by others who share one's faith in the ineffable goal—the faith that arts and crafts are as meaningful as home runs, stock market profits, effective deodorants, blue ribbon hogs, test tubes or our numerous other supposedly winning strategies. Unquestioning faith in macaroni may be enough. "Use your noodles," the teacher had instructed the kids.

Rick rests for a moment on a bench and notices that, three floors above him, there's an office in which ghostly fluorescent lights are still burning, creating a bright patch on the otherwise black grid. Within it, he can see the top half of a lone worker rise from his desk and move like a golem from a cabinet to water cooler to file cabinet to pencil sharpener to waste basket before returning to a desk laden with paper purpose. Seated again, the worker folds his arms into a nest and settles his head in it. Sleeping? Weeping? Dreaming? If dreaming, dreaming of what? Paper?

The others who brushed past Rick on his path home were barely blips on his screen, but the desk jockey above him makes him wonder. Does that worker suffer under a burden as impersonal and degrading as his own? Office environments are considered by many to be more respectable than The Sizzler. The salaries earned within them are higher than his own, the shirts and ties worn there are more esteemed by society, and the world considers sheets of paper more significant than burgers or bratwursts. But do those differences make a difference? Do they lessen the toll on souls who play white-collar games? Ask the man whose head is on the desk, minding his p's and q's. And zzz's.

Or ask the man who's nearing the end of his long walk home. A destination is a purpose of sorts. It fills an hour or so worth of void. But now that the goal's achieved and the sweetrolls are gone, there's nothing left but the bus he'll take tomorrow—it'll get him back to within three blocks of The Sizzler—back to eight more hours of "What'll it be, Bud?" and another walk home.

Rick kicks off his shoes, collapses in a chair and turns on the television. In ten minutes, he's asleep. The machine continues to "entertain" the unconscious pawn, offering remedies for every flaw known to man—cancer, dandruff, mesothelioma, B.O., obesity, acne and diseases the names of which nobody knows. "Don't take this wonder drug if you've ever had endocranial neoplasia type two," the TV warns. Rick has no idea if he has or hasn't, and he doesn't care. The TV goes on to show cars speeding through deserts and up mountain roads, kicking up clouds of dust. It shows people who live lives as good as goods can offer, free of those unsightly hemorrhoids. It shows people gathered in laughing groups of friends.

Even if one is conscious, the cures, goods and services offered don't do anyone much good. None of them clarify the nature of the game. Few offer any information, but all threaten potential side-effects. And, although we, who remain at least semiconscious, remain uncertain of the rules of the game, it isn't a game of solitaire. The lone hand loses, Bud.

Our Hearts May Attack at Any Moment

In July of 1995, more than seven hundred Chicagoans died as a result of a four-day stretch of hundred-degree-plus temperatures. I was almost one of them. Because I was delirious during some of the early parts of this story, my memory of some events is spotty, but here's what I've retained.

On a Thursday night at the beginning of the heat wave, I went to a play at The Spikey Saddle, one of Chicago's many little theaters. I don't recall the name of the play, but I do remember that it was a shrill pro-abortion rights argument.

Now, I almost always find myself on the left of most issues, but abortion makes me uncomfortable. I have no idea when life begins. I do feel that women should have control over their own bodies but, given the number of abortions performed annually, I'm convinced that many people use abortion as alternative birth control. That, as far as I'm concerned, takes terminated pregnancies beyond freedom of choice and makes them tantamount to murder. Usually, though, I keep my mouth shut, knowing that America's pro and con minds are made up.

During the play, the owners of the theater had set up a buffet of hors d'oeuvres in the lobby for post-play snacking, so a lot of the audience hung around to chat and chew longer than is customary.

During the chatter, Sheila Zimmerman, the director of the play, reiterated the playwright's stance loudly and angrily enough that I couldn't keep quiet. When she said, "Well, if you don't believe in abortion, just don't have one," I was aghast at how thoroughly her statement ignored the moral implications of lives at stake. I tried to clarify the opposing point of view in terms she could understand. I said, "And if you don't believe in killing Jews, just don't kill any. That's insufficient."

Ms. Zimmerman sputtered and made it clear that she hadn't understood the parallel. I could tell I was no longer welcome to snacks or opinions, so I split.

Once back in my hot apartment, I didn't feel well. I was weak and dizzy and vomited several times. Being a diabetic, I was afraid I was becoming dangerously dehydrated and lowering my blood sugar levels, so I drank orange juice. I vomited again. I drank some more orange juice. Still feeling ill, I went to bed but I had trouble sleeping. I got up several times to stick my head in the bowl, always following the adventure with an orange juice chaser.

In the morning, I was awakened by a phone call from Myra, a girlfriend who lived nearby.

"I can't talk," I said. "I'm too sick. I have to lie down."

"I'm coming over," she said. "You sound terrible."

"No, don't do that. I'm good for nothing today. I'm going back to bed. Bye."

But twenty minutes later, Myra was at my door. I barely had the energy to let her in, stagger back and flop into bed. She took a look at me and said, "I'm calling the hospital."

"No! I don't need the hospital. I can't afford it. I just need some sleep."

My speech was slurred and I had trouble keeping my eyes open. The next thing I knew, paramedics were carrying me down the three flights of stairs on a stretcher. Before we reached the ground floor, I began gasping desperately for breath. When they got me into an ambulance, they put an oxygen mask on me and began pumping me full of fluids.

I awoke in a bed in an Evanston hospital. I was breathing again and feeling normal. I lay there, ready to go home but mystified about what had caused my emergency. I suspected that the food in the hot theater lobby, having sat around unrefrigerated during the play, had been responsible for sending me from hospitality to hospital, but the docs didn't leap to that conclusion so, for the time being, I was held simply "for observation."

The next day, Myra came by to do her share of observing and ordering me to relax, relax, relax. I tried to reassure her that I felt fine.

"You saved my life, hon," I told her.

"So it turns out you could afford the trip after all," she said, remembering my protestations.

I was confident that it had simply been a case of low blood sugar and that, once that had been addressed, I'd be as good as new. I said as much to the docs, who told me how wrong I was. When I'd been admitted, my glucose level had been dangerously *high*—nine times normal levels, which had resulted in my inability to breathe. I'd misjudged the effect of vomiting. Dehydration causes the proportion of sugar in the system to go up, not down, and each time I gulped orange juice I was exacerbating the situation.

"The condition you had was extreme ketoacidosis," I was told. "Blood sugars as high as yours can trigger pulmonary problems. Once we lowered your blood sugars, you could breathe again, but we think you may have had a heart attack as a result of the high. We should hold you a while to be sure you don't have another."

I had nothing to do but wait for them to give me an all clear.

* * *

Being in a hospital while you're feeling fine, not awaiting a surgery, is an odd experience. The novelty of the surroundings quickly wears off. Ambient sounds drift in from other rooms and nurses' stations, augmenting the frequent beeps, buzzers and alarms—the hospital equivalent of muzak. Monitor numbers tic up and down, signifying whether you're doing well or poorly, but you have no idea what they mean. I spent the first day feeling as if I was nothing more than a thing passively awaiting direction from my puppet masters.

I woke from an afternoon nap on the second day to find that I'd acquired a roommate. He was a black guy about ten years younger than me who, like me, wasn't awaiting surgery. Nor was he in pain, so we introduced ourselves to each other. His name was Charlie Parker—the same as the greatest jazz saxophonist who ever lived. I wasn't sure I'd heard him right. I own almost every recording Parker ever did, so I ran through all the questions that I'm sure he'd answered hundreds of times. This, most definitely, would be a story I'd tell my fellow jazz fans. Unfortunately, Bird didn't live in my roommate's heart as he did in mine, so we soon exhausted the jazz topic.

Which brought us to the topic that preoccupies all us bedridden types: What's your ailment? My own wait-and-see diagnosis didn't provide me with much to tell. Charlie's story was far more interesting.

"I feel okay now, but I was electrocuted. I work for the CTA. Six hundred volts of electricity run through the third rails to move the trains. But rails have little gaps between sections. If a subway stops at just the wrong spot, trains can't start again. When that happens, an employee uses a long pole with a three-foot aluminum cross piece on the end of it to reestablish the connection. You touch the cross piece to the rails to bridge the gap and the train can start again. I was the guy who had to do that. Well, I did it, but current ran up the pole and electrocuted me. It knocked me out and threw me against the back wall of the platform."

"Oh my God! Why didn't it kill you?"

"I don't know *why* it didn't. Six hundred volts is plenty enough electricity to do the job. But it cooked me. You know how, when you cook a piece of meat, juice comes out of it? Well, the juice came out of my body's meat. The docs say I'm probably gonna have a heart attack as a result."

"That's why I'm here, too. I mean, not 'cause I was electrocuted, but they're waiting to see if I'm gonna have a heart attack. How soon will they know about you?"

"No telling."

The first news Charlie got came not from doctors but from a phone call he got from a fellow CTA employee.

"He said the CTA is claiming the accident was my fault," Charlie reported. "They say I didn't follow proper procedures for completing the circuit. But I did."

"They tend to blame accidents on employees," I said. "Remember that el car that fell off the trestle at Wabash and Lake? A few cars were hanging off the track, threatening to fall to the ground. It was pretty dramatic seeing cars dangling off the track at a forty-five-degree angle. I can imagine the terror the passengers in those cars were feeling. The CTA claimed the motorman had taken the curve too fast. But later, they built a tall barrier wall right where the accident had happened. How would a wall prevent another motorman from driving too fast?"

"They're afraid I'll try to sue them," Charlie said. "I probably could do that."

"They'd probably win," I said. "I'm sure they have a bunch of high-powered lawyers. And you already have an idea of how they'd approach it—claiming it was all your fault."

Neither of us really knew anything about how courts work, so our speculations were brief. We talked a little about this and that, but both of us were thinking primarily about our possible heart attacks. Those thoughts filled our quiet hours. Lub-dub, lub-dub. So far, so good.

The next day—again, for no reason we could explain—Charlie was released. There was still a possibility that he'd have a heart attack, but doctors felt it was no more dangerous for him to have it at home than in the hospital. So, good luck to you, Charlie. It's been nice having you stop by for a pointless visit. Ron, stay where you are. Read another book and we'll see what happens. Lub-dub.

* * *

My time in a private room didn't last long. I was awakened from an afternoon nap by my new roommate. Saul Resnick, a guy in his mid-sixties, was yelling at a lady with a food cart.

"You make sure the next meal is made to *my* specifications. I've been in this zoo for three days, and not one bit of food I've been given has been what I need! I can't eat *this*."

"I bring only what doctors say you can have. I don't decide."

"Doctors! Feh! Don't talk doctors! Never has there been such a collection of schmucks as I meet here! They got no idea from kosher, they sneak whole milk into the mashed potatoes, salt into everything and by the time anything gets to me, it's cold. Hear what I'm saying, for God's sake! I can't eat that stuff."

I kind of doubted his assessments. All the food I'd been given had been salt-free. The woman who'd brought the food cart waved her hand dismissively and left. Resnick turned to me.

"This place is gonna kill me. I know what I can eat and what I can't. I'm sorry. I demanded to go to the kitchen so I could give 'em instructions in person, but they wouldn't let me do it. I can imagine what the kitchen looks like."

Finally he calmed down enough to say, "My name is Saul. What's yours?"

"Ron. So, what do the doctors send you that you can't eat?"

"I can't have whole milk. It's gotta be skim. They gave me mashed potatoes that had whole milk in 'em. And I can't have salt. I been on a salt-free diet for years. They send me all kinds of little packets of this and that. Who knows what's in 'em? I'd just like to get a nice piece of fish."

"My only complaint is that the food's too bland," I said. "Of course, at home, I probably put too much salt on everything. A lotta pepper, too."

"Well, I should know if there's salt in what they give me. And cottage cheese! All cottage cheese got *tons* of salt. I complained to one of the doctors but he wouldn't believe what I told him. I said, 'What's your name?' I wanted to report him to the administrators. He wouldn't even *tell me his name.* Dr. X, he tells me! Can you believe? Dr. X! I'm not gonna let that go. I know what he looks like."

His complaints were interrupted by a visit from his cardiologist, who overheard the tail-end of his tirade.

"Listen, Saul," the cardiologist said, "you've got to calm down. You've given yourself three heart attacks already, and your constant fury is working you up to another one. The next one's likely to be your last. There's no point in my fixing you up if you insist on raging at everything in sight."

"It's this cockamamy institution drives me crazy!" And for an example of the irritants, he told the cardiologist the story of the supposedly outrageous Dr. X.

"There's no secrecy involved," Resnick was told. "That was Dr. Xenophanes. Everyone calls him Dr. X. because so few people pronounce Xenophanes correctly."

"So he can't wear a badge or something? How's a man to know what's going on if he don't say? He's hiding something. He wants to keep me from reporting him. And he didn't listen about the food. What excuse for that?"

"You're getting the food you're *supposed* to get. Again, I tell you—calm down or else it'll be that's all, Saul! The top of your head's gonna blow off."

'You people got no idea of what I'm supposed to get. My lawyers are gonna hear about this mishegoss. When I get outta here ..."

"If you don't kill yourself, your lawyers will. I've said my say, and I have other patients to see to. So goodbye. I'll see you again tomorrow. Call your lawyers if you want and then call the undertaker."

* * *

I can't say I was happy to be in the hospital, but I didn't agree with my roommate that the hospital was the cause of all my woes. If I'd been in the habit of monitoring my blood sugars instead of using my intuition, I wouldn't have wound up in this situation. I resolved to be more thorough in the future. My only beef with the hospital was that nurses would wake me up every three hours to give me blood tests. That and the frequent beeping of various alarms. The food was passable.

An even greater annoyance was Saul's unending complaints about hospital food, room temperatures, funny smells, lumpy pillows, nurses' inattention, doctors' malpractice and the crappy quality of current television programming. Not even the weather or the lousy view out our window were exempt, despite the fact that neither of us had access to the outdoors.

I was therefore happily surprised to get a respite.

"Seen any good movies lately?" Saul asked.

"Not any *new* good movies, but I've rewatched a couple of my favorites—Felini's *8½* and Brando's *On the Waterfront*. I've seen both of them so often that most of the lines are in my head."

"*On the Waterfront* I know. I agree with you on that one. Kazan's a genius. I don't know from the other one. My own personal favorite is *Judgment at Nuremburg*. Everything about it. It shows so many shades of the German population's responsibility for the Holocaust—the judge played by Burt Lancaster, who thinks he's remained an honorable man, the Marlene Dietrich character who thinks her social class and so-called sophistication are enough to make her an acceptable companion for the upstanding judge played by Spenser Tracy. Guilty, guilty, guilty! *All* of 'em!"

"And the tragic figure played by Montgomery Clift! Oy! It made me weep. What performances!"

We were in complete agreement about the power and justice of the film. That topic sustained us for half an hour. But then it was time for the food cart again. Time for another tantrum.

"Who ordered this?" Saul exploded. "Not me, obviously. Meat and dairy on the same tray? Not for any Jew I know. I suppose they expect I should wait six hours to finish the meal? And which is the dairy silverware? Anyone in food prep ever hear of kosher? Or maybe I should convert while I'm here? It wouldn't surprise me to know you inject me with pork chops while I'm sleeping. Is there a rabbi on staff? I'd like to have a little chat with him."

While this was going on, the doctor who'd visited that morning, perhaps attracted by of Resnick's loud complaints, stuck his head in the room. He didn't say anything. He jotted something in a notebook and disappeared. So did the lady who'd delivered Resnick's lunch.

Soon after the food was taken away, a nurse appeared with a pill for my roommate.

"Am I gonna get maybe some lunch now?" he asked.

"No," she snapped. "You're gonna take a nap." She gave him an injection.

"I don't want a nap. I'm hungry."

Hungry though he may have been, a few minutes later, Saul was sound asleep. I finished my own lunch and read for a while now that our room was silent. Then I, too, took a nap.

* * *

I awoke to another newcomer—a sixty-something woman sitting at the foot of Resnick's bed. She was watching him sleep.

"Hello," she said. "I'm Marla Resnick, Saul's wife. He told me about you. Said you're a good roommate. I hope he hasn't been too difficult to put up with."

"No, no. We've talked about our favorite movies."

"The doctors knocked him out with some heavy tranquillizers or sleeping pills. He wasn't talking about movies with *them*—just his complaints. He's an angry man."

"I noticed. Things here aren't as bad as he probably told you they are. He disapproved of the food he was getting. I have no idea what his needs are or what he's used to having at home . . ."

"Oh, it probably has nothing to do with the food. That's just the way he is about everything."

"They tried to convince him that his menu was dictated by

doctors' orders, but he didn't think much of the doctors, either. Does he have a special diet at home?"

"He pretends that he keeps kosher, but he doesn't really obey those rules either. He argues with the rabbis as much as he does with doctors. He argues with *everybody*."

"He talks about lawsuits a lot. Does he really sue people as much as he says he does?"

"It makes me sick. He sues *everybody!* It's driving us into the poorhouse. I can't even keep track of it all—neighbors, the post office, the gas company, the police, the gardeners, a roofing company . . . I'm surprised he hasn't sued *me*. Not that he trusts lawyers. He thinks *everyone* is out to get him."

"One of the doctors told him it's his anger that's overtaxing his heart. Have his doctors at home warned him about that?"

"The only warnings he believes are the warnings he gives himself, and he warns himself about everything. Most of it's imaginary. We've been married for thirty-two years. He wasn't always like this. He used to be happy, friendly. The anger started about five years ago and it's getting worse all the time. I have no idea what caused the change."

Saul began waking. "What caused what change?"

Mrs. Resnick went to the side of his bed. "Hi, Honey. You were a long time asleep. How are you feeling? Anything I can get you?"

"Yeah. You can get me out of here."

"You're not ready to go home. You just had another serious operation and you'll be here for at least another week. We don't want you should run another risk by straining yourself. They gotta keep a close eye on you to be sure . . ."

"Every day I'm *here* is a strain."

We got to hear an exhaustive repetition of Saul's litany of complaints. Even the story of Dr. X., despite the fact that the mystery of X. had been explained. I kept quiet while Mrs. Resnick did her best to fend off the swarm of her husband's angry bees. It was hopeless. When she couldn't take any more, she kissed him and left. Tomorrow, there'd be more.

Saul was quiet for minutes when he was alone again. Then he said, "She's a wonderful wife."

"She seems like it." After a bit, I said, "You know, she lives in the same world you do. She puts up with the same people you do, deals with the same problems, but she sees things differently. She told me about some of your legal issues. They cause her a lot of worries. You'd both be happier and you'd be healthier if you could let some of those problems go."

He waited a long time before saying, "I suppose you're right. We none of us gets justice in this world. So why me, I guess."

"Right! It's nothing personal, Saul. Everyone—you included—dishes out some bullshit to anyone who's handy. Most of us ignore it. So what?"

* * *

Perhaps as a reward for my dishing out advice, later that night, a nurse arrived to tell me that I'd be going home the next day. Apparently, my non-crisis had passed. And, as an appetizer to that festive event, I got to sleep through the night without being awakened for blood tests. The next morning, I was up early to dress, pack my suitcase and sit on the bed awaiting the all-clear.

"So. Another miracle cure from modern medicine," Saul said.

"Yup. Back to the wonderful world of forty-hour work weeks, cooking for myself and fighting traffic. It's good to be alive. Truthfully, I can't wait. I don't like being here any more than you do."

"Well, it's been nice meeting you," he said calmly. "You know, I feel better today. Maybe these klutzes have done me some good after all."

"To hear their side of it, they even saved your life."

"Yeah, that too. Could be. Could be."

I phoned Myra to tell her I'd be needing a ride sometime that day—who knows when. Then I settled back to see if I might finish the novel I'd been reading, but I couldn't concentrate. Thoughts of blood sugars future, the electrocution of Charlie Parker, the secrecy of Dr. Xenophanes, Saul's tsouris and Mrs. Resnick's suffering kept me from concentrating on the book. And, I kept checking my watch and visiting the nurses' station to ask repeatedly, "Any word? Any word?"

It wasn't until three o'clock that I got some papers to sign and a packet of take-home instructions. With that, I called Myra, grabbed my suitcase and headed for the door. For some reason, the staff insisted I be put in a chair and wheeled to the parking lot. On my way out, Saul silently raised his hand in farewell. In one of my infrequent flashes of inspiration, I dipped into my shallow pool of Yiddish to wish him farewell.

"Zeyn gezunt, Saul." (Be healthy.)

Touring the Detours

When me and Marlene had both turned eighteen, we decided we'd had enough of St. Louis. Hey! There's a little poem in the middle of that—Marlene, eighteen. We'd never slept together or even spoke about it in so many words, but we kind of knew that that's what we'd do (another poem) whenever we got to wherever we were going. Denver sounded as good as anywhere to settle. We took off.

We'd been driving the long way across Nebraska for about two hours, not saying a word, the neither of us. Out of nowhere, she says t'me, "Say something."

"What d'y' want me t'say?"

"Something philosophical."

"I don't even know what that means."

"I mean something that makes you stop and think about something you never thought before."

I tried to satisfy her by saying the first silly thing that came to mind.

"Crocodiles are green, but they sleep on the bank."

"What's the philosophy of that?" she asks. "It doesn't make any sense."

"Philosophy often doesn't. And you never thought about *that* before, right."

"Maybe not, but I've thought of lots of things that don't make sense."

"See? You're already seeing something like you've never seen it."

There wasn't another word for a hundred miles. I glanced at her to see if the quiet was due to her being mad, but it wasn't. She was seriously thinking about what I'd said. That got me to thinking too. Not about crocodiles or philosophy, but about how little we say that makes sense. Me or her or anyone.

There wasn't a reason we aimed at Denver. Just to go somewhere not St. Louis. St. Louis wasn't anywhere. Our families were down on us, especially my step-dad. Our friends were pretty worthless and we had no jobs. They call Missouri the Show Me State, but as far as we could tell, there was nothing it could show us. They also call it the Gateway to The West, so we decided to open that gate and get to somewhere something might be happening.

I thought we'd begin to see mountains by western Nebraska but even eastern Colorado was just more flat. The whole Nebraska'd been too much of that. (That, flat—another accidental poem! I dunno what's got into me.) I was feeling like a marble on one of those tilt boards where you twist knobs to avoid falling in the holes. Except no knobs in Nebraska would tilt the board, so we were like going nowhere. I started to think we'd made a mistake— like we'd of been better off sleeping on the bank like crocodiles. Instead, we were sleeping in the car. We couldn't afford motels. Sometimes the cops would tell us that wasn't allowed and they'd make us leave. I couldn't see that we were hurting anything. When that happened, we'd just move to another spot.

"This sucks," I told Marlene. "Why'd we go west?"

"Where else would we go?"

"There's three other directions I can think of," I said. "Pick one and we'll go there."

Real quick, she said, "South. From what I've heard about New Orleans, it sounds like fun."

"How do we get there?" I asked. I never had much sense of direction and no gas stations give out maps anymore.

"We just go back to the Mississippi and follow the river allaway down."

"What? Drive through Nebraska again? I'm not doin' *that*!"

"There's gotta be other ways. Turn around here and make a right first chance you get. That'll be south."

Pretty soon, we were in Kansas and I headed east to hit the river. Omigod! Kansas was as bad as Nebraska. I don't understand why Dorothy ever wanted to get back from Oz, Auntie Em or not. If there's no place like Kansas, I say good!

Again, we drove and drove without a thing to look at until we came to a place that used to be a town. It used to have a name and people used to live there, but, before we got there, a tornado had turned it into a pile of planks, little pieces of glass and upside-down cars. I saw a toilet up a tree. I couldn't imagine anyone would live there again. Not if y'gotta climb a tree to take a crap.

I thought for a minute that we should stop there and maybe I could earn a few bucks by helping to clean up. We were running out of money. But then I figured that the townsfolk there were broker than we were and were only interested in volunteers. So we drove on.

I feel bad about saying the junk pile was the only thing worth seeing on our whole trip so far. If I was killed in a tornado, I wouldn't like someone lookin' at my corpse and sayin' it was interesting.

As we drove on, I got to thinking about people who live in wiped-out places. Why do they stay for another round? I wondered. Once you've been through one forest fire, earthquake, hurricane or tornado, why not move to higher, drier parts of the country? One tsunami or mudslide should be warning enough that it's time to pack up whatever's not soaked or broken and beat it. But then I

thought, where would you go? Underground? There's no place I
know of where bad stuff never happens. What weather's expected
in Shangri La?

Finally, the river. I always thought the Mississippi was the only
good thing about Missouri. There's something about water, especially rivers, that gives a place a sense of adventure. Rivers cause
they're moving, always *going* somewhere. Like railroads. The tracks
may be laying still, but they wouldn't be there at all except they're
commanding something to *move*, out of sight to somewhere. Carrying loads of needed stuff—wood pallets, fuel oil, poisonous
chemicals, marshmallows, animals, whatever—and carrying the
gibberish spray-painted on the sides of boxcars off to people who
might know how to decode the paint. I like that. I'd like to get to
somewhere where people could understand *me*.

Y'know, I once read a book by Mark Twain called *Huckleberry
Finn* where Huck and a black guy named Jim took off on a raft
down the river. They had left Missouri just like Marlene and me,
getting away from lives they didn't like. Along the way, they ran
into all kinds of stuff they'd never seen and people they couldn't
have expected. I could never put that book out of my mind. It told
about life how I think it should be, with surprises every turn of the
river, newness everywhere.

Most of my life I'd bumped into walls, one day like another. I
wanted to bust through those walls and get to the so-called Land
of the Free. Same way for Marlene.

By the time of our trip, there were no more beatniks. Marlene
and me, I guess, were kind of like them. Except for the ones who
wrote about the beats. They had money, but none of the rest of 'em
did, and neither did we. We weren't beatniks or bums, just had to
be moving, had to see what roads do over the next hill. At least St.

Louis *had* a few hills. I wonder how the beatniks got around no money. At least Marlene and me didn't need to buy dope.

When we got to Arkansas, I knew we were getting close to where we were headed, but now the money was almost gone. We wouldn't have enough for gas to New Orleans, never mind food. I figured I'd have to get some sort of job there to fill our tank.

"What would you do?" Marlene asked. She didn't think I had any marketable skills, and I guess she was pretty much right.

"Maybe I could be a bicycle jockey."

When we got to Little Rock (the first thing that looked like a city), I stopped by a place that called itself a bicycle club, but nobody there knew of companies looking for messengers. I don't have much imagination about looking for jobs. Next, I stopped by a half dozen businesses, but none of them even knew what I meant by that. On my seventh try, I found one that did, but they expected a guy to have a bike of his own. Obviously, I don't, so that shot that down.

I wound up with a job as a cook/waiter at a little restaurant called Maid Rite. A Maid Rite is a sandwich of loosely packed ground meat. The little pieces of meat don't stick together like a burger when you eat it. To cook it, you just throw the meat on a hot griddle and sprinkle water on the grill. It doesn't take any skill. You put it on a bun with a couple pickle chips and that's it. The place had only ten tables, so I could both cook and serve without much trouble.

The sign outside the place had a sign that said Maid Rite in big letters and above that, Eat, and below it, Eats, so that the thing entire read, "Eat Maid Rite Eats." I got a laugh out of that.

A fringe benefit of working there was that I could eat lunch for free. I didn't much like Maid Rites—I'd rather of had a burger— but two Maid Rites would fill me up. It was like three bucks on top of my pitiful salary.

The most memorable thing about the job was that the boss, a guy named Dwight, was missing a hand. In place of that, he had a metal hook! He liked to show off to customers by sticking the hook into boiling water to hook 'em a hot dog. The regulars were used to it, but it creeped me out.

Meanwhile, Marlene got a job in a drugstore, working the register and restocking shelves. It didn't pay much either, but at least it was something, and she kind of liked talking to the locals. She's really attractive, so the locals liked talking to her and flirting, too. I don't have that leverage to get my foot in any doors.

All the time driving, I worried that something would break on my old Dodge. Even back home, that always worried me, but there, I could tap my friend Ellis for freebies. He'd rather work on cars than loaf, so alls I'd have to pay for was parts. And while he was fixing whatever it was, I could get another friend to give me a loaner for a few days. No such friends on the road.

My first glimpse of New Orleans was kind of disappointing. I guess I expected the Mardi Gras, but it wasn't like that in August. No parades or girls flashing their tits to get someone to throw 'em beads. The only good thing was lots of street musicians. There was plenty of music everywhere and people dancing. My first earful of zydeco. Wow! And there was every *kind* of people—blacks, whites and what the locals call yellows. Not like Chinese—they were what folks back home call mulattos. Some of 'em speaking strange languages and wearing strange hats.

And *food!* Etouffée, jambalaya, bouillabaisse, po' boys, alligator jerky, gumbo, and pralines! We couldn't stop ourselves from stuffing our limited bankrolls into our mouths. This, at last, was what we'd come for!

Marlene right off felt at home and happy. So much that I kind of felt I'd lost our connection. Even though I loved the New Orleans food, I, after a month there, was feeling jumpy. By this time Marlene and me'd become bed partners and I certainly didn't want to leave *that* behind, but I still wanted to see around the corner. Not that I liked the prospect of life on the road. Another thousand miles of driving would make me want to stay wherever I was. What to do to get it all together? I first had to bounce the question off Marlene.

Turned out, she was game. Maybe not immediately, but she wondered if another New Orleans was waiting. If so, she, as much as I did, wanted to taste it. For a week or more we readied, slowly pulling up our shallow roots, guessing where to go and wondering how many more miles the old Dodge would last. What would we do if it gave out in some dull version of Nebraska?

The lobby of our first motel had a rack of postcards of various places, including some Florida ones that made it look cool, and Florida wasn't as long a drive away as we'd already come. It showed palm trees, Disney World and beaches full of bikini women. And I mean bikinis that'd be arrested in St. Louis! Marlene punched my arm when I remarked on that, but she wanted to drink out of a coconut with a pineapple and umbrella in it. One man's tourist attraction isn't like a woman's.

Traveling through Alabama and Mississippi's not a trip I recommend. The people there have cleaned up their attitudes since the early sixties, I guess, but there's still plenty of ugly left. It's mainly conversational, not lynch mobs. Blacks are allowed to drink from any fountains and go in swimming pools with anyone else, but you don't wait long to hear "nigger" coming out of them. It rocks a Missouri boy's mind off kilter like it would if you saw Egyptian pharaohs or Ben Franklin walking down the street or Adolph Hitler in the grocery store, the return appearance of a Model T. Those two states are like a time machine to nasty days. Deja I don't wanna vu.

But we got through that and wound up in Florida. We didn't stay long in Orlando cause we couldn't afford to get into Disney. Too bad. They call it "the happiest place in the world." I should have guessed that that much happiness would be expensive. I doubt I'll ever have a bankroll to finance that much happy, even if I wished upon a star.

So we headed farther south and hit some beaches. The postcards weren't lying about the bikinis. We even went to one beach where everyone but us had forgotten their suits. I took me time to lose my hard-on, but the naked guys didn't seem to have a problem. Marlene, who was dressed the same's she woulda been up north, gawked as much as me, but both of us were uncomfortable.

"You wanna take off your suit?" I asked her.

"No," she said, and that was the end of that. The beach had a bar, and Marlene got to have her umbrella drink. The naked barmaid didn't ask her for I.D. Maybe in Florida you don't *need* one. If you don't need a bathing suit, who knows?

One thing you should know about Florida—it's *hot!* And *humid.* So was New Orleans, to tell the truth. Up north, that sounds like a plus, but there's such a thing as too much. We were so desperate for air conditioning that we hung out a while in hotel lobbies. We were still sleeping in the car, which was steamier than doing that in Nebraska.

Another reason to leave the state is all the stuff the postcards don't show you. Snails, kudzu, trailer parks and herds of old folks playing mahjong. It does differentiate there from home, but not in a good way.

The trip north out of Florida's a long one, too, but the scenery's better than it was in the grain belt. Lots of palms and tropical plants. Then through Georgia and the Carolinas. The Blue Ridge mountains were real pretty.

In Virginia, the Dodge gave up the ghost in a little town called Ettrick. Stranded! By amazing coincidence, Ettrick was where my Mom had lived during WWII, while dad was at Fort Lee in the army. (He was alive then.) Worse than being deprived of transportation was the fact that we lost our bedroom, and Ettrick didn't offer many jobs. It looked like we'd be there for a while.

Thank goodness Marlene didn't take long to work her magic charms on a man who did the hiring for a bank. It wasn't easy cause her only credential came from Little Rock, but the bank guy called there and they had nothing but good to say about her. The salary was better than she had expected. Better than Little Rock, too.

It took me longer (as usual) but I finally got a job in a lumber-yard, taking stuff off the racks with a forklift and delivering it to customers' trucks. You might think that would be strenuous, but it wasn't. I worked there two weeks before I spilled a load of plywood and they laid me off. In other words, fired. The only other thing I could find was driving a truck on a long rural postal route.

We rented a bedroom in someone's house. Cheaper than a motel, and our landlady included a supper in our rent. I'd been afraid the landlady, Mrs. Brockwell, would turn us down on account of us not being married, but she was lonely, so our presence gave her something besides money. It was like a fair trade. We were doing better than I thought we could do. Things were hunky dory. In fact, I'd say we were more comfortable there than anywhere since home.

Being in a good mood, one day I decide to write home to tell Mom where I was. I described all the presentable stuff we'd been through and asked them to drop a word to Marlene's people. Much to my surprise, about two weeks later, Mom sent a check for fifty dollars, which I gave to Marlene to start a checking account. We felt like we were respectable and rich, and it started us on a habit—a little deposit every week.

Mom also told me to say hello to her old friends in Ettrick, but, of course, I had no idea who they were. She didn't clue me in to any of their names, and probably most of 'em were senile or dead.

On a lark, one weekend we took a trip to Washington, DC. It was only a hundred-thirty-mile trip. The postmaster, a good guy, Lenny Tropper, let me use the truck. In all our travels, we'd never been much for touristy sites, but in DC we did it—the White House, Mt. Vernon, the Washington monument, the Capitol, the tomb of the unknown soldier— and bought a mittful of postcards. DC was the most expensive place ever, so we slept in the truck, which wasn't as comfy as the old Dodge had been. Marlene had to sleep in the back of the truck on a pile of bunched-up mail sacks.

It wasn't a big deal as far as most "vacations" go, but when we got back, we were pretty ragged out. We agreed that DC would be our last vacation. Neither of us was cut out to be that kind of tourist. And when we got back, we tossed the postcards.

By living tight, Marlene and me managed to bank twenty bucks a week, so at the end of six months, with the fifty Mom had sent, we had $570—as much as I'd ever had at one time, even back home. I could start to think about buying a used car and, beyond that, where we'd go next. We'd have to rack up more savings to travel, cause even with a car, that takes money.

I noticed that whenever I talked about where to go next, Marlene was mainly quiet.

"Whatsamatter, babe?" I asked. "Don't have no ideas?"

"I think I've had enough of the road. I been thinking I might like to go home."

"You mean St. Louis? I'm not sure I'm ready for that."

"Not necessarily St. Louis, but just somewhere we could settle down."

"You mean get married?" That shut my mouth a while. I'd never thought about that. Not exactly. But when she put it in my head, it seemed pretty good. I guess I'd been thinking for some time that we were kind of married already.

"Maybe married or maybe not. Just somewhere we could stay a while. Somewhere to feel like we belonged and connect to people we'd get to know well, y'know."

Like so often happened on our travels, sometimes I need Marlene to say a thing to let me know what I think.

"Yeah, I know, babe," I said, and was quiet a while. I slept that night at Mrs. Brockwell's, allatime pondering what Marlene'd said. By the next morning, I'd firmed it all up. At least as much as I ever do.

"I'm ready, Marlene. Let's do what you say. I'm even ready to get married if that's what you want, but let's wait to see how we feel when we're home. But I'm kind of tired of seein' the world. It's not as different from St. Louis as I thought it'd be. We've seen a good chunk of the U.S. and A., and it's all got to feelin' kind of familiar. Let's hit our last road and go home."

She kissed me and I started to shop for a car.

Those kind of decisions aren't easy to make, especially when the deciders aren't very articulate. For which I apologize. It can't have been comfortable to let me lead you through our wanderings.

It wasn't always so for me either, but I'm glad I did 'em. I don't believe life's supposed to be easy.

Again, I got lucky. Mr. Tropper told me about the local police department's car auction. It's got cars they nabbed from legal
wrong-doers, and the cars don't have set prices. If no one bids higher then you, you can buy 'em cheap. Well, I went to check it out
with my $570 in my pocket and bid on a few. Much to my amaze-
ment, I drove away in a three-year-old Pontiac that I bought for
five hundred. For which Marlene kissed me again, this time bigger.
First thing we did was take Mrs. Brockwell for a ride.

Next thing up was the old problem of what route to take. You'd
think any fool would know how to get home, but home was quite a
ways off—a thousand miles or more through three states. We took
more than a few wrong turns and accidentally saw more sights than
we'd intended to.

I once heard a proverb that says, the journey of a thousand
miles starts with one step. I'm here to say that the proverb's true. So
off we stepped, and three days later, we drove under the arch.

I can't say my step-dad was glad to see us, but Mom was, and I
was glad to see her, even though she was awkward about Marlene.
She said, "I never thought you two would keep together."

Marlene said she hadn't been so sure either. We stayed at Mom's
house for a week, visited friends and dropped in at some of our
old haunts. Getting back in touch with a place you've lived in for
seventeen years felt a little like getting acquainted with some of the
spots we'd seen on our travels.

But we were kind of spoiled by having been around. St. Louis
wasn't as bad as we used to think, but it was too familiar. We still
hankered for some novelty.

"What do you say, Marlene? One more trip to look for our
settle?"

"Why not?" she asked. "I know it's not St. Louis. What say we try St. Paul, Minnesota? I've heard good things about it, and we'd still be living with a saint. Ha ha."

Both of us had gotten good at snap decisions and good at agreeing when to hop, so after a week of preparations, we were in the Pontiac and back in the wind. A day later, St. Paul, which we liked right away. It was obviously hipper than St. Louie—it seemed there were young folks all around, easy to be friends with, open minds, lots of folk music, some jazz, little theaters and our old pal, the Mississippi, washed its shores. It's not as expensive as a lotta places we tried, and we found a nice apartment we could afford. Three rooms on the second floor above a bakery, a balcony that looked out on a bustling street . . . Just the kind of nest we'd imagined.

So did we get married? No, not yet, but we're closer than ever. I can't imagine life without Marlene, and she says the same about me. We have memories in our heads that no one else has, which makes it feel that if we didn't have the other one close, we'd lose half our brains. Speaking for myself, I don't exactly have enough brains to spare. I do have a lot more than I had when I left home, headed for Denver.

Actually, that's a laugh—headed for Denver. As if any of us knows where we're headed. I'm just glad I mostly know where I *am* and know I don't know about tomorrow. Tomorrow, I'm sure, will take care of itself. It's always just around the corner.

Coffee with the Disbelievers

First the bad news. The government doesn't want you to know it, but there's a network of catacombs under our city's streets—tunnels used by military men who come up from under our feet to watch our every move. The Joint Chiefs of Staff would have us believe the tunnels have something to do with national security. That's a lie. Sources have revealed that they were built to prepare for a takeover of government by the militia. In a moment, I'll tell you how I found out about it.

Before I tell you, though, let me insert some good news. There *are* people who know the real truth. Assuming there *is* such a thing as truth. These people have looked in the horse's mouth, they've put their fingers in the wounds, they've counted the angels dancing on pinheads and have remained skeptical about even experiences they've lived through. They've arrived at realities they regard as indisputable.

* * *

A Hundred Cups is so named because one can choose from that many variations on your basic cuppa joe. The conversations available there are equally diverse. Politics here, history there, art over by the window, family matters near the counter, jokes, travel plans, family matters, television, crossword puzzles, cosmology—all over the place. Topics shuffle like seats on a carnival ride. They whirl and vary from day to day, as do the participants. It's all good, as is the silence at tables where someone may be in the mood for reading, writing or meditation.

Last Tuesday, I was in the mood for silence. I had started writing a short story Monday night and had progressed past the first of the many stumbling blocks to come. Pen in hand, paper spread before me, I was on a roll, brimming with what would come next.

But Braden Travers came next. He's a sixty-three-year-old guy who's our house conspiracy theorist, always ready to reveal facts known only to him and his fellow insiders. He reveals them to whoever is willing to listen and anyone who isn't, oblivious to whatever else they're doing. Oblivious. That, definitely, is who he is. He's oblivious to his own statements, to reality and to any input from outsiders who doubt his wacky theories but fall prey to his apparently innocent openings. His opening on Tuesday came from the day's newspaper.

"Did you see this?" he asks, pointing to a story I can't see from where I'm sitting. I look up from my work. "What?" I foolishly ask.

"They've appointed a group to investigate the reelection committee. I think they're gonna subpoena the chairman and the president's lawyer. If the lawyer admits he took a check from him any time after he was in office, the lawyer will go to jail and the president will be impeached because it's clear that one of them directed him to pay off that woman and someone was in cahoots with the Russian ambassador over the vote fraud. Congress will have to take . . ."

I faded him out. I've heard him report too many similar "news" stories in the past. This time, as far as I could make out, someone had done something wrong and someone else is planning to make someone pay for whatever it was. Who was who and what was what wasn't clear. I made my first effort to dead-end his story.

"No, I didn't see it."

"Well, they've got the actual checks. See? They're pictured in the newspaper. Isn't that against the Constitution?" Braden asks.

"I don't know anything about the Constitution," I say, making another try.

"It reminds me of that guy in the Eisenhower administration who took a vicuña coat from someone else. You can't get involved with stuff like that. Or Gary Hart. And *he* didn't have any foreign enemies goading him on. It was just some domestic bimbo selling her brand of blue jeans."

Now I'm really confused. Which president when was doing what to whom and who was going to pay the price? Which bimbo? What jeans? And Braden is just getting started.

"The only reason the public doesn't hear about these things is that the FBI and the Russians keep them quiet. Lyndon Johnson kept his hands on their throats to guarantee his election. There was a memo they found in his desk that as much as confessed to the coverup."

"Waitaminute!" I say. "What coverup are you talking about? And who found what? In whose desk?" My head is spinning. "Whose throat was Johnson keeping his . . . ?"

I should have known better, but I'd been sucked in again, responding as if I were talking to a reasonable person. Mercifully, Braden suddenly discovered that he was due to be somewhere else.

"I gotta go," he said. "See ya next time."

* * *

The next time Braden came in, I was sitting with Jerry and Lois. Jerry's the host of a morning talk show on radio and Lois, his wife, is a grade school teacher. Both of them are in their mid-forties. Their presence didn't deter Braden from joining us, uninvited. Braden didn't notice, but Jerry was in the midst of beefing about his station's management.

"Ratings serve a purpose, I guess. Advertisers always want to hear numbers. But at our place, the bigshots are over-sensitive to any change. They view a one-percent drop in share of market as a threatening trend, ignoring the fact that shares bounce up and down all the time. We're tops in our time slot. Changes doan mean nuthin'.

"But they're not happy unless they've got their fingers in the pie. 'Add more jokes, don't work so blue, play more music, tell 'em the time and temperature more often, maybe we should add traffic reports . . .' I tell 'em 'Nothing is broke, so you guys can go to hell.'"

"If you ask me," Braden offered, "it's because your station doesn't cover the real news."

"What real news?" Jerry asked. "We cover the same news everyone else does."

"That's what I mean," Braden said. "The mainstream media conspires not to talk about it."

"Well, first of all, what do you mean by mainstream media? And what do you mean by 'it'?"

"Major media is almost every newspaper, magazine, TV network and radio station. They put out the official line on almost every topic and *ignore* things they don't agree with."

"If there's one thing I can't stand it's *ignor*ance," Jerry said. I knew he wouldn't contain his sense of humor for long. "Well, tell me, friend, where do you get the information you trust?"

"On the radio? There's only one dependable station: WACK."

"I should have known. And what stories do they cover that we don't?"

"You know about Area Fifty-One, don't you? The Air Force has a lot of practice keeping things under wraps. They don't want to panic the public. It's in the national interest. If everyone knew what was happening, the Mexicans would try to break into the hangars where experimental aircraft are being kept. Once that happens, the national security will go up in smoke. Everyone will know about it then, but it will be too late.

"So what do you think?" he asks Jerry. "Is it extraterrestrials or foreign enemies?"

"I'll put my money on the extraterrestrials," I said. "They have more experience."

Braden didn't ask experience at what? He seemed to know. "There was a story about that in the paper today," he said. He shuffled the paper for five minutes but was unable to find it. Inexplicably, Braden was carrying a *mainstream* copy of the daily lies.

"They always bury stories like that," he said. "The advertisers don't want the public worrying about such things. It isn't good for business. If people have their eyes on the skies all the time, they won't have time to spend money. They won't even have time to pay off their credit cards, and then national security would fall apart. Credit card companies would go out of business.

"El Chucho was involved, too. Because of the cocaine. Probably the Venezuelite president, too. There's a lot of money in cocaine, so he showed the Mafia how to dig long tunnels under our cities as a means of bringing drugs to the United States. They were built during Prohibition by bootleggers as a way of subverting Michigan. The gangsters covered the noise of their project by claiming they were going to create a transportation system like Chicago's subways, so even the city government agreed to haul dirt away from the tunnels. There are miles and miles of tunnels under all the major cities here, and . . ."

"Under Cincinnati?" Jerry interrupted.

"Even Milwaukee."

"Under Portland, Oregon?" Jerry asked.

"Yes, and . . ."

"Under Tucson?"

"Under almost every U.S. city."

"Under Keokuk, Iowa?"

"I don't know which cities, but . . ."

"How about Mashed Potato Falls, Idaho, or Horsebreath, Montana, or Tittickler, Tennessee?"

Braden looked at Jerry quizzically, wondering if the rapid-fire questions were sincere or whether they were mockery. He couldn't make up his mind, so he gathered his scattered newspapers into a ball, glanced at his watch and did one of his hasty exits, off to attend to another mysterious duty. As he passed the other coffee drinkers on his way out, I saw a number of them nestle deeper in their booths, hoping to duck notice. They need not have worried. Like the Lone Ranger, Braden galloped out of sight without so much as a goodbye.

So that's how I learned of the secret tunnels. And that's all I'll tell you about them. You already know as much as I do.

* * *

Lois, always a calm, thoughtful and quiet lady, had been quiet during Braden and Jerry's back-and-forth. Now it was her turn.

"You guys weren't very nice to that crazy guy. The world overloads him with information. It's more than he can handle, so he mixes it all up and gets gunned down in the crossfire. No one escapes without wounds, but that guy is obviously a victim."

"A victim of what?" Jerry asked. "His own stupidity?"

"We're all victims of our own stupidities. He's just farther gone than most of us. I hope. But all of us have been painted into our corners by neglect, outside pressures, injustices, genetics, physical disabilities, cruelty or whatnot. It's not that any of us chooses to be stupid. The most blame you can lay at any of our doors is that we're lazy. We choose circuses over bread, cotton candy over sustenance, spectacle over substance and wind up with freight trains full of fool's gold. We're easily distracted by shiny objects and are easy marks for snake-oil salesmen."

"Phew!" I said. "You've given me a whole new view of Braden. A new view of all of us. I'll have to think about that."

"Believe me," Lois said, "I think about stuff like that every day. My classroom has the full spectrum of kids—stable kids, wild ones, smart ones, stupid ones, inspiring ones, pathetic ones, and some who have a lot to teach me. I have about seven hours of contact a day. I can't help but ponder what makes the difference. Where do the winners acquire their coping skills? My feeling is that those who fall short have almost always been handed the short end of the stick—some form of suffering or deprivation."

"That's me," Jerry said. "Suffering and deprived."

"If you've had to take it, I assure you, you've dished it out, too," Lois said. "Sometimes I think a lot of your listeners are masochists," Lois said. She may be quiet, but when the situation warrants, she does a great job of speaking up.

* * *

I began to wonder, though, what put Braden aboard *his* runaway train? One day I realize that I'm the one in the best position to find out. The next time he checked in, I began my investigation.

"Does your family live in the area?" I ask him. I expect a yes or a no before a quick transition to the day's gibberish, but no. It seems I've knocked on a door Braden's been waiting to unlock.

"Not anymore," he says. "They did for a few years before my mom and dad died. Before that, we lived in Hibbing, Minnesota, but we had to move. My dad had worked twenty-five years in a lumberyard up there. When a palette of plywood sheets fell off a forklift and crushed his leg, he couldn't work anymore. His bosses said he hadn't loaded the forklift right, but it was really 'cause a strap broke. He tried to tell 'em what really happened, but they wouldn't believe him. I think it was prob'ly they were afraid they'd get sued, and the lumberyard owner was a friend of the governor. They fired dad. He couldn't get work after that.

"Times got pretty hard then. My folks hadda sell the house and move down here. It made my dad ashamed, but there wasn't anything we could do about it.

"I wasn't sorry to leave Hibbing. When my dad got fired, one of his best friends, Critsman, zipped in and got his job at the lumberyard. Critsman didn't even put in a good word for my dad. You think you know someone, but wait. Sooner or later, you find out about their real selves. There's more skunks in the woods than you think. Not just in Hibbing.

"So we had t'come down here. My dad couldn't get a job here, either, 'cause of his leg. He was never the same after that, he was so ashamed about being unable to work and about having to live with my aunt. Two years after that, dad died. My ma died soon after that.

"Doctors told her she had diabetes. I didn't think that was it. She lost a lot of weight and she was funny colored. I knew a bunch of other people who had diabetes and ma didn't look like them. I kept asking the doctors to double check, but they didn't pay any attention to me. They kept saying it was diabetes. Much later, they said it was pancreatic cancer, but, by then, it was too late to do anything about it. She died before the year was out. The doctors never admitted their mistake.

"So it was only my brother and me living with my aunt for a while. We were really best friends in those years. Then he married his girlfriend and she moved them to Santa Fe to be close to her family. It was pretty lonely then. I was only nineteen, but my aunt told me I could stay there as long as I wanted. When she died, though, she left the house to one of her sisters and I hadda find somewhere else to live. I been living in an apartment over on South Street for years. It's okay, I guess, but I don't know many of the people there."

* * *

My one question about family had shed more light on Braden's mindset than I'd hoped. When you can't trust your employer, your dad's best friend, doctors or your aunt, you're off to a shaky start. I can see how such a history might lead one to become mistrustful of official versions of what's what. But why turn to hoodoo and hobgoblins as your alternative? What made Braden choose to fly with the ancient astronauts, listen to whisperings of the dead and blame backaches and dandruff on the Masons? Two plus two doesn't add up to swamp gas. Not even in Irish neighborhoods on St. Patrick's Day does one see mobs of mischief-loving leprechauns. So why walk the wiggly way? I didn't have to wait long for an answer.

* * *

At our next encounter, Braden introduced me to his friend Theodore. Theodore's a guy about the same age as Braden. I know I'd never seen him before because if I had, I'd have remembered him. A haystack of gray hair ballooned out from under his knit cap, matching his full mountain man beard. His most riveting feature, though, was his laser-beam eyes scowling out from under Andy Rooney eyebrows. It was hard to imagine he wasn't aiming death ray weapons at me.

"Hi," I said. No response.

"Theodore lives in my apartment building. He's our resident intellectual."

Theodore snorted.

"By that, I mean he's a student of how the world works. He's opened my eyes to a lot of things."

Theodore went, "Mmmff."

"I notice you've got a big bag of lemons, Theodore," I said. "Where'd you buy 'em? I don't know of a grocery store within a mile of here."

"I know a place," he said, and squinted at me. I wondered if I had asked him to reveal classified information.

"Lemons," he said. "No one gives 'em the credit they deserve."

What could I say? I had no clue about what credit lemons *do* deserve. Braden explained.

"Theodore eats lemons all the time."

"Y'gotta," Theodore said. "It's the only way to perteck yerself from the drinking water."

Me, I use them to make lemonade or to squeeze a wedge over fish. I doubt the Lemon Man uses them for that. I bet he eats 'em whole, right out of the peel.

"Ever since the Truman years, our water's been loaded with chemicals, and you can see what it's done, mainly cuz of radiation. The national IQ has been going down, down, down. I call water 'stupid juice.'"

I thought I'd see if, behind all that hair, Theodore might have a sense of humor. "Bartender!" I called. "A round of stupid juice for the house."

Nope. No sense of humor. Theodore didn't say a word. He just glared at me. Braden tried to reanimate his buddy.

"See, that's what I mean, Ron. How many people know about the water? I wouldn't except Theodore told me."

"So do *you* eat a lot of lemons, Braden?"

"Not as many as Theodore," he says. "I don't really like 'em. But you can't be too careful."

"I'm not," I say.

Theodore jumps in. "You probably believe what the government doctors tell you."

"I didn't even know the government *has* doctors."

"You're kidding! Why do you think drug prices keep going up?"

By that point in the conversation, I knew I'd met the gardener who was watering the hemlock seeds in Braden's garden. But where did *Theodore* get his ideas?

"He buys most of the stuff he reads at a used book store in Milwaukee. A lot of 'em he wrote himself," Braden said.

That figures, I thought. I might have guessed that Theodore's main source of wisdom would be the writings of Theodore. Reading one's own writing is enough to drive *anyone* nuts.

One morning Braden showed me a dozen issues of publications from the Theodore library. Among them, a monthly magazine with the lengthy name *What They Don't Want You to Know*; a photocopy of an article called *Look to the Skies*; the premier issue of *UNCLOUD YOUR MIND*; an eight-page magazine that claimed to be The Journal of The Worldwide Clarifiers, and two broadsheets: *The End Is Eminent* (sic) and *Who Have You Elected*?

"Have you *read* all these?"

"I don't remember. Some are pretty old. But I've got boxes of them. Theodore always gives me copies when he's done with 'em."

I flipped open *The End Is Eminent*. The first thing I noticed was the author's fondness for imaginative spelling. The second thing was the shocking prediction that the world would end on February four, nineteen ninety-four. I would love to have seen that year's March issue. I couldn't resist questioning Braden about that.

"Why are we still here?" I asked. "Now that we know the hidden truth, I would think we'd have carried it to our graves. What gives?"

"The comet that was heading toward the Earth took an unexpected turn," Braden said.

"Naw, naw, naw," I said. "Doomsday prophets since the world began have been predicting its end. Guys who say stuff like that make money by pedaling fear. And they know that when their predictions don't come true, guys like you will make up excuses for them."

"Everybody makes mistakes," Braden said. "How many times have you heard weathermen predict snow and then no snow falls. And, you've heard TV predict wrong election results."

"The difference is that people who make those predictions can explain how they do it. They see weather to the west of us, account for wind patterns and pressure systems and tell you the percentage of likelihood the storms will hit us. They know routes past storms have taken for a hundred years. They know that this year's storms will probably behave the same way.

"And don't get confused. When a weatherman says there's a forty percent chance of snow, he's saying there's a sixty percent likelihood that it *won't* snow. When I hear a prediction that the world may end on a given day, I think there's a zero percent chance that it will. So far, I've been one hundred percent right."

"Well, Theodore says . . ."

"See, Braden, that's where you take the first wrong step. Theodore eats nuts for breakfast, lunch and dinner and more nuts for between-meal snacks. The publications he depends on are full of comets that don't destroy us, conspiracies that don't overthrow governments and spacemen who never abduct us. Look at back issues of those magazines and you'll see that I'm right. If you continue to bet on long-shots, you'll usually wind up a loser. That's why they're called long-shots.

"Let me ask you this, Braden. How do most people respond when you tell them all these doomsday predictions and conspiracy theories?"

"They're surprised. They never realized what's really going on."

"Do they believe what you're saying? Do they want to hear more? The next time they see you, do they come over to your table and say, 'Hi! How are you?' or do they avoid you?"

Braden was silent. His sad face was his only answer.

"Your beliefs drive people away. Think about it. Look around this place and you'll see people gathering in friendly groups, talking about things they've done, people they know, things they've seen . . . No conspiracies or evil underground forces that are controlling our minds."

"That's because they don't know about them," Braden offered.

"No, that's because *nobody* knows about them. They don't know about them because they don't exist. You can't see them, feel them, hear them or smell them. I'm not saying there aren't evil people or harmful institutions in the world. I'm not saying there aren't things we don't understand. But that's no reason to imagine there are bogeymen from the great beyond. No reason to think Mata Hari and the Rosenbergs are plotting with Boris Badenough."

I felt pity for Braden. He's not a bad guy. I kept trying to redirect him.

"Pick some topic people don't know about. Maybe something Theodore told you about."

He thought a moment. Finally, "Bigfoot."

"Okay, now let me ask you, have you ever seen a Bigfoot footprint? Has anyone ever seen a baby Bigfoot? Has anyone ever found Bigfoot droppings? I'll bet the answers are no, no, no. Why not? What evidence of his existence can you offer?"

"I can show you photos of him and a lot of articles . . ."

"But you always tell me not to believe what I read. What makes *your* magazines and newspapers more credible than mine?

"Mine aren't published by some big corporation. They're by people like you and me"

"So if *I* put out a magazine you'd believe *me*?"

No answer.

"Well, if you wouldn't believe my *magazine*, would you believe lies I told on the internet?"

"Wup!" Braden said. "I didn't realize how late it is. I gotta run. See y' next time."

* * *

Someday, perhaps, reporters from *Time*, CBS, *The New York Times*, *The New Yorker* and *The Washington Post* may see the light and begin leaking the names of Kennedy's killers, the whereabouts of Hoffa's body, Elvis's new address and the truth about Queen Elizabeth's drinking problem. But even if that day never comes, there will be those who scamper after bullshit like lab rats hustling through a maze, madly searching for chlorophyll gumballs that don't exist. They'll continue to wonder if the scientific method is a path to truth or just so much jiggery-pokery.

How does *any* of us decide what's true? Is *anything* unquestionably true? How do *you* spell bologna? How do *you* spell summerogna sausage?

* * *

The next time Braden came in, I was with Jerry and Lois again. Braden greeted all of us and started with, "Hey, Ron. I've got a question for you. Do you believe in atoms?"

"I do."

"But you've never seen them. And your common sense tells you this table and this cup are solid, not swirling masses of little balls."

"No, but the world works as atomic theories say it should. There's plenty of evidence that the little balls are swirling. And no one says I'd be able to see them."

Jerry spoke up. "I *ordered* a cup of swirling balls with a shot of espresso."

"I suppose you believe in the Eiffel Tower, too. Have you ever seen it?" Braden asked.

"I've seen pictures."

"You know pictures can be faked. Maybe someone's putting one over on you."

Lois pitched in. "I've actually seen it. I guarantee it's there. It's made of billions of atoms."

Surprisingly, Braden said, "I believe in in atoms and the Eiffel Tower, too. I was just curious about how you decide what's true and what's not."

"That's a good question, Braden. It's not an easy one to answer.

Generally, I'd say that if you doubt something or if you believe something, look for proof that you're wrong. We're all very good at fooling ourselves. And be careful of taking anyone else's word for what's what. They're good at fooling themselves too. Even Theodore. I mean *everyone's* good at fooling Theodore *and* Theodore's good at fooling himself."

"I agree with you, Ron. I've even stopped eating lemons. Thanks for that. I hated 'em."

Lois laughed and said, "And even without the lemons, I think your IQ has gone *up* a few points." I could have kissed Lois.

This time, Braden joined in the laughter—the first time, I think, that I'd ever heard him laugh.

"Congratulations, Braden. Now that you've seen some light, I'll bet if we ask Jerry nicely, he'll make time for you on mainstream radio. Unless he gets abducted by his own station's management. Y'know, they've been on this planet before."

"There's no reason to abduct Jerry," Lois said. "He's been living on a distant planet for years. Go ahead, Jerry—tell us something in your native language."

Ball of String

My beater rattles across campus, past classroom buildings, the student center, the dorms and field house, over the river and past trailer parks and a few dark outposts beyond the academic world.

"Jesus!" Harper says, "If this guy is such a jerk, why are we going this far to go to one of his parties?"

"Wine, women and song," I say. "and maybe some Yahtzee if we're lucky. Plus, somewhere during the course of the evening, you'll get to witness a social phenomenon that will amaze you."

"What?"

"I don't want to spoil the surprise. You'll know it when you see it."

"You'll be sorry if you're setting me up for a joke," he says. "I'm not in the mood to waste a perfectly good Friday night on some snipe hunt."

But here we are. A two-story, four-unit apartment building out in the middle of nowhere. It sounds like the party is in progress. We're greeted at the door, not by our host, but by a good-looking coed who neither of us knows.

"Hi. I'm Mary Ellen. Who're you?"

"Ron van Rioux and Greg Harper. Friends of Mike's. We brought a case of beer to add to the stockpile."

"The fridge is already loaded. Just put it on the floor next to the fridge and c'mon downstairs. There's a game of Twister starting."

Downstairs is an enormous party room surrounded by several smaller rooms. In the main room are a wet bar and a dart board, sports posters and pin-ups tacked to the walls. About a dozen people are busy around the Twister mat, where one couple is mutually contorting and about ten people are lounging on couches around the perimeter.

Mary Ellen and I retire to a spectators' couch and Greg disappears with a girl he knows. Some of the other partiers arrived as couples and those who arrived as loners have been hunting new partners, trying to appear casual about it. Mike, our host, never one to be subtle, is now on the Twister mat, his nose already in his partner's crotch—more or less the purpose of the game—and his partner, a well-known bimbo named Alice, is giggling.

After Mike and Alice collapse, Mike comes over to greet me.

"Hey! Glad you could make it. I see you've already met Mary Ellen. This is Alice. There's beer in the fridge. Make yourselves at home."

"I'll wait a bit. Got a heavy weekend ahead of me. Physics midterm on Monday. I don't wanna sleep till noon tomorrow."

"You know the old theory: If you don't know it now, you'll never know it."

"Yeah. That's a theory."

"Hey! Donna! I thought you were going home for the weekend," Mike hollers at a newcomer.

He leaves Mary Ellen and me and goes to give Donna a hug.

"He sure is a social butterfly," Mary Ellen observes. "As a host, he's the busiest! He pays the ladies special attention. I've been here about an hour, and I've seen him hit on at least a half dozen."

"You've got that right. The thing is . . ." I hesitate, deciding whether or not to confide my real opinion to a girl I just met. I decide to go ahead.

"I know Mike because we're both journalism majors. Naturally, that means we're around a lot of talk about newspapers, magazines, writers, editors . . . It's pretty wide-ranging. Some of the folks in our department focus on newsy stuff, some on sports—pick a field. And some of us identify ourselves as writers, some as editors, some as reporters. But not Mike. Mike's vision is focused on his idol— Hugh Hefner."

"Hugh Hefner! What about him?"

"*Everything* about him! Mike's a wannabe. He thinks of himself as a Hefner clone."

At that, Mary Ellen looks across the room at the actual Mike Felscher, who, at the moment, is playing beer pong with three of his guests. Any resemblance to Hefner is hard to spot.

I say, "I think he actually takes *notes* on Hef's clothes, his opinions and his vocabulary. Craziest of all, I'll bet Mike's the only guy on this campus who's actually *read* the Playboy Philosophy. Myself, I take philosophical looks at the magazine's pictorial content, but I can't take that pretentious horseshit seriously.

"Personally, I think Hefner's kind of an anachronism—like a World War II pilot with pin-up decals on his plane. Like guys who still say, 'Woo! Woo!' or wolf whistle when they see a pretty girl. But I know girls on this campus who don't see it that way. They'll try to sell the idea that he's a women's libber, freeing women to express themselves by taking off their clothes.

"Don't get me wrong," I say. "I'm all for women who express themselves. And what's more expressive than taking off your clothes?" Mary Ellen jabs me in the ribs with her elbow. "But Hefner as a liberation ally is ridiculous. How liberating are those bunny costumes?"

"I look at those things and I can feel the wires cutting into my whole body," Mary Ellen says.

"Yeah, but I'd call those cute little tails a bit of re*butt*al." Another elbow jab. "Frankly, I see the whole Hefner persona as ridiculous.

How is it hip to hang around all day in your bathrobe even if you do call it a smoking jacket? The pipe, the Pepsi, the fancified vocabulary like 'posh,' 'yclept,' 'urbane,' 'ribald' and all that. He's a cartoon character even if he *is* surrounded by naked women."

"Most women would agree with you. I had no idea that any *guys* felt that way."

"Well, Mike definitely doesn't. He parrots Hefner's so-called philosophy, imitates his wardrobe as much as his limited budget will allow, and reports on all the celebrities who hang around the guy, never realizing that the shine around bunnyman is mainly reflections of their own glow."

"I don't see it. Just between you and me, I think he's kind of a goof. Mike too. Same reasons. I probably shouldn't say that while I'm enjoying his party and drinking his beer."

"So you're enjoying his party?"

"Welll . . . I've enjoyed talking to *you*."

"Back atcha. As for the party, it's pretty much what I thought it would be. Pretty much what all Mike's parties are—heavy on the booze and the babes, just like Hef says they should be. Oh, I almost forgot—there's another constant at Mike's parties that I specifically brought my friend Greg to see. It should be coming up soon, so I should give him a heads up. I'll bring him back here. I think you'll get a kick out of it too."

A few minutes later, I return with Greg and his friend, Sherry, who, it turns out, came with Mary Ellen. The two of them begin to chatter and, for a few moments, forget that Greg and I are there.

Greg whispers to me, "So what's the big secret? When's the reveal? Will I know it when I see it?"

"You don't have to whisper. Mary Ellen is waiting to see it too. And, believe me, you'll know it when you see it."

The girls include us back in their conversation which, it turns out, is pretty interesting. They've known each other since high school, so they've got a lot of shared history, including a European trip. They reminisce.

"That trip sparked my interest in architecture," Sherry says, "and I've continued to study it ever since. Not just European architecture or the buildings of several hundred years ago. I'm crazy for contemporary buildings that aren't just cubes—the ones that seem to undulate and flow like water. The Guggenheim, in New York, for instance. I wish Wright had ignored his severe boxes more often.

My favorite architect at the moment is Zaha Hadid, an Iraqi woman. All of her buildings are so sensuous they're like living things. Curves and swirls and swoops all over the place."

"I remember how excited you were by Frank Geary's place in Spain," Mary Ellen says.

"Yeah! The City of Wine Complex! That's what I'm talking about! For me, that was one of the highlights of our trip. I mean, all the castles and cathedrals laid me low, too. The architects, engineers and contractors of way-back times were such innovative scientists and artists—the technological discoveries. They take my breath away. But *now* is the time I live in. I can't help but value the architects who can envision the future."

Now *that's* the kind of stuff that, for me, makes a great party! I made a mental note of some of the buildings Sherry had raved about. I want to look up pictures of them. Better still, I'd love to travel the world as the girls had done.

But the time I'd been waiting for had come.

"Perk up, guys 'n' gals. You're about to see what I prepped you for."

Mike rolls a three-foot diameter ball of string into the room.

"I got this at a garage sale," he introduces his toy. "It only cost me five dollars."

"What's it good for?" a pragmatist asks.

"I'll show you," he says. He moves the partiers back from the center of the floor, forming a circle of spectators around the vacancy. No spotlight is necessary for Mike to be *in* it, the center of attention.

He steadies the ball of string a bit and leaps aboard. And *stays* aboard for about five minutes, shifting his feet to roll the ball all around the ring, waving his arms to maintain balance and aiming stupid grins at all observers as he arrives at their hours on the clock. He'd obviously put in a lot of practice time.

I was impressed by his skill, but, to me, his moves resembled an epileptic's marionette—more clowny than balletic. I subtract more points for his awkward dismount. He lands off-balance and sprawls into the ring of spectators.

But I've never been a typical observer of *any* performance. I see buffoons where others see genius, I see buffoonery and this party crowd is a prime example. They erupt in applause and laughter, and many of them reward the saltimbanque with handshakes, high fives and claps on the back.

"Anyone else want a try?" Mike asks. A few of them volunteer, but most of them can't even mount the ball.

"Well," Greg says, "that was novel, alright. I'm sure Mike is even better at that than Hefner is."

"Hefner would be working at a disadvantage," Mary Ellen says. "It would be a tougher act with a pipe in your mouth."

Comments like that earned Mary Ellen more points in my book. I casually put my arm around her shoulder, hoping to demonstrate a bit more than fondness, but she shrank from it. Too soon I guess.

"Weird though that was," I say, "the string dance wasn't the phenomenon I was promising."

"It'll do till the next circus comes to town," Greg says.

Greg, Mary Ellen and I go back to talking about our interests that have nothing to do with Mike's performance, and Sherry has disappeared. The ball of string has rolled offstage, and the spasm fans drift back to their beers and hookup hunting.

"Sherry's pretty interesting," Greg says to Mary Ellen. "Does she have a boyfriend?"

"Not at the moment," she says, "but you'd better make your interest known quickly. She goes through boyfriends like a parakeet goes through cuttlebones. That's been true as long as I've known her, but, since Europe, she's more insatiable than ever. While we were there, too.

"I should shut up. I don't want to give you the wrong impression. She's such a good friend and she's really a sweet girl."

"How did you two come to get a European trip?" I ask.

"It was part of a student exchange program. She spent her junior year of high school living with a family in Spain and I spent a year in Germany. In exchange, students from those countries lived with families in our home town. It was the best year of my life."

"Did you choose Germany or did you have to go wherever they sent you?" I ask.

"The organizers of the program told me they had an opportunity available in Germany, so I took it. I could have said no and hoped for something else to be offered, but I didn't really have a preference. I did know a little German because my mother's parents speak it most of the time."

Greg and I continue to question Mary Ellen about her time in Germany for about half an hour when she realized that we hadn't seen Sherry recently. Mary Ellen took a walk around the room and checked the bathroom, but no Sherry.

"Do you think she left without telling you?" Greg suggests.

"No. I drove both of us here," Mary Ellen says. "I'm gonna ask Mike if he knows where she went." She makes another circuit of the room and comes back. "No one's seen Mike recently either," she says. "They must have gone somewhere together. Maybe they made a liquor run."

"I doubt that," I say. "The kitchen is still stocked to get us through the winter. I think there's a more likely explanation. It's what Greg and I came to witness."

"What?" Mary Ellen asks.

"This is gonna sound strange. It's strange to me, too. It has to do with the ball of string,"

"*What?*" she asks again.

"I apologize if I'm off base here, but I've been at quite a few of Mike's parties and he almost always dances on that ball of string. I know the three of us think it's a stupid stunt, but not everybody does. In fact, a lot of women find that Mike's ability to dance on it is an aphrodisiac. Usually it's brainless chicks who fall victim to its 'charms', but not always. Did you check the bedrooms?"

Mary Ellen gasps, "You think that Sherry is screwing the circus bear?"

"I didn't hear her say anything that would rule that out," I say. "I've seen it work that way on two previous occasions. The stunt seems to wipe out every inhibition, every social reluctance. Not just with women Mike knows. I've seen it work on total strangers, including women you'd never suspect. *That,* in fact, is the surprising social phenomenon I told you you'd witness. The aphrodisiac powers of dancing on a ball of string."

Through our conversation, Greg remains silent. I had seen that Greg was thinking he was off to the races with Sherry. He had no reason to think of her as "his girl," but neither did he have reason to disqualify her. Now he was sitting with us in an empty barn, looking like cattle rustlers had made off with his herd. And he couldn't really *say* anything about it. He hadn't brought his brandin' arn.

"I mean no offense to your friend, Mary Ellen," I say. "There's a mysterious magnetism involved, and Sherry wouldn't be the first to fall under its spell."

"I don't know what to say," she says. "I don't know why *I* should be embarrassed, but I am."

Trying to lighten up the conversation by returning to a subject that she and I had agreed on, I say, "I guess some women go for the Hugh Hefner type."

Success! A smile returns to Mary Ellen's face, and she says, "We'll see. If, the next time we see Mike, he's wearing a posh velvet smoking jacket, we'll know you called it right."

* * *

So, Greg and I drive home unaccompanied by any new acquaintances. Past trailer parks, over the river, past the field house, dorms, student center and classroom buildings.

We're silent through much of the trip, but, finally, I risk asking, "Whutcha think?"

"For starters," says Greg, "I have to revise my previous assessments of what females want. It isn't, after all, good looks, brains, money or a good personality. It doesn't even depend on having a snazzy sportscar. No one imagines Mike has any of those things. One can get laid, maybe even establish a meaningful, lifelong relationship, without any of that claptrap. I see now that all it takes is a ball of string. That's my version of the new Playboy Philosophy."

"So, the night wasn't wasted. You've learned a new, mysterious fact of life. If you don't know it now, you'll never know it," I say, trying to rescue a moral of the story.

Not long after the event described above, Greg and I got news that, at one of Mike's parties, his act ended prematurely. Mike fell off the ball and, with an urbane splat, broke his arm. It's tough to maintain one's balance or an aura of savoir faire with one arm in a cast. But who knows? Maybe he wound up getting an ER nurse in the sack even without the ball of string. Maybe he just returned to campus, a sadder but wiser clown. Somehow, I doubt it.

Long after the party, I continued to think about the effect that Mike's dance had on females. Or, I should say *has* on females, for, as soon as his arm healed, he was back in the arena, performing his mating dance.

I began to realize, though, every creature on the planet attempts some sort of outlandish ritual in order to preserve its genes and, usually, it appears foolish to non-participants. Peacocks spread their tails, bower birds build their love nests, penguins have their mounds of pebbles, mountain goats do their head-butting (who wouldn't be attracted by *that*?), poets have their poems, athletes have their muscles, businessmen have their bankrolls, models have their makeup, primitives and soldiers have their enemies' heads on sticks . . .

Whatever Lola wants, guys. When inept, do as the Eptians do.

My Intellectual Property

In case you missed it, at the front of this book, there is a message prohibiting you from reproducing or transmitting in any form or by any means, electronic or mechanical, including photocopying, recording or by any information storage and retrieval system without permission in writing from the publisher. In other words, you may not mimeograph, ditto, photograph or commit to memory anything you see before you and, before it was published, there was nobody to whom you could turn for written permission. The material currently in your hand is destined to be its single iteration before extinction.

The same is true for the works of most authors. They imagine they've protected their genius from theft by unscrupulous authors and publishers when, in fact, there are no banditos lurking in the underbrush. And why should there be? There was never any commercial potential in budding writers' unlocked cars, unsecured homes or the briefcases they forgot on the bus. If you think my writing is likely to bring you more fame or fortune than it brought me, you're likely to be disappointed.

There's a caveat, though: You *may* reproduce small chunks for the purpose of review or just for the hell of it. "Call me Ishmael," for instance, is yours for the taking. You should know, though, that Ishmael didn't earn Melville a whale of a lot. And you may swipe "It was the best of times" without penalty, though, these days, who would want it? It doesn't accurately reflect the tenor of our times. Few would call them the best.

For some reason, publishers persist in threatening plagiarists despite the fact that few works stay off the remaindered table for long. There's no reason to invest in acid-free paper to print first editions of supposed masterpieces that won't live to see a second edition. Most of them have the life spans of fruit flies, and their primary financial potential lies in their possible value to collectors, especially if they're bound in old Moroccan grandmother.

There's some fascinating folklore surrounding light-fingered literati who have dabbled in borrowing from the greats. There's the tale of James Joyce's maid who came across the manuscript of *Finnegan's Wake* while dusting Jimbo's desk. She submitted the novel to a publisher, claiming it as her own. Without the imprimatur of Joyce's name on the work, the publisher took a pass. "This is rubbish," he said. "It doesn't make any sense."

Then there was the sad case of Leonard Fillibrand, who claimed to have written *Lady Chatterley's Lover.* The novel was published under his name, with the result that he was jailed as a pornographer. He served five years before Lawrence was revealed as the actual author. Fillibrand was released. By that time, public sensibilities had relaxed, so no further punishments were meted out. Supreme Court Justice Potter Stewart echoed the public consensus, saying, "I know smut when I'm fortunate enough for it to come into my hands. This book isn't pornographic but it *is* pretty dirty." He followed up by dog-earing several pages and highlighting some of his favorite passages with a yellow El Marko. In years to come, the public's judgments on clean or dirty continued to loosen up. It turned out that the novel wasn't dirty at all.

I must confess that I'm often unsure about whether my own thoughts are truly my own or inadvertent borrowings from my predecessors. I'm pretty well-read, so the attic of my memories is crowded with the wit and wisdom of writers wittier and wiser than

I'm likely to ever be. The perfection of their writing sticks in my mind but I don't always remember the source of the nuggets I've unearthed. Before I know it, I've reproduced or transmitted a borrowed masterpiece. Imagine my disappointment when I realize my genius is second-hand. My only consolation is that I am, at least, able to recognize quality when I see it. I steal only from the best. No shades of gray for me.

I've alerted my publishers to keep an eye out for suspiciously familiar passages in my work, but they're as fallible as I am. My *Canterbury Tales* was in its second printing before a sharp-eyed reader recruited lawyers to get the thing pulled from the shelves. I should have realized what I was doing when I found myself writing in Middle English. Oops! Suddenly I longed to gone on pilgrimages.

I do think we should be slower to brand literary "coincidences" as plagiarism. The world in all its bare-assed glory is observable by all, and, given writers' shared genealogy, it's only natural that two or more of them will overlap in what they chronicle, even if their approaches to punctuation and spelling differ somewhat. The fact that, in the aforementioned *Canterbury* opus, I wrote, "Whan Zephirus ake with his sweta breth" and Mr. Chaucer had spelled it out differently didn't hinder the lawyers' case against me.

Honestly, I hadn't even remembered reading Chaucer's tales, but, obviously, I must have. Had I not, I couldn't have concocted such stuff. Not my bailiwick. I could have avoided all the legal unpleasantness that ensued if I'd followed that ancient advice, "Write about what you know."

The trouble with that is, I don't *know* anything. I get ideas, sure, but before I begin to weave them into stories, I'm forced to do a lot of research to come up with details. So it's off to the library and the internet, where I encounter thousands of other people's words and ideas laying around loose, ripe for the picking. I pick, and, well-supplied with my harvest, I'm able to pass myself off as a tightrope walker, an opera singer, a heavyweight boxer, an international diplomat, a great writer or a worthless rummy. I can even fool myself into thinking I know about the lifestyles of such people. On occasion, I gather enough second-hand "knowledge" to pass myself off as a woman, a wolverine, an extraterrestrial, a paleolithic fossil or a bowl of pudding. The stories I've written from those perspectives have been praised for their original points of view.

Another piece of advice that causes me to scratch my head is, "Make it new." What's new? After all these centuries, not much. Generational points of views of questors after novelty have pretty much drained the cup. Read Joseph Campbell's *The Hero with a Thousand Faces* to get an impression of how miserably authors have flunked the test. One can create a character who paints his face blue or one who fights with a light saber but you're just warming up yesterday's hash. Do we really need another "good guys vs bad guys" epic?

Or another love story? Romeo and Juliet haven't stopped writers from retreading that well-worn turf. Over and over, boy meets girl or vice-versa and everybody kills each other. What else is new? A rose by any other name is still what Gertrude Stein says it is.

Even if you restrict yourself to autobiography, you're probably repeating the life experiences of folks who lived before. You may change the names to protect the innocent (if there *are* any), but everybody is the same. There's even a rumor that the Everly Brothers were one guy, doubled by electronics in the studio. Or was that you?

Generally, I've found that it's a good idea to ignore the theoretical rules of writing. For instance, "If you hang a gun on the wall at the beginning of a story, it's got to go off before the end." I tested that theory.

"Paul hung the shotgun on the wall, locked the cabin and started the Jeep. An hour later, he was at the airport, bound for Vienna. He would never see the little cabin again.

"That winter, eight-foot snowdrifts piled against the shack. It was late April before they melted completely.

"Suddenly, the shotgun went off."

My editors didn't like it. They questioned my sanity. I told them about the rule I was attempting to obey but they weren't impressed. "We have rules too," they said, and fired their own shotgun, ending any possibility of getting that story published.

Writing is a risky business. When one commits his thoughts to print, he reveals his intellectual bank account. Myself, I'm no Jeff Bezos. Too many of my stories prove that I'm living on pocket lint and, often, even *that* intellectual property isn't really *my* property—it's *rented.*

But, as far as my day-to-day life is concerned, it gets me by. I change my socks, check the mail, clean the gutters and do fairly well with the opposite sex. None of that requires any intellectual capital. Life accepts Monopoly money and never bats an eye. It's not until one tries to *create* something— fiction, poetry, films, paintings, etc.— that the public holds the currency up to the light, looking for counterfeits.

Be warned: the public is highly suspicious of anything that's labeled intellectual. They can smell intellectual stink a mile off. If they suspect that a bowl of corn flakes is *intellectual* corn flakes, they won't eat them, even if you put sugar on them and include a toy in the box. "Intellectual" is pure poison. Even "intelligent" they approach with caution. Safer to dine on unthreatening mush.

Public scrutiny is one (fairly inconsequential) thing. More important is the squint one gives oneself. Few people, I find, question the value of their own information or opinions. The result is that the strength of their convictions and the weakness of their facts grow proportionately. I strongly recommend self-doubt. It's my most valuable intellectual property, and I encourage one and all to steal some of it.

By the way, you may also steal the prohibition against stealing or reproducing in any form that appears at the beginning of this essay.

Fade to Black

My eyes are ready for sleep. My body is weary and, if the clock has any authority, it's time to leave the conscious world. So I undress and lie down in bed, but soon after I close my eyes, the bees in my head begin to buzz. They remain in frenetic pursuit of their cryptic daytime goals, the individual bees, each in thrall to its instinctively programmed specialty—protecting the hive, tending to the queen, making honey or dancing out the codes known only to bees. Those specialties send them in all ten theoretical directions of space. I can't watch them all, can't follow any logic nor understand the flow. And none of this is tranquilizing.

The bees buzz about the major or minor encounters I've had with random people throughout life—business contacts, lovers, family, friends, coffee house acquaintances, street faces recognized on second encounters, fictional characters who've transitioned from art to become parts of my psyche . . . Situations they played in my life at the time. Items checked off on my list of things to do, items ignored and the repercussions of doing or not doing. Sensory memories—tastes, touches, smells. Historical events, political opinions, scientific theories, word combinations, the "what if" game, animals, jokes, toys of my childhood, places I've been or haven't been and things I don't know, buzzing, buzzing, keeping me awake.

I lay there, wishing I were a bee-keeper. Instead, I'm kept. I'm kept awake, considering, revising, speculating, roiling in nostalgia, ignorance, aspiration, regret and other ragged preoccupations I wear during the day. I long for escape. Oh, let me sleep!

I must smoke the bees, get them calmed to zero with a lullabye more soporific than any chant or chemical agent. I begin with what I remember of meditation practice. I lay on my back, arms at my side and try to ignore what each part of my body is feeling. I must remain immobile, breathe evenly. Let the sensations in each body part fade, beginning with feet and working their way up. I count my breaths to dull the buzzing hive . . .

Inhale   exhale   one   inhale   exhale   two   inhale   exhale three   inhale   exhale   four   inhale   exhale   five   inhale exhale   six   inhale   exhale   seven   . . .

While I learn to do this (it *does* take practice), the bees interfere, making me lose count, often early in the count . . .   Eight inhale   exhale   nine   inhale   exhale   ten   . . .

The bees intrude: "Why is there an almost universal consensus that the world's mathematics use a base ten system? Is it because we have ten fingers? I remember learning about other systems. Base twelve, for instance, adds T (ten) and E (eleven) to the familiar numbers, and when numbers are high enough to require a second place, each is worth twelve. A two in the second spot is worth twenty-four. The third place is twelve squared (one forty-four) A two there is worth two hundred eighty-eight. A T there (ten) is worth fourteen hundred and forty. An E equals fifteen hundred and eighty-four," the bees inform me, keeping me awake. But they continue:

"The most useful alternative base is base two, which uses only ones and zeros. The fact that each place is occupied by one or not makes it easier for computers to talk to each other. They need only be on or off, firing or not firing, impulse or no impulse, and via long strings of yes or no, complex information can be communicated."

I remain awake, fooling with the concept. Which makes me

lose count of breaths and makes room for another bee to sing its song: "The man who taught the math course in which I learned about other bases was a bald-headed milquetoast who, at age forty, still lived with his mother. Many of my classmates would take pleasure in tormenting the man. Behind his back, they called him Scaldy-Baldy Chrome Dome or called him by his first name. 'I just saw George in the rest room. He was combing his hair with a washcloth.'

Once, our class was thrown into chaos by a window being pierced by a hunting arrow shot from the playground. A joker hollered, "They're after your scalp, sir!" Another joker yelled, "They're too late!" The memory of all that keeps me from fading into unconsciousness.

And leads to another topic, sometimes related to the first—to other teachers from my past, for instance. The ones who continue to impact my present and, rarely, the ones who failed to make an impression except for their physical appearances or quirky verbal presentations. Sometimes the bees abruptly change their tune, making dizzying apiary leaps among non-sequiturs.

Start the lullaby again.

Inhale exhale one inhale exhale two inhale exhale three inhale exhale four inhale exhale five inhale exhale six inhale exhale seven inhale... Until I get to sixteen. When I was that age, I was having one of the happiest years of my youth. All the events, people and emotions from that wonderful year became another buzz: The girl I thought I loved, the oblivion I felt when she turned her back on me, the heady liberation of a driver's license, a battle with acne, the dizzying prospect of completing high school and fear of what might follow...

But practice makes . . . Well, not perfect. Not having an end-point, counting breaths *has* no perfect. But I improved my control over the bees. I began to count many more breaths than I could as a beginner. Before long, I was able to reach three hundred without interference from bees. As I approached three hundred, Morpheus would pull at my sleeve, blurring the numbers. Ah! I'd soon be gone.

However, having realized that three hundred was almost always my outer limit, I found myself thinking of that as my goal and I'd keep track of how close I was coming. At first, I'd mark only fifties. At fifty, I'd be sixth of the way; one hundred, a third of the way; one fifty, I'd be halfway home. Every three brought me one percent closer to three hundred: eighteen equals six percent; forty-eight, sixteen percent; eighty-four is twenty-seven percent. I developed the ability to keep track of percentages without losing track of the count itself. I was now so efficient at this that I could recognize multiples of three without having to do any calculation.

At the same time, my concentration and patience were improving. I became able to count to four hundred or, occasionally, to five hundred. Along the way, I began to wonder how closely I was approaching those new potential goals. Three breaths were no longer equal to one percent. But I couldn't switch from threes to fours as I passed three hundred. Too complex.

Ach! My once-neutral numerical mind-block was beginning to resemble beesong! They'd found a way to defeat the lullaby and prevent me from losing consciousness. I had to get rid of numbers. No more counting.

But breaths are good. Now I'd inhale   exhale   one   inhale exhale   one   inhale   exhale   one . . . Nothing to keep track of, just deepening, deepening.

At some point, I realized that the position my body was maintaining—immobile on my back, legs straight, arms folded on my chest—was identical to the way corpses are positioned at a wake. And my bedclothes felt a lot like the satiny décor morticians arrange to display a body. Just enough cushioning under the neck to elevate the head for viewing, just enough covering for the lower extremities to keep mourners focused on the face, crenulations of surrounding fabric arranged to be pleasingly symmetrical and funereal. Something likely to be eternally comfortable.

Inexplicably (in my current state, I'm incapable of explaining *anything*), the body in the casket isn't mine. A beloved U.S. president has recently died in office and is now neatly packaged in a coffin, the coffin being transported by train from D.C. to his unidentified home state for burial. The train is, perhaps, indicative of the era in which this is taking place. It isn't a diesel—it's an old-fashioned steam locomotive with smokestack, cow-catcher and an array of wheels of various sizes.

The coffin is positioned in one of the cars so that the president makes his way, head leading his body west across the nation, his feet pointing back to his successor's office and the bureaucratic minutiae that are the capital's stock in trade.

The train passes through major cities, small towns and farmland that grows many of the crops that rarely come to mind when urban dwellers think of agriculture—oats, nectarines, okra, sorghum and such. There's one farmer frustrated by his inability to produce a decent crop of cloves. Past wind farms that didn't exist when steam locomotives ran the rails. Vigilant wind farmers in their propeller beanies stand by, puffing as they nervously await harvest of their expected crops—bushels of air, waiting to be harvested and converted into electricity to feed our toasters and televisions. The train passes feed lots, universities, defunct gas stations in near-ghost towns, vacant motel rooms, burger joints, barrooms and billboards.

A bee reminds me of trains that passed near the playground my friends and I frequented in the mid-fifties. Then we had a game that, when we'd hear the rumble and whistle of an approaching train, required us to stop whatever we were doing and scramble to get "higher than the ground" (the name of the game) before the train was alongside the playground. Anyone who didn't was a loser. I don't recall there being any consequences beyond that. When the train was past, we went back to doing whatever we'd been doing before. And once the memory was past, I went back to trying to achieve sleep aboard the train that bore the ex-president's corpse.

Had this been a whistle-stop campaign, the train would have been decked in red, white and blue with well-meaning local musicians honking upbeat anthems as the train passed their bandstands. This is not such an occasion. The train wears black crêpe, and citizens who line the tracks are not cheering. They're pondering their participation in an historic moment and are wearing faces prepared to be seen in possible photographs. They appear to be somber. They've come to claim they saw the great man pass as if they'd actually seen the man.

Which they have not done. They saw the train that pulled the car in which the casket in which there are remains of what was once the leader of the land. Who's no longer present, however cushioned his body may be. He's an emptiness. The flesh and bones in the box are insensate, on their way to terra incognito, beyond agendas. No one is running for office now. Citizens watch the train in the absence of the ex-president, satisfied that, in seeing the train, they have seen the man.

Humans don't insist on much to define what happens as an

event. The passing of this train has qualified, and the trackside crowd has participated. The hidden dead man has rescued attendees from the purgatory of their mundane lives.

I sense that the ex-president and I—two absent figures—move in the same cosmic direction, following Edwin Hubble, one of the bees' non-sequiturs. We find our eyes at the eyepiece of the telescope named for him (which *has* no eyepiece. It wasn't intended to fit to an eye). But there we stand, empty shell and I, looking through the device at the universe Hubble imagined. Lo! The breathless accuracy of many of his guesses! The night sky's fuzzy blurs that consensus had previously guessed were stars, blurred only by their distance from earthbound viewers, Hubble had told us were galaxies. I see he was correct.

The billions of stars we had counted in our minds are, he told us, *hundreds of trillions!* And now I move among them, passing planets, stars, nebulous gas clouds and spiraling whorls of multicolored plasma spheres. I move among them, passing into black holes and (yes!) out of them, arrow through the Dagwood sandwich of multiverses, observe the nervous jitter of tangled strings performing the unpredictable ballet of the cosmic genome. I pass planets that host molecules just beginning to arrange themselves to create life, planets where those molecules have mastered the trick, planets where life once crawled, stood, walked, run and flew to thrive too well, developing technologies that contributed to their extinction. I also pass diverse afterlives enough to satisfy those who believe in every blotch on theologians' palettes. I experience the vacuums that many imagine constitute space.

A flock of toasters from the distant past flutters across my computer screen—the bees' last futile effort to keep me awake.

My speed increases, but, regardless of my speed, the space before me and everything in it recedes before me. The way ahead expands faster than I. Theoretically, nothing travels faster than light, but as I approach that supposéd limit, no edge of anything becomes apparent. If it's all expanding, expanding into what?

I'm now neither energy nor matter, not ever having been a conscious man, never fighting to achieve sleep. There are no more bees. Their little wings, their threatened stings can't keep up. I leave whatever self I had to the wakeful world and its concerns. No numbers, no train, no ex-president, no Hubble. I'm dark energy itself. Successsssssssssssssssssssssssssssssss...............

I have finished with the dessert spoon and put it in the sink.

About the Author

Ron Gillette was born in 1944. He spent most of his career as the editor of several trade magazines and, in that capacity, wrote and reported hundreds of articles on business topics. Once retired, his creative life saw him first as a poet. He's had several dozen poems published in the little magazines and, in 1984, a collection of his poems, *Hardware and Variety*, was published by Erie Street Press. In the eighties and nineties, he turned from the printed page to performance poetry and was an early collaborator with the Poetry Slam's founder, Marc Kelly Smith.

Much to his surprise, in 2018, short stories began to appear and, since then, they've become his only writing. As he imagines is true of all stories, his contain a lot of fictionalized autobiography in a stew of knowable and unknowable ingredients. The carrots and potatoes in it are the people who have played roles in his life.

Gillette is a widower with two adult children, Meghan Lane and Jason Gillette, and four grandchildren. He lived the first half of his life in Chicago and currently lives in New Berlin, WI.